The Meissner Effect

The Meissner Effect

The Adventure Begins

R. Grey

Printed in the United States of America
10 9 8 7 6 5 4 3 2 1

ISBN-13: **9780998383309**
ISBN-10: **0998383309**

For
BJ

PREFACE

This story contains many footnotes, which is unusual for a work of fiction. Although these footnotes are not critical to following the story, they provide historical, political, and scientific information that will increase your curiosity and enjoyment while reading. I encourage you to take advantage of them.

—R. Grey

PROLOGUE

Jeff Catson, ex-gang member and US Army Special Forces decorated combat veteran, was hidden in the trees next to the Copperfield ski run at Copper Mountain Resort in Summit County, Colorado. He had been spending a few hours each afternoon for the previous two days shadowing Senator Gregory Welsh, and he knew the senator always took his last run of the day on the Copperfield trail.

Catson was tired. He was also pissed. It had taken a lot of manipulation and planning to sneak away from his detail in Denver to get to the resort. So far, no one had suspicions. He hoped it would stay that way. He had been forced into this assignment. With his experience, he was able to plan it carefully but hastily. That last part he didn't like.

Nevertheless, his adrenaline surged. His mind sharpened. His hearing became crisp and clear. His breathing softened. His body was poised and ready. He missed this kind of excitement and welcomed the rush of action. This assignment was different, though. A smile crept across his face. Yet, he would never admit this feeling of joy to the person who had blackmailed him into this mission. *Someday I'll get even*, he thought.

His dark-brown eyes narrowed as he scanned the ski run. *Damn goggles.* He preferred sunglasses, but the dark-green goggles hid his face better. He was getting impatient. He raised his goggles to get a clearer view.

Catson was a good skier, and he would have enjoyed spending these days on the slopes while secretly watching Welsh, but his mind was on other things. His day job kept his past well hidden, until now. It had finally caught up with him, and here he was. Though this mission was right up his alley, he didn't appreciate being forced into it.

His six-foot, 180-pound muscular frame stood out in a crowd, so he hid in a patch of thick blue spruce and douglas fir covered in a blanket of fresh snow. The only sound he heard was the occasional soft thump of snow as it fell from a tree bough. It sounded loud to him. He was more than ready.

He had bought a light-gray ski parka especially for this occasion. It matched his ski pants, and it was a common enough look on the slopes that he'd be just another skier. He would never admit it, but it was the red stripe circling each sleeve that persuaded him to buy it. The stripe reminded him of the red-band symbol of the 5SD gang of his youth. It gave him a sense of pride.

It was a cold twenty-two degrees Fahrenheit, and the sweat that had developed underneath the warm jacket began to chill him. He would much rather have been moving. *Soon*, he thought. He needed to get back to Denver.

Senator Gregory Welsh was on a well-deserved vacation. He loved skiing but didn't get the chance to do it often. In fact, he had not been on a slope in more than three years. *I should retire*, he thought for the umpteenth time as he whooshed through the fresh powder.

He was the senior senator from Montana and a Democrat. "How long have you served now, Senator?" the ever-present press would ask.

They knew the answer. "Too long!" he always said.

He loved his job, and Montana loved him. He'd had a distinguished career of more than four decades, though the past several years had been challenging. His wife contracted breast cancer, and the last year of her life was hard on both of them. She'd died two years ago, and he had buried himself in his work as a means of recovery. That work led to his latest accomplishment, and he felt certain he would triumph. All he needed were just a few more votes to get his Meissner bill passed.

As he approached his final run of the day, his face was beaming. The day of powder skiing gave him some well-deserved joy, and he knew the research results of his bill would be a boon to society as well as the highlight of his career.

He was in good shape for a seventy-eight-year-old, but still an old-style skier. He had learned on long, skinny skis ages ago in his youth. His first couple of skis were wooden, and he'd managed to break them in record time. He remembered his father just shaking his head while looking at the second pair.

He finally got a pair of metal skis: Head giant slalom race skis. He loved them so much, he never got rid of them. They were old and beaten up and brought a lot of stares when he had to stop to catch his breath in the high Copper altitude. Some even took out their cell phones to take photos, but he didn't care. He knew he looked a bit old-fashioned, especially with his one-piece ski outfit and old-style ski poles. It didn't matter; he would just smile and ski away, thinking how things had changed.

It was a beautiful, bright, sunny day. *Hope my sunscreen is still working* was the thought that passed briefly through his mind as he made his way over to the Copperfield trail.

For Kevin Hall, the day was epic. It had snowed more than a foot during the night, and today was what skiers called a "bluebird day": clear blue sky with a bright sun and a foot or more of fresh powder. According to legend, Eskimos had different descriptive words to describe the various types of snow. In English, the snow today would be called a "light powder." It had been advertised on the radio that morning as "champagne powder," although that term was often overused and misused to promote skiing.

In all his years of skiing, Kevin had experienced champagne powder only once. He had been a kid at Eldora Mountain Resort, west of Boulder, Colorado, and it was one of the most memorable days of his life. He remembered putting his mouth close to the surface of the snow and blowing an eighteen-inch-deep hole. That was champagne powder. In those days, one skied on long, narrow skis, which sank deep into the powder; in very deep powder, a snorkel was needed in order to breathe. Today's fat skis float more or less on top of the snow, producing a slightly different feeling but still thrilling. The snow today wasn't quite "champagne," but it was good enough for Kevin.

Kevin Hall was a fully certified ski instructor, a PSIA level three,[1] with six years' teaching experience. His mountain of choice was Copper Mountain Resort, just west of the town of Frisco in the Colorado Rocky Mountains. Its base sat at 9,712 feet, while its highest skiable peak reached 12,313 feet, well above the tree line—the elevation above which the climate was too harsh for trees to grow. Copper Mountain was voted the locals' choice year after year. Originally, the area housed a booming mining village, and some of the old buildings were still standing. Centuries earlier, Ute and Arapaho Indians hunted there. In 1971, construction began on what now consisted of 2,490 skiable acres, and Kevin was trying to take advantage of all of them.

His scheduled morning private lesson had canceled. He didn't know the reason, but the cancellation gave Kevin a free morning to try out his freshly tuned and waxed skis. He had spent a half hour the previous night preparing his skis, and he couldn't have been more excited to use them.

He kept to the less-tracked back bowl of Copper. At the top of the bowl was a view of the snowcapped peaks of several other mountains. He specifically liked the pyramid-shaped Pacific Peak, which stood out easily in the Tenmile Range. At 13,950 feet, it was just shy of being one of Colorado's "fourteeners."[2]

---

1 PSIA stands for Professional Ski Instructors of America. A level-three certified instructor is considered fully certified and is recognized worldwide.

2 According to the Colorado Geological Survey, there are fifty-eight mountains that have topographic elevations of more than fourteen thousand feet in the state. But if measured by topographic prominence—they must be three hundred feet above the nearest fourteener's connecting saddle—then there are only fifty-three.

"Wow," Kevin said as he paused before a thrilling descent into the deep powder.

He remained in the red ski-school uniform because he was on call for the afternoon lesson lineup—a call he ended up missing. Later, he would claim he never got that call. That would be true; he was also well aware there was no cell signal in the back bowl. He'd probably get a lecture from one of the supervisors about his responsibilities: "We're a guest-orientated resort." But it was a rare powder day, and he figured his instructor seniority gave him enough clout to get away with a little recreation of his own.

At nearly five foot eleven and 158 pounds—more or less—Kevin was athletic and fit. He knew every bit of this mountain, and he skied all of his favorite runs before nearing the end of the ski day. He decided to take a cruiser down the Copperfield trail to the Timberline chairlift, where he would ride back up and finish on the High Point and Vein Glory trails. There was a shortcut he could take at the bottom of the mountain that led across a frozen stream and back to the instructors' locker room.

The Copperfield trail, a blue-level or intermediate run,[3] was generally groomed and considered a "cruiser" because it required little effort for an advanced skier. There was no other skier in sight on the run, and Kevin gleefully set out on a fast carve along the less-tracked tree line. He had wanted to teach skiing since his first lesson at age six. He also wanted to teach the ancient tradition he had been brought up in, but he had

---

3 Skiing trails in the United States are rated green for beginners, blue for intermediates, black for experts, and double black for advanced experts.

to do that on the sly because of his grandfather's warnings. Yet right now, he wasn't thinking of anything as he laid deep tracks in the snow.

About a third of the way down the Copperfield trail, where the bottom of the Tempo trail intersected from the left, he stopped to rest. He moved to the side of the trail closer to the trees so he wouldn't be in the way of others who might be racing down. Normally, he could ski the mountain top to bottom without stopping, but he had been skiing all day and was tired. Besides, it was worth stopping just to take in the view.

As he stood resting, taking in some extra oxygen and brushing snow off his jacket, a lone skier appeared above him and continued down past him. His out-of-fashion one-piece outfit was a dead giveaway to his skiing style. He used a braking technique to slow his turns instead of finishing them, and his skinny skis were too close together, indicating he had probably learned to ski a long time ago.

Analyzing a skier's technique was a spontaneous and sometimes annoying characteristic of an experienced ski instructor. Kevin's friends would tell him to stop the instructor stuff. "Let's just ski, OK?" But in his head, Kevin would be thinking, *She needs to learn to release that downhill ski. Her technique would be so much better.*

About a hundred yards down from where Kevin was resting, another skier suddenly raced out of the trees from the right side of the run. As the new skier caught up to the man in the one-piece ski suit, he appeared to pull out what looked like a gun. Kevin heard two muffled bangs, and the man in the one-piece suit hit the ground and slid a few yards to a dead stop, leaving a trail of red on the snow.

"Shit!" Kevin yelled.

Catson, hearing the yell, turned his head and spotted Kevin up the hill. *Damn, where did he come from?* Quickly stopping and regrouping, Catson raised his gun to shoot the red-suited witness, but Kevin had disappeared. *What the hell?*

That quick disappearance momentarily confused Catson, as Kevin had seemed to literally disappear. He considered chasing the witness, deciding he must have gone into the trees, but it was more important to finish the execution. The witness appeared to be a man wearing a ski-instructor uniform. That narrowed the identity. He would handle the problem later.

Crap! Denver will have to wait.

PART 1

The Washington Gazette

WASHINGTON, DC, FRIDAY, FEBRUARY 6, 2015

SENATOR WELSH SHOT DEAD
By Abe Southerly

Senator Gregory Welsh (D-MT) was shot while skiing at Copper Mountain Resort, Colorado, on Thursday, February 5. An anonymous male witness called the ski patrol at approximately 3:30 p.m. and reported that he saw a man shoot someone on the Copperfield slope. John Abernathy, head ski patroller, responded to the call and ordered the immediate evacuation of the victim, who was rushed to the hospital at the Summit Medical Center and pronounced dead. The body was subsequently identified by authorities as Senator Welsh. The FBI has been called in to help with the investigation.

CHAPTER 1

"Kevin, Kevin. Don't try so hard. It doesn't happen through effort." Grandfather was being as encouraging as possible but was also a little upset with himself for pushing too soon.

"I don't get it," his eleven-year-old grandson said.

"There's nothing to get," Grandfather told Kevin, patiently and softly. "Let's continue another day."

It was the day after the murder, and Kevin Hall was sitting in meditation. His childhood memories were distracting him from the horror he had witnessed and drifting him in and out of deep silence. He was the latest in an ancestral tradition of a secret meditation program. As the story was told to him, a long, long time ago, members of a secret club learned how to develop special abilities. Those abilities were passed down through generations of families in the club.

At the time, Grandfather felt this was the best way to explain the tradition to Kevin. As Kevin grew, so did his curiosity, and his grandfather told him the full story: "It's about the Holy Grail. Today, it's believed to be a fictional story, a legend of ancient times. Actually, the Holy Grail is not a thing at all. It's consciousness itself—pure consciousness."

The understanding came from early Christianity. Grandfather would read Kevin the following parable attributed to Jesus:

> Whosoever drinketh of this water shall thirst again: But whosoever drinketh of the water that I shall give him shall never thirst; but the water that I shall give him shall be in him a well of water springing up into everlasting life.[4]

Grandfather explained that the Grail was historically believed to be a chalice or dish that the disciple Joseph of Arimathea had used to catch Jesus's blood. Today, some believe it was Jesus's DNA that he passed on to Mary Magdalene by giving her a child. The proper translation, Grandfather told Kevin, was that the Grail was a hollow vessel—an open, pure nervous system that "catches" pure consciousness, the "water" of life.[5] Joseph of Arimathea received from Jesus the knowledge of how to experience pure consciousness: the Holy Grail of life, the essence of Jesus. The experience of pure consciousness would consecrate one's vessel and make it holy. Thus, the nervous system and the experience would become one: the Holy Grail.

Kevin learned from the many conversations with his grandfather and mentor that this knowledge was closely guarded by

---

4 Gospel of John 4:13–14, King James Bible.

5 The concept of a nervous system was known as early as the third century BCE through the teachings of Alcmaeon of Croton, Paxagoras of Kos, and Herophilus of Chalcedon.

a tight circle of Jesus's disciples. Over time, however, its use and understanding became slightly twisted. It was no one's fault. Once the master was gone, individual ideas started to creep in. Followers of the Gospel of Thomas were believed to have kept alive the correct understanding of how to experience pure consciousness and the benefits and abilities one gains from its practice.

These followers passed on the knowledge to a special group: the Knights Templar. Some believe the Knights Templar had contact with traditions of India, just as some believe Jesus once spent time there. According to the Holy Grail tradition, it was that connection that begot a more universal understanding of Jesus's teachings beyond common Christianity.

As Kevin grew older, he began doing his own research and learned that the Council of Trent officially accepted the four canonical Gospels of Jesus (Matthew, John, Luke, and Mark) on April 4, 1546, by a vote of twenty-four for, fifteen against, and sixteen abstaining. The council formalized what various synods had accepted from 382 to 419 CE (Common Era). Christianity placed a high value on these gospels, but many scholars believed they were not historically or factually correct. Some even went so far as to call them propaganda. That thirty-one members of the council had voted against or abstained was, for Kevin, a strong statement that other understandings had existed.

Kevin learned of many unofficial gospels of the Christian faith, including the Jewish-Christian gospels, the Gospel of Peter, the Gospel of Judas, the "Q" Sayings Collection, the Infancy Gospels, the Harmonies, Marcion's Gospel of Luke, and the Gospel of Thomas. The Gospel of Thomas consists of

114 sayings that emphasize direct experience versus church doctrines. It teaches that internal insight beyond duality is the way to enter the kingdom of God, whereas the canonical gospels talk about entering via "grace."[6] This is why those of his Holy Grail tradition believed that the followers of the Gospel of Thomas passed on the true understanding to the Knights Templar.

Kevin knew that experiencing the Holy Grail required an innocent, inward experience accomplished via correct meditation that produced an inner singularity known as pure consciousness. It was this experience that drove him to learn more about his tradition.

In 1120, nine men formed the Knights Templar for the sole purpose of preserving the knowledge of the Holy Grail. Hugues de Payens was credited with creating the Knights Templar, but it was the unknown ninth knight who had the correct knowledge of the Holy Grail and who inspired Hugues de Payens to form a group to protect and secretly promote that precious knowledge.

The Holy Grail by this time had grown into a legend of its own accord, and the Knights Templar encouraged that legend to keep the true understanding a secret. The Roman Catholic Church officially endorsed the knights, whose mission it

---

6 This understanding was further promoted by the celebrated discourse *Gratiæ per silentium* (Grace by means of silence) by Duca Calogero di Francescantonio (c. 1297–1350). The duca was a wealthy, respected citizen of a flourishing Florence. He interpreted *silence* to mean prayer, and thus the path to grace was through the silence of prayer. In truth, the silence of pure consciousness spontaneously blesses one with grace. An interesting irony is that in 1872 the *Consulta Araldica* (College of Arms) posthumously granted di Francescantonio the title of duke in recognition of this unprecedented scholarly work.

believed was to protect pilgrims traveling to the Holy Land. The church did not know the organization's true purpose: to protect pilgrims "traveling" to pure consciousness and to keep them from persecution.

In 1139, Pope Innocent II exempted the Knights Templar from obeying local laws by issuing the *Omne Datum Optimum*, a papal bull.[7] This gave the knights unprecedented powers and privileges. From their point of view, it allowed them to perform deeds in accordance with the laws of nature, God's absolute laws. They also sought out worthy individuals to enlighten them in the correct knowledge of the Holy Grail. The knights had to report back to the pope, who had final authority, and the arrangement eventually led to mismanagement.

The organization grew large over time, with the main body performing the official role of the church. But a small inner circle kept the secret role intact and quietly initiated a select, dedicated few. In 1307, King Philip of France had them arrested for what he called witchcraft and idol worship. Most were burned at the stake, but 108 knights managed to escape via eighteen ships to what is now known as the United Kingdom, eventually settling in Scotland. This was known from statements by Jean de Châlon, which many historians claimed to be false due to Jean's other wild claims of the Knights Templar's special abilities. Yet, it was these special abilities that allowed those 108 knights to escape.

Kevin's tradition further maintains that the knowledge survived through the eventual formation of two groups: the Illuminati and the Freemasons.

---

7 A papal bull is an official charter of the Roman Catholic Church issued by a pope and sealed by a *bulla*, a bubble of lead used as a seal.

Small groups of the Templars renamed themselves as the Knights of Christ and were able to merge back onto the European continent. It is not clear how the knowledge passed from them to the Illuminati because of a large gap of time. The term *Illuminati* means "enlightened." The group's original mission was to oppose abuses of power.[8] Kevin's understanding was that they accomplished this via the special abilities they had developed through their Holy Grail practice. In 1785, they were officially disbanded and scattered to many places, including the United States. Some believe they still exist.

According to Kevin's grandfather, their family's heritage came from the society of Freemasonry. In an attempt to prevent their knowledge from being lost, the Templars created the Halliwell Manuscript,[9] which in secret, symbolic form described how to develop pure consciousness. These Templars became known as "masons," the lineal ancestors of the modern Freemasons. In 1717 they created the Masonic Grand Lodge of England, where key members kept the purity intact. Like their predecessors, they also allowed misinformation—what today would be called "alternative facts"—to be propagated to keep the true understanding secret and available only to those who proved worthy. Schisms eventually emerged, and the Freemasonry branched in many directions, including the British colony in America.

---

8 This is clearly outlined in historical documents.

9 The Halliwell Manuscript (c. 1390) outlined a "craft of masonry." Its sixty-four pages of rhyming couplets on the surface outline the geometry of construction. In truth, to those of the HGT knowledge, it describes the process of constructing the experience of pure consciousness.

Though many of the nation's founding fathers—including George Washington, James Monroe, Benjamin Franklin, and Paul Revere—were members of the Freemasons, it is not known which of them were keepers of the Holy Grail knowledge. Yet, it is believed that the Eye of Providence—the all-seeing, all-knowing, divine eye of God, part of the great seal of the United States—was designed by keepers of this knowledge in 1782.

The ancestral ties were lost over time, and the families who were the keepers of the knowledge dispersed. For Kevin, the fact that the true knowledge of the Holy Grail—the ability to experience pure consciousness—survived through the ages proved that the secret heritage of the Illuminati and Freemasons was genuine.

Kevin's grandfather knew only these stories of the Holy Grail's origin and a few unsubstantiated rumors passed down from his parents. He knew of no other keepers of the knowledge. Yet, both he and Kevin believed there were other keepers, and rumors to that effect intrigued Kevin.

Several of the rumored keepers were authors and poets. Kevin enjoyed descriptions of their experiences. In particular, he liked the writings of William Wordsworth (1770–1850) from England. His poem "Lines Composed a Few Miles above Tintern Abbey" hints that he possessed this knowledge:

> That blessed mood...
> The breath of this corporeal frame
> And even the motion of our human blood
> Almost suspended, we are laid asleep
> In body, and become a living soul.

For advanced practitioners of the Holy Grail meditation, the breath slows and at times is suspended. Heart rate is minimal. The body is as if asleep, while the mind is infinitely expanded.

Henry David Thoreau (1817–1862) from the United States is another author rumored to have been a keeper and was a favorite of Kevin's. Thoreau wrote in his journal:

> If with closed ears and eyes I consult consciousness for a moment, immediately are all walls and barriers dissipated, earth rolls from under me, and I float...in the midst of an unknown and infinite sea.

While his high-school class was studying Thoreau's book *Walden*, Kevin was mocked by his fellow students and even a little by his teacher when he stood and read his book report. He knew the story was about experiencing a higher state of consciousness, losing it, and not understanding how to get it back. To substantiate his understanding, Kevin gave examples of other historical figures who had had similar experiences.[10] Unfortunately, his fellow students and teacher had no ability to grasp the concepts Kevin knew so intimately.

Kevin continued deep in meditation, drifting in and out of his memories. His grandfather had taught him this sitting technique when he was ten. According to the tradition, that is the age when the nervous system is developed enough to

---

10 Kevin's research uncovered many such individuals. He would have been thrilled to have read the *Supreme Awakening* by Craig Pearson, Ph.D., MUM Press, 2013, where the experiences of over eighty such individuals are described.

experience pure consciousness. Over time, it simply became known as the Holy Grail technique. Thus, the name of the experience and the name of technique became synonymous.[11] Kevin called it the HGT.

The memories continued mostly in silence—the deep experience of consciousness by itself, pure consciousness. Then his cell phone rang.

Kevin nearly jumped out of his deep meditative state. He had forgotten to silence his phone. He tried to ignore the ringing at first but peeked at the caller ID. As a senior instructor, he had the phone numbers of many of his coworkers.

"Hi, Sheely."

"Did I disturb you? You sound tired," Sheely said.

"No," he lied.

"I'm having a small get-together next Friday evening to celebrate Paul's birthday. Can you come?" Sheely asked.

"Ah, sure. What time?"

Kevin finished the conversation as quickly as he could without being rude. He wanted to get back to his meditation. He couldn't. The images and feelings of yesterday rushed into his consciousness at the sound of Sheely's voice.

---

11 This was what also happened to the ancient tradition of Yoga, which Kevin was soon to be introduced to. The word *yoga* means *union*. It is a comprehensive philosophy for unlocking inner, untapped human potential. There is a distinction between the experience of the "state of Yoga" and the "practice of yoga." The experience is that of an unbounded state of pure consciousness known as *samādhi*. The practice consists of ways of behavior, *asanas* (physical postures), breath exercises, and meditation. Both are called yoga.

CHAPTER 2

*Y*esterday.

When Kevin returned to the instructors' locker room, he was at a loss. The killer would surely have spotted the bright-red uniform of a ski instructor. If he spoke to the police, even anonymously, the information he could provide might make it easier for the killer to discover his identity. He sat on the bench and stared blankly at his locker. His heart was pounding.

The locker room was split into halves, and the entrance and exit doors opened to a small lounge in the center. The narrow passages between the lockers barely allowed two people to pass, but the space was fully functional, with natural light from several windows to create a cheerful atmosphere. At the moment, though, Kevin wasn't feeling cheerful.

"Kevin, are you OK? You look burned out." Kevin looked up. He hadn't noticed Sheely's approach. Sheely Shannon was one of the newer instructors at Copper, and unknown to Kevin, she had a crush on him. There was just something about him. She couldn't put her finger on it, but it was very attractive to her. With a five-foot-five athletic frame, she was considered a knockout, yet she was humble and sweet. She wanted to spend time with Kevin, and it bewildered her that he did not seem to take notice. Several times during the season, she had stopped to say hi to Kevin. Sometimes they would have a brief, polite conversation, but mostly the greetings were just said in passing. So today she had taken a gamble and had walked to his locker.

"Oh, just a long day of skiing," Kevin replied in a half truth.

"Several of us are going to Endo's to have a beer. Why don't you join us?"

"Um…all right. I'll be a few minutes."

"Great. I'll see you soon." She walked away with a smile.

What should I do? Kevin slowly undressed and absentmindedly hung his uniform in his locker. He wanted to report what he had witnessed but was afraid for his life. He remembered the killer pointing the gun at him. *What if he decides to eliminate me?*

He slipped his jeans over his long johns, grabbed his jacket, and stuffed his gloves and helmet liner into his backpack before carrying his ski boots to the dryer on the other side of the locker room.

Copper hired more than ninety instructors in anticipation of a great season, thanks to a new publicity firm, so the boot-dryer racks filled up quickly. Kevin found a few empty spaces near the top of the third rack to leave his boots. He turned around, walked past the small lounge, and exited through the twin doors into the hallway that led to the lobby.

"Damn." Panicked and confused, he had forgotten to put away his skis. He walked back into the locker room, exited through the outside doors, and grabbed his skis from the racks. He had a personal slot in the full-time instructors' ski-storage room. Depositing his skis, he headed to the lobby.

Inside the lobby of the Edge, there was considerable commotion. The Edge building housed Copper employees, the instructors' locker room, and an employee cafeteria. It was once a Club Med facility, but the small rooms were much better suited to the dormitory life of young employees than hotel guests. The lobby held the registration desk but was large enough for a TV, a few couches, a ping-pong table, a pool table, and a foosball table. It was always busy, now even more so. Several police officers were talking to a couple of patrollers and the ski-school director.

"Why are the police here?" Kevin asked another instructor, though he was certain he knew the answer. After all, he had anonymously alerted the ski patrol about the shooting.

"There was a shooting on the hill."

"No kidding," said Kevin, pretending to be surprised.

"Apparently, it was a senator," the instructor said.

That was a surprise. Kevin continued feigning ignorance. "When did this happen?"

"Don't know. I guess that's what they're trying to figure out."

"Did they catch the shooter?"

"I haven't heard for sure, but the rumor is the killer is still at large."

Kevin watched the scene. About six feet to his left, he spotted a man in a light-gray jacket with red stripes on the sleeves walking toward the police and patrollers.

That looks like—he couldn't finish the thought. The man he spotted now wore jeans and a Broncos ball cap, but the jacket was a dead match to the one the killer wore. Kevin gasped. He sensed the man's mind and the energy pattern around him—an ability his grandfather had taught him. *It's him.*

The man began talking to one of the police officers and showed him a badge. *Holy crap! He's some sort of cop.* Kevin quickly left the Edge and headed toward Endo's.

Endo's Adrenaline Bar and Grill at the bottom of the mountain was a favorite hangout for the instructors. After entering, he paused to gather his thoughts and emotions as he panned the room for his fellow instructors. A group of people who know one another form a bond that creates a physical vibration. Kevin knew how to sense it and quickly spotted his friends.

Kevin's extraordinary life training began early, as soon as his paternal grandfather saw an eager sparkle in his eyes. At the time, Kevin was small for his age. But from the first whisper, his grandfather knew he was mature enough to learn their tradition. Kevin continually grew in knowledge, consciousness, and stature. Today, he was strong, fit, and uniquely mindful.

"Hey, Kevin, thanks for coming," Sheely said with a smile. "Is everything OK? You still look stressed out." Sheely was driven by her heart, giving her the ability to sense the emotions of others.

"Yeah, you look like you need a beer," Paul said. He turned and yelled to the bartender, "Hey, Pete, get a beer for Kevin, will you?"

"I'm OK. Just a hard day of great skiing," Kevin said.

"You didn't teach today?" Paul asked.

"No, my private canceled, and it was too late for the morning lineup. I sort of missed the afternoon one." Kevin laughed.

"You'll get some flak for that," Sheely said.

"Yeah, I've been avoiding the sups," Kevin said. The supervisors were responsible for assigning all lessons.

The group chatted at the bar for about an hour. Sheely was pleased that she finally got some time with Kevin, even though he seemed distant. *Maybe I'll call him and invite him to my party*, she thought.

Kevin carried on a conversation as best he could, but he had retreated into his inner self. Though the depth of his consciousness was an unusual advantage, he had just witnessed a murder and was a little shaken. Fortunately, Sheely's warmth had helped settle his emotions. He now knew the decision to stay silent was the right one—at least for the moment.

CHAPTER 3

While Senator Welsh was vacationing in Colorado, Andrea Locker, vice-president of the United States, was sitting in her office, reading his bill S. 362:

114th Congress   Calendar No. 2
SENATE
==
MEISSNER STUDY

November 12, 2015

Mr. Gregory Welsh, from the Committee on Science, Technology, and Infrastructure, submitted the following:

R E P O R T

Together with
MINORITY VIEWS

The Committee on Science, Technology, and Infrastructure having considered the same, reports favorably on an original bill (S. 362) to approve the Meissner Study[1] and recommends that the bill do pass.

PURPOSE

The purpose of this measure is to approve funding for the Meissner Study.

BACKGROUND AND NEED

Although the federal government, through the mainte-nance of the country's infrastructure, promotes the stabil-ity, efficiency, and security of the US transportation and commerce, it by association also promotes and maintains the overall health of society.

Studies[2] have shown that when the infrastructure fails or is in great need of repair, the overall health of the society declines. Hospital visits increase, arrests increase, accidents increase, and the overall feeling of the city involved is one of discouragement.

This study expands the term "infrastructure" to include all aspects of life that affect the health of society. A prelimi-nary study, done in June 2013, showed that a Consciousness Generated Field Effect[3] (CGFE) could reduce crime by 24 percent. This scientific technology represents a break-through in promoting the coherence of life in society and should be studied on a broader scale.

"What nonsense," VP Locker said out loud. She was reviewing the bill so she could counter any push from inside the committee. She was counting on the operation currently in progress to help but was taking precautions on her own. She continued reading.

COMMITTEE RECOMMENDATION

The Committee on Science, Technology, and Infrastructure, in an open business session on September 8, 2015, by a majority voice vote of a quorum present, recommends that the Senate and House pass an original bill, as described herein.

"Of course it was approved by the majority liberal Democratic assholes of that committee.[12] And what are all these goddamned footnotes?" she burst out angrily. Frustrated, she decided she'd better read them and skipped ahead to the section labeled Footnotes.

FOOTNOTES

[1] In physics, the Meissner effect is a phenomenon in which a coherent state repels any negative influence. The Meissner study is an attempt to apply this technology to society as a whole. Success would set a new scientific paradigm via the use of the Consciousness Generated Field Effect.

[2] Many societal studies have been done after infrastructure failures. Three leading ones clearly document the societal effects. One report was produced after the bridge on I-40 collapsed in Webber Falls, OK, in 2002, killing 14; another after the bridge failure on I-35 in Minneapolis, MN, in 2007 that killed 35 and injured 145; and the third in 1994 when the disastrous Northridge, CA, earthquake had a death

---

12 The Committee on Science, Technology, and Infrastructure was formed in February 2010 to bring the resources of modern technology and modern science to all aspects of the infrastructure of the nation. Due to its importance, it was manned by both houses of Congress, a precedent-setting historical first.

toll of 57, with more than 5,000 injured. In each of these studies, the crime rates, reported sicknesses, and overall tensions in the cities affected increased dramatically. These studies can be requested from the Government Accountability Office.

[3] The Consciousness Generated Field Effect was first predicted in 1960 by a little-known Indian Vedic scientist and proven in a study done in 1974 on eleven cities that had 1 percent of the population practicing the technique. The crime rate decreased by 16 percent.

Why are footnotes always so damn small, Andrea thought and went back to reading where she left off.

SECTION-BY-SECTION ANALYSIS

Section one recommends a study of a city with a population of approximately one million. The analysis of a larger population would give greater credence to the results. It further recommends that two independent groups be assigned to gather and analyze the data to give further validity to the outcomes.

Apparently, some early studies have proven to be scientifically valid. So I hear, Andrea thought grudgingly. She didn't know that more than fifty such studies had been conducted.[13] That was

13 These little-known studies used sophisticated time-series intervention analysis and transfer-function analysis to minimize any trends or seasonal cycles in the data that could skew the results. These studies scientifically validated the unified field effect of consciousness. New evidence has shown that an advanced CGFE produced by as little as the square root of 1 percent of a given population could generate the same effect.

information Senator Welsh was keeping in his back pocket, to be used as necessary. To her, the studies were a bunch of crap, but she couldn't let them be distributed. She knew that the power the Republican Party held over the country depended upon the chaos the country was in, and she was secretly a Republican.

Locker skimmed through the rest of that section and continued to the next one.

COST AND BUDGETARY CONSIDERATIONS

The following estimate of the costs of this measure has been provided by the Congressional Budget Office:

MEISSNER STUDY

In June 2013, a private firm submitted an application for a presidential permit to allow it to implement a controversial program that would study the societal effects of a Consciousness Generated Field Effect on a New Mexico Native American tribe.[5]

Among other findings, this preliminary study showed a 24 percent drop in crime during the period of the Consciousness Generated Field Effect. The cost of this study was $750 per person. There were eighty individuals involved, approximately 1 percent of the total tribal population of approximately seventy-eight hundred. The total cost was $60,000. The funding for this study primarily came from private donations.

It is estimated the cost to do an expansive study as proposed by the Meissner study would be $7,500,000. This would allow the training of ten thousand individuals or 1 percent of a city with a population of one million.

Andrea skipped ahead, ignoring the footnote.

MINORITY VIEWS

Under existing law, any study must first obtain a permit from the president of the United States. In 1984,[8] the president's authority to issue such permits...

"Blah, blah, blah," VP Locker said out loud. She abruptly stopped reading and closed the bill in disgust.

CHAPTER 4

"**F**lex your ankles." Kevin was following closely behind Carolyn as she skied down an intermediate slope, talking loudly enough but without yelling so that she could hear. Most students didn't like instructors yelling at them. Besides, it was nearing lunch, and she was probably a little tired.

Kevin was back to teaching skiing. It was Saturday. He had called in sick on Friday, the day after the murder, to get his mind and body back into balance after witnessing such a tragic event, but he had to get his life back to normal—well, as normal as possible.

Kevin was doing his best to be instructive without being overbearing, but the private lesson with the couple from Los Angeles wasn't going well. Both of them, especially the woman, were set in their ways, and they weren't listening to his instructions. He was frustrated and needed a different approach.

"Carolyn, let's stop. Come over here by the side of the trail. How are you feeling?"

"My thighs are tired," Carolyn said.

"Do you know why?" Kevin asked.

"Because it's time for lunch?" Carolyn joked.

"I'll go along with that," said her husband, Glenn.

"Yes, that too." Kevin laughed. "But actually, Carolyn, it's because you're sitting back."

"What do you mean?"

"Here, let me show you." Kevin demonstrated a stance in which the skier sits, as if in a chair. "Now you do it."

Carolyn copied the move.

"How do your thighs feel?" Kevin asked.

"Like it's time for lunch. OK, I get what you're saying. It tires my thighs to have a stance like that, but how should I stand?"

Kevin demonstrated a stance in which the angles of the joints—ankles, knees, hips—were equally bent. "We call this position *stacked*. That is, I'm using my skeletal structure rather than my thighs for support. You want your hips over your feet and your knees over your toes."

"Oh." Carolyn seemed somewhat defensive, but Kevin could tell by her tone that it made sense to her.

Kevin had been emphasizing this point all morning and even demonstrated it earlier, but as with many students, it needed repeating. Alignment is important, especially in life. Kevin learned this lesson early on through considerable training. Alignment with the laws of nature is critical. It is impossible to break the laws of nature, but it is possible to resist them. Nature, driven by the force of evolution, always pushes one forward in a positive, fulfilling direction. Resisting nature feels like swimming against a current: in Kevin's case, the current of life.

When a person is less evolved, resisting nature feels like swimming against a slow-moving current. When a person is highly evolved, the resistance is strong—more like swimming against a swift current. Being highly evolved, Kevin struggled for a while before he truly understood this concept. In skiing, the same principle applies: the law of gravity wants to move you down the hill. Experienced skiers work with that force. Skiers still learning tend to resist it, and one of the most common forms of resistance is sitting back.

"Let's try something different," Kevin said. He pulled out four trail maps from his pocket. "I'm going to slide these maps into the back of your boots. What it will do is force you to have more forward lean in your ankles. May I put these in your boots?"

"I don't understand, but yeah, OK, you can do that," Carolyn said.

Kevin lifted the hems of Carolyn's ski pants over the tops of her boots.

"No funny business now," Glenn joked.

Kevin tucked in two small map booklets per boot and told Carolyn to ski. She skied down about a hundred yards and stopped.

"Did you see that?" Kevin asked Glenn.

"See what?" Glenn didn't see anything different.

They skied down to where Carolyn had stopped.

"Ah, I see that look on your face," Kevin said confidently. "What are you feeling?"

It took a few moments for Carolyn to gather her thoughts, or maybe she was hesitant to admit that Kevin was right. "My thighs didn't get nearly as tired, and my turning seemed easier."

Kevin saw recognition in her body language and said, "Your ankles were more flexed, which kept you more upright—that is, more stacked—and the added pressure on the front of your boots transferred to the front of your skis and made it easier to initiate your turns."

Carolyn gave a hesitant but clear nod of understanding. This was why Kevin taught. It gave him a wonderful sense of satisfaction and accomplishment. He wished he could be as direct in teaching his HGT knowledge, but he had to be careful about that.

"That's very cool. I can see that now," Glenn admitted. "Do I need to stand up more?"

"No, you're doing fine. Let's ski to lunch."

At the bottom of the mountain, they put their skis in one of the racks and walked toward Copper's Center Village cafeteria. It was a typical ski-area cafeteria: large, but not large enough to fit everyone. Carolyn grabbed Glenn's arm as they funneled their way through the chatter, clatter, and shuffling of people, tables, chairs, and trays. Finding a place to sit was always a challenge, but Kevin was focused. He spotted several people about to leave and hurried to claim their chairs. Carolyn and Glenn followed.

Relieved, they took off their jackets, helmets, and gloves. Carolyn and Glenn entered the food court to buy lunch. Kevin took out the sandwich he had prepared at home and watched over their belongings. Once the couple returned, Kevin did his best to start a conversation.

"You guys are from Los Angeles, right?" he asked. Outside of teaching, Kevin had little to say. His friends would sometimes make fun of him: "You don't have to be so shy." Kevin didn't consider himself to be shy; he had more reasons to be quiet than his friends could ever understand. But when teaching skiing, he stepped into a more talkative role and changed his personality. It was a challenge for him but a necessary skill for teaching.

"Actually, we live in Long Beach, which is just outside the city," Glenn said.

"Isn't that what they call the harbor region?"

"That's right. Have you been there?" Glenn asked.

"No, I wish. I read about it somewhere. It's one busy place."

"You can say that again."

They went back to eating their lunch. After several minutes of silence, Kevin felt pressured to get a conversation started again.

"How long are you here for?" he asked.

"Just three more days. We go back on Wednesday."

"Much too soon," Carolyn added.

"What do you do in Long Beach?" Kevin asked.

"We both work out of LA. I'm with the FBI, and Carolyn is a detective with the LA police," Glenn said proudly.

"Uh oh! I'd better not do anything illegal," Kevin joked. An idea popped into his head. "I'm reading this book about a guy who saw a murder take place," he said before expanding upon the fabrication. "It turns out that a high-level, important person was killed, and the killer turned out to be a policeman who was living a double life. There was a witness to the murder who got away. The dilemma is, should the witness go to the police, which most certainly would put his life in danger, try to figure out what's going on himself, or not do anything at all? I haven't read any further, so I don't know what happens, but what would you recommend if it were a real situation?"

"Sounds like what happened here the other day," Glenn pointed out.

"I know. It's spooky," Kevin said.

"The news on that certainly broke fast. Were you here that day?" Glenn asked.

"Yes, I free skied. It was a great powder day. I learned about the senator at the end of the day."

"So, anyway, back to your book. You're saying there's probably a hidden agenda somewhere, a bigger picture that could seriously put the witness's life in danger?" Carolyn asked.

"Yeah, something like that."

"Well, speaking officially, it would have to be reported. The police would want to question the witness. Unofficially, my advice would be to report it anonymously."

"Go to an outside agency would be my advice," Glenn added.

"What do you mean by 'outside agency'?"

"Well, if the character really felt his life would be in danger by reporting it to the local police, maybe he has a friend he trusts in some other law-enforcement agency. Together, they could work quietly to solve the case."

"What? I can't believe you said that," Carolyn said.

"Hey, it's fiction," Glenn said with a shrug.

"You guys are too funny." Kevin chuckled. "Anyway, I'm curious to see what happens in the book—to see if the author is in agreement with either of you."

After lunch, Carolyn caught on to ankle flexion. Glenn needed just a few minor adjustments, and the day ended on a good note, with both of them smiling and looking forward to getting into the hot tub at their lodge.

"Thanks for the great lesson, Kevin. It was expensive but turned out to be worth it. I learned a lot," Carolyn said.

"I agree. Thanks," Glenn added.

"You're welcome. Will you be coming back?"

"Boy, I'd love to bring my girlfriends here and have a girls-only vacation," Carolyn said with a smile.

"Yeah, all of you would end up drinking, not skiing," Glenn joked.

"Ha-ha." Carolyn hit him gently on the arm.

Kevin got a fifty-dollar tip. A nice tip, although instructors always hoped for a hundred-dollar tip for a private lesson. Private lessons cost upward of five hundred dollars—more than eight hundred at some ski areas. If a skier could afford that, instructors felt, they could easily afford a Benjamin. Occasionally, instructors got skunked by guests who didn't realize that instructors received an hourly wage regardless of the price of the lesson. If the guest wanted a certain instructor—a "request private"—then the instructor received time and a half, but tips were still important to an instructor's pay. Even though it wasn't what he had hoped for, Kevin was grateful for the tip.

He was also grateful for the advice he had been able to glean from them clandestinely, but he didn't yet know how he would be able to use it.

CHAPTER 5

The FBI was called in as soon as the victim was identified, and it did not take long for them to get organized. Now they had the witness to the senator's murder. At least that was what they thought.

"So, what you're telling us is that you saw someone come down the hill shortly after you heard the gunfire?" the FBI agent asked.

Owen Baker, a Copper ski instructor, was sitting in the Frisco police office surrounded by the police chief, the Summit County sheriff, and two FBI agents. It was Sunday, and he was supposed to be working, but he felt what he had to say was so important that it gave him the right to skip out.

"Yes, that's correct. I wasn't sure it was gunfire, as it was a muffled sort of sound, but it was unusual enough on a ski slope that it raised my curiosity."

Owen hadn't worked on the day of the murder. It was his day off, and it was a bluebird day that he couldn't resist. He was skiing down Windsong, the trail just to the right of Copperfield, when he heard what sounded like gunshots. A patch of trees separated the two trails. He and a few other skiers on the trail stopped after hearing the gunshots; others just kept skiing.

Not hearing anything else after a couple of minutes, the other skiers continued on. But Owen was still curious; he skied carefully through the trees on his left and entered the Copperfield trail. Down the hill, he saw what appeared to be a man skiing.

Word had spread that the authorities were looking for the witness who made the call to the ski patrol. Owen wasn't the caller, but he was at the scene and heard the shots. He thought he should at least report what he heard and saw. *An excellent excuse to skip work.*

"But you didn't see Senator Welsh lying in the snow?" the agent asked.

"I didn't even know there was a murder until it hit the news," Owen admitted. "And no, I didn't see a body. It must have been in a hollow or something. Maybe I saw a ski pole sticking up in the snow, but I'm not sure. I came out closer to the bottom of the run, and it sounded like the shooting was higher up. But yes, I did see someone skiing away about fifty yards or so below me. It looked like a man."

"Can you describe him—height, weight, the color of his jacket, anything?" an FBI agent asked.

"He appeared to be of normal height. Not short or tall, maybe somewhere around six feet. He also appeared fit, at least from the rear. You know, maybe 170 pounds? And he was making good turns. So, he was probably an advanced skier."

"Do you remember the color of his ski clothes?"

"I think he had a beige or gray jacket."

"Was it beige or gray?" the other FBI agent asked.

"I don't know. He was too far away. It was a light color. I don't remember the color of the pants," Owen said.

"Anything else? Type of skis? Markings on his ski suit? Anything at all?"

Owen thought for a moment. "There may have been some red on his jacket. I can't remember for sure. Oh, and I think his boots were green. You know, that bright fluorescent sort of green. Yeah, they were green, and he was arcing his turns, so he probably had a modern ski."

"OK. If you think of anything else—"

"Yes! He wasn't wearing a helmet—just a hat. I don't remember the color."

"Thanks. If you think of anything else, please contact the chief here," the FBI agent said. "Also, please keep this to yourself. This is an ongoing investigation."

Owen left feeling proud of himself. His ego sometimes irritated his fellow instructors. He felt he now had a way of boosting himself even more in their eyes. He would tell them just enough to make them envious while obeying the FBI's demand to keep the information to himself. Yep, he had met with *the* FBI.

CHAPTER 6

"Where have you been?" William Benn demanded of Jeff Catson, who had just walked into his office at 7:34 a.m. on Sunday, February 8. "You were supposed to report to me yesterday."

"Hey, I had to finish up my security preview assignment for the VP in Denver, and I didn't get home until late yesterday."

Benn didn't respond and waited for more.

"OK, I should have called." There was a reason he didn't call: he didn't want to.

"You left a witness."

"There were some complications," Jeff said.

"Complications? You call a witness 'complications'? This was supposed to be completely covert and untraceable. What the hell?"

"I triple-checked; the slope was empty. Somehow, I missed seeing him. He was a ski instructor," Jeff replied.

"You're a skilled combat vet, and you missed seeing him?"

Jeff stayed silent.

"I don't care who he was," Benn nearly yelled. His face was turning red. He had a strong Brooklyn accent and was known for his outbursts and for taking a "my way or the highway" approach. Although he was balding and had a middle-age belly, his height of six foot five could be intimidating.

Jeff rarely flinched, but even he felt some tension in Benn's presence.

"I want him taken care of. Is that understood?"

"Yes sir," Jeff answered.

VP Andrea Locker was entering her office when the phone rang. She had just left an early Sunday morning emergency meeting with the president and chief of staff to develop an executive response to Senator Welsh's murder.

Running to her desk and attempting to remove her coat at the same time, she nearly tripped over her trash can. She kicked it out of the way and grabbed the phone.

"Locker."

"Andrea, this is Senator Benn. We need to talk."

"No shit! I've just come from a meeting with the president. Have you seen today's *Washington Gazette*?"

"No, I haven't seen a paper yet this morning, but I read the Friday article on Welsh."

"Well, Senator Welsh made the front page this morning. The article documented his career and raised a lot of questions."

"Questions?" Benn asked, confused.

"About why he was killed. What else would they be questioning?" *You idiot!* "And there was a witness. We agreed that this activity would be off the grid. That's a complication we didn't need. If that witness can identify…Shit."

"Your phone is encrypted, yes?" Benn asked.

"Of course, you idiot." This time she said it out loud.

"Just checking," said Benn, doing his best to ignore the insult. "Jeff told me the guy came out of nowhere and then completely disappeared. But he was in a ski-school uniform, so we have a lead. I've directed Jeff to handle the situation."

"OK." Locker was starting to calm down. "At least we've taken care of the primary objective. If that study passed, we would have a major issue. Jill—Jill what's-her-name from Utah and John Moore were involved with Welsh in promoting that study. We need to get to them."

"It's Jill Hill, and I'll handle it," the senator said.

"Well, at least now that damn study will most likely be buried along with the deceased senator," Locker said.

"I agree," Benn said.

The vice-president hung up. Though the color in her cheeks was returning, she was still frustrated. She pulled and twisted strands of her blond hair. She and Senator Benn had carefully planned this event but left the killing details to Catson. She couldn't afford anything to go wrong. That would be more than embarrassing; it could put her in prison.

Locker was numb to criticism from the press and the frequent blond jokes about her. Little did her critics know the brilliance of her mind. She had an ego as large as Senator Benn's, and they often played against each other. At five foot eleven, she was no pushover physically either.

She took a deep breath and settled into the day. After clearing a few documents that required her immediate attention, she began once again looking into the status of the Meissner study—that absurd project that the now late Senator Welsh wanted commissioned.

"How can anybody in their right mind buy into that stuff?" she said out loud. The possible impact of that study was completely unacceptable to her.

Andrea Locker had earned a master's degree in public administration. Though she carried a 4.0 grade-point average, she was always more interested in promoting herself than paying attention to her classes. In her Ethics in International Relations class, she befriended and eventually seduced the young associate professor. Thinking of that A+ always made her smile.

In her senior year, she ran for the class president. After she lost the election, she claimed the young man who won had raped her. It became a she said/he said confrontation. Using a Title IX defense, she successfully had him expelled from the university. Later, he was eventually sentenced to community service. Locker still did not get the presidency, but the fact that her opponent would forever carry the stigma of being a sex offender gave her great pride.

After graduation, she took a year off and did some traveling. While visiting a girlfriend in Palo Alto, California, she checked out Stanford University, as it was her first choice for graduate school. As such, she knew a thesis was in her future. Thus, she took some time at the Stanford library researching theses and dissertations. She wanted to know the level of excellence the school required. She copied several that caught her interest for future reference.

As it turned out, Stanford didn't accept her. She wasn't happy about that, and through confident, arrogant irony, she got revenge. When it came time to present her graduate thesis at her second-choice university, it was hard for her not to smile. Her "original" research was pirated from one of the copied Stanford PhD dissertations she still had in her possession. She tweaked it to meet her thesis needs and was confident it would never be discovered—who'd search for obscure data from a dissertation done years ago clear across the country? The adrenaline that surged through her as the attending professors and guests applauded her presentation gave her one of the biggest rushes of her life. *The fools!*

She had considered going for a PhD, but several key Democratic leaders had taken notice of her and persuaded her to go into public office. With the help of her Washington mentors, she became the youngest person to hold a legislative position at the state level. Later, with several years of experience under her belt, she was elected as her district representative to Congress. Her rapid political rise was inconceivable to most, but not to her. She deserved it. In fact, she believed she should be the president.

Vice-President Locker was elected on the Democratic ticket along with President Wilson. But she was no Democrat—at least not any longer. As a House Representative from Maine, she had become disenchanted with the direction of the Democratic Party. She approached and confided in Republican Senator Benn.

Benn was at first put off. Outside pressures were threatening him. He didn't need anyone else involved, but after some additional thought, he saw potential for both of them. They worked out what they called a patriotic placement plan, or "Triple P." The goal was to put Locker into the White House so they could have greater leverage. Now, six months into her term as VP, the plan was working. She and Benn were able to refine the details of keeping the country in line with their vision of controlled chaos. Unbeknownst to Locker, this also served Benn's hidden agenda—assignments he was being forced to fulfill by others above him.

They believed the citizens of the United States were primarily ignorant and should be kept in place through the authority of their leaders.[14] Early in her career, Locker suspected that the true leaders were not the elected government officials. Instead, she sensed that the country and the economy were really controlled by an elite privileged few. These leaders were able to manipulate Congress and the Republican Party into passing bills that favored their financial status. Keeping the country in a relative state of chaos was key, so the public would need Congress to act on its behalf in an attempt to fix problems.

"Fixing" problems required bills to be passed, bills that had the backing of lobbyists, hidden money, and corporate interests—all of which were clandestinely influenced by this small, elite group. On the surface, it appeared to be a policy of smaller government. In reality, it was smaller government only as long as that government did what the elite few wanted. It was an economic, self-perpetuating circle of greed that Senator Welsh saw and to which he sought a solution. The Meissner study was

---

14 Andrea Locker's and Senator Benn's opinion of the American public was validated a year later by two political scientists from Johns Hopkins University in their book *What Washington Gets Wrong*. They interviewed the political establishment. Their conclusion: "They think Americans are stupid and should do what they are told."—Alex Thompson, "Washington's Governing Elites Think We're All Morons, a New Study Says," *Vice News*, September 30, 2016, accessed October 3, 2016, https://news.vice.com/article/washingtons-governing-elites-think-were-all-morons-a-new-study-says.

the result of those efforts, and others in his party were beginning to buy into the idea. That was when the leverage that came out of Triple P paid off.

On Locker's way up, she quickly grasped what she suspected was true: that the state of the union—the chaos that permeated the country—greatly benefited a few powerful individuals. She had no idea who they were, but Senator William Benn appeared to be one of them. He had sponsored a jobs bill that was popular among both parties in Congress. The day it passed, the Dow rose by 254 points, the highest increase of the year. This caught Locker's attention. It didn't take much research to find out which company benefited the most. A little more digging to find out who the major stockholders were, and lo and behold, there was Senator Benn.

Locker spent a couple of days digging and asking around, and a few things about Senator Benn just didn't add up. She began to suspect his background included illegal activity, but she wasn't able to uncover any specifics. In addition, she discovered several unsubstantiated rumors of sexual assault by the senator.

Interesting. He seems to have the character I'm looking for. The potential conflict of interest with the senator's stock holdings was enough to start Andrea Locker's partnership with Senator William Benn that led her to the White House.

CHAPTER 7

Jill Hill, democratic house representative from Utah, had been trying unsuccessfully to get Congress to pass a funding bill to benefit the National Park Service in her state. Utah had thirteen national parks, multiple national landmarks, monuments, and trails that had more than ten million visitors each year. Repairs and updates were badly needed just to maintain the safety of the parks. Funding for all parks nationwide had been dramatically cut by the Republican-dominated Congress, and the conditions at Utah's parks were among the worst. Jill was also trying to get funds to expand the parks.

She walked into her office Monday morning to discover a request for a private meeting with Senator Benn. *Why would he call and leave a message on a Sunday?* She wasn't happy about it. Benn was a Republican senator from New York and chairman of the Senate Finance Committee. He was a driving force behind cutting government programs and a major headache for Jill.

"Time for your meeting, ma'am," her assistant announced.

"Where's my bulletproof vest?" Jill asked.

"You'll do fine," the assistant encouraged.

"If I'm not back in an hour, please contact the Capitol Police," Jill said, only half joking. She walked down the hallway

of the Cannon House Office Building, descended to the base-
ment, and traversed the underground tunnel that connected it
to the Capitol. Along the way, she looked at the collection of
high-school students' projects from the annual Congressional
Art Competition that hung on the walls. It was a nice diversion.

Once at the Capitol, she found her way to the tunnel connection to the Russell Senate Office Building.[15] She took the
open-air subway car rather than the nearly one-thousand-foot
walkway. She had lingered too long admiring art, subcon-
sciously stalling. She tried to visualize a positive meeting but
did not have much success. Her five-foot-five, middle-aged
frame didn't help her against Benn's six-foot-five presence.
That one-foot difference was intimidating, but she didn't get
into Congress by being weak, she told herself as she exited the
subway and headed toward Benn's office.

"Good morning, Ms. Hill," one of Benn's assistants
announced as she walked into the outer office. "He's expecting
you. Please go right in."

"Ah, good morning, Jill," said Benn, rising out of his chair
with one of the phony smiles Jill hated. "Please have a seat."

Representative Hill sat silently while Benn came around to
the front of his desk to sit in the chair next to her.

"First, I want to offer my condolences for the loss of your
friend and my colleague, Senator Welsh. He was a respected
lawmaker." Benn paused. "Now, you're probably wondering

---

15 The Cannon House Office Building lies just south of the Capitol, and
the Russell Senate Office Building is just north of the Capitol Building. Both
are connected via an underground network of tunnels. It is not unusual for
members of Congress to get lost in the Capitol's massive underground system of tunnels and walkways.

why I asked you here this morning." He smiled again. "Well, I have a deal for you."

"Continue."

"You still want to fund an expansion of your state parks?"

"*Our* national parks," she replied with irritation. "What's really needed are repairs not only for the parks in my state, but also for the fifty-nine parks across the nation, which are part of the four hundred and nine national areas managed by twenty-two thousand employees of *our* park service. Your party's cost cutting has hurt every location in the nation, including the twenty-six in your state."

"A matter of opinion, but anyway, I wanted to get your opinion on a deal I'm willing to make."

"Continue."

"You and Representative Moore have been proponents of Senator Welsh's Meissner study, yes?"

"You are well aware of that." Jill was chairwoman of the Committee on Science, Technology, and Infrastructure, which was proposing the bill to fund the study. Representative John Moore was a key member of that committee.

Benn got up, strolled back to his desk, and sat down. "OK, here's the deal. I'd like you and John to kill the bill and proposed distribution of those preliminary studies. I don't want those results known, especially the new advanced techniques, programs, or whatever the hell you call them. Personally, I think it's a bunch of science fiction, but there are too many people who will fall for it, and that will have a negative effect on the finances of our country."

"You mean your own and your cronies' finances," Jill retorted.

Benn ignored her jab. "If you do this for me, and you get John to buy in, then I'll make sure you get the funding for the parks."

Jill was boiling inside.

"Look, you have virtually no chance of going forward and promoting this Meissner effect, as you call it, regardless of the outcome of that study. Without my support, you will never get the funding for your parks or get that bill passed. This is a one-time offer."

Jill entered politics to help her state, and it was a role she hoped to play since her college days, when she volunteered for several social service organizations. There was so much the government could do at so little expense. She thought she was ready for the politicking required to get things accomplished in Congress, but the surprising number of dirty deals disgusted her. Now she would have to make a lousy deal herself to get a bill passed to improve the parks in her state and in the rest of the nation. She hated it, and she hated dealing with Senator Benn. Her jaw tightened.

"OK," she said, aware that she might regret the agreement at some point. *But for the good of the whole*, she thought.

CHAPTER 8

That same day, Jeff Catson was back on a plane, flying to Denver. "What have I got myself into?" he mumbled to himself. He had just caught United Flight 1062 from Ronald Reagan Washington National Airport to arrive in Denver at 6:11 p.m. Jeff was on his way to clean up the "situation."

If that bitch Locker hadn't blackmailed me, I wouldn't be in this situation. Oh well. Just get this thing done. He settled back into his seat to get some shut-eye.

That "bitch" had been cunning enough to check out the Secret Service agents who were assigned to her. One of them was Jeff Catson. After the revelation about Senator Benn, VP Andrea Locker felt it wise to be more cautious about the people in her life. She asked for and received the background reports of each agent. She was pleased to learn their accomplishments and skill levels, the names of their spouses and kids, if they had any, where they lived, how much money they made, and, of course, their work schedules. Given her position, she was able to acquire detailed financial information as well, and this surfaced an anomaly.

It's always the money, she thought at the time. There were suspiciously large deposits into Jeff's local bank account, large enough compared with an agent's salary to raise questions. Jeff was single and an orphan, so immediate family could be ruled out as the source of the funds. Andrea looked deeper into Jeff's early background and found it to be a little sketchy. It reminded her of Senator Benn's.

Continuing her research, she discovered that the funds came from a bank in the Cayman Islands, immediately raising a red flag in her mind.[16] Unfortunately, that was all the intelligence on the account she could acquire. She couldn't discover the balance without raising suspicion. Even if she tried, she probably wouldn't get it anyway.

Sometime later, as she was again reviewing Jeff's file, she took the time to read a reprint and discussion of an old *Army Times* newspaper article about Jeff saving the lives of a family in Iraq. Another article on the page caught her eye. It described how $3.5 million had been stolen from the US Army base in Fort Carson, Colorado.

Andrea remembered that Jeff had been stationed at that base. *Was that the money in the Cayman account?* Going back through his file, she saw that he was stationed at the base at the time of the robbery. Her suspicions grew. Further research revealed that the money from the base was never recovered and that two military police officers were killed during the robbery.

---

16 The Cayman Islands has a large banking industry with over two-hundred banks generating billions of dollars for its economy. It is well known as a tax haven for both legal and illegal financial activities. An estimated $1.9 trillion of US money is stashed there.

If Jeff was responsible for that robbery and the killings, then she could use a man like him under her control. *What a boon that would be.* She devised a scheme to trap Jeff into confessing, if he was the culprit.

She asked Jeff to join her in her office and asked him about the questionable deposits into his Wells Fargo account. Jeff lied and said they were from a trust fund that a distant uncle had set up for him. When Andrea countered that he had no relatives and that she knew the money had come from a Cayman account, Jeff became noticeably nervous. He didn't have a clear explanation, and that was enough for Andrea.

She lied and told him she knew the account had been opened with $3.5 million within days of the Fort Carson robbery. She added that the bullets in the gun he so proudly carried probably matched the bullets removed from the two MPs who were killed. It would be easy for her to get a court order, she hinted.

Jeff was silent. He knew his service weapon was not the gun he used at Fort Carson. Also, the amount of the deposit was only $3.4 million and took more than a few days to set up. A technicality, but still…

He hesitated a moment, trying to find a way out of this, but if the VP could figure it out, so could the FBI. "What do you want?" Jeff finally asked her.

She had him. It was dumb luck, but she had him.

In Denver, Jeff picked up his rental car: a four-wheel drive Ford Explorer.

Jeff knew the area well from his stint at Fort Carson. He checked into his reserved room at the Days Inn near the airport. He had the beginnings of a plan, but first, he needed some food and a good night's rest. The next day, he would drive up to Copper Mountain Resort and take a ski lesson. He was on vacation, after all. At least that was his cover story.

CHAPTER 9

Secret Service Agent Jeff Catson arrived at Copper Mountain for his ski lessons. As a youth, Jeff was fortunate enough to be chosen to join a youth ski club. A former star basketball player for the Chicago Bulls, who grew up in the Chicago area where Jeff lived, formed a charitable ski club for disadvantaged children. Jeff was a perfect candidate and was quickly accepted. The group took regular bus rides to Alpine Valley, a small ski area about two hours north of Chicago. It survived mostly on man-made snow, but Jeff didn't know the difference anyway. He had caught the ski bug. While in the army, stationed at Fort Carson, he took up the sport again. He quickly advanced and was able to handle most ski-area trails.

Seeing all the instructors lined up at the lesson area triggered his memory. *He had a gray helmet.* Seven instructors were wearing gray helmets. Five were men. One seemed too small to have been the witness. That left four.

What if today was his day off? Jeff decided to take an indirect approach. He got into a class with a female instructor to see what intel he could pull out of her. Jeff knew he had good looks and figured a little flirting could loosen her up. He had to lie about his skiing ability to get into the lower-level class.

Unfortunately, he wasn't able to get information of any real use. He didn't even score a date. What he did get was a reprimand from the instructor that he should be wearing a helmet. Jeff didn't own one and didn't want to rent one. He was a combat vet, after all. He didn't need a helmet. He was also wearing his favorite sunglasses and his new ski jacket. The odds of the witness recognizing him as a student taking a ski lesson were nil, he told himself. Besides, he liked his new jacket.

Jeff showed up at lineup the next morning not even wearing a hat. He was tough. The cold didn't bother him. Besides, he wanted to annoy the female instructor even more. He succeeded at that and smiled at the disgusted look on her face. He was assigned to a different instructor that morning, but he still didn't have any luck finding out who the witness was. But to his surprise, he improved his skiing. The gray-helmeted instructor, Robert, took a video of each of his students skiing. Jeff did not want to be on camera, but everyone else in the class did. He would just ask the instructor to delete the video afterward.

They viewed the video during lunch, and Robert made comments. Jeff saw for the first time that he initiated with his upper body instead of his legs when turning left. But on his right turns, he did just the opposite—he initiated those turns by moving his legs within his hip sockets and allowed his upper body to follow. The explanation Robert gave—why his turns to the right were the correct method—made perfect sense to him. He was actually enjoying the lesson. Unfortunately, he was so intrigued by what he saw on the video that he completely forgot to ask to have it deleted. Also, he wasn't able to determine if Robert was the witness.

On his third day—this time wearing a hat—he chose another gray-helmeted male instructor. This was the top-level class, but he felt he could keep up with the group. Unfortunately, the supervisor switched the instructors at the last moment, and Jeff ended up with Robert again. He was not happy.

During the usual chitchat while riding the lift, he changed his strategy and opened up a little. He said he was a police officer. He was hoping this would get a reaction out of Robert, leading to a conversation about the shooting.

The morning provided no additional clues for Jeff, but Robert opened the lunchtime conversation with, "So, what sort of police work do you do?"

"I'm an investigator. Primarily homicides," Jeff answered, hoping to steer the conversation.

"No kidding," said Sally, another student in the class. "Did you hear about the murder that took place right here at Copper?"

"I think the whole world heard about that," Jeff said.

"No kidding," said Robert, mimicking Sally. Both of them laughed, as did several others in his class.

"Have you guys heard anything more about it?" Jeff asked Robert. "There must be some rumors floating about. Being in law enforcement, I'm curious."

"I haven't heard any rumors, but one of our instructors apparently saw something and talked to the police about it."

Damn, he talked.

"Wow," Sally said. "What did he see?" All the students turned their attention to Robert.

"Well, he won't talk about it. He said he was asked by the FBI not to say anything because it was an ongoing investigation," Robert answered.

Jeff needed to know more. "Surely you guys must have some ideas."

"Nope, we keep bugging Owen, but he won't budge," Robert said.

"Can we ski to where the murder took place?" Sally asked excitedly.

"That run has been roped off, but we can check. We can at least see the top of the run," Robert said. "Is everyone up for that?"

Jeff finished the lesson with a smile on his face. He now had the name of the witness, and the only thing he needed to do was to locate him. He recalled all the name tags the male instructors wore, and none said Owen. As it turned out, Owen was attending a PSIA clinic at another ski area, but he was at lineup the next day with a gray helmet.

His name tag said, "Owen Baker." Owen was assigned to teach a beginner class, and since all the instructors knew Jeff was more advanced, he would not be able to get into Owen's class. So, he saw no reason to stay. He feigned illness and left early. Owen went off to his lesson without recognizing the guy wearing green boots, a light-colored jacket, and no helmet who left because he wasn't feeling well.

Back in his room, Jeff was satisfied with himself. He would show up when the lessons ended and follow Owen. In the meantime, he had plenty of time to take a nap.

Ski-school lessons generally ended at 3:30 p.m. At 3:15 p.m., Jeff left his room on the third floor of the Copper One Lodge for the short five-minute walk to the lesson area. He took a seat on the outside patio of Jill's and ordered a beer. The main cafeteria at Center Village has an inside bar called Jack's. Jill's was open only on nicer days like this one. Although the temperature was in the freezing range, the sun made the dry Colorado air feel comfortable even though clouds were starting to move in.

From the patio, he had a direct view of the ski-school meeting area where the lessons ended. He watched several classes end their lessons. The ski lifts closed at 4:00 p.m., and by 4:15 p.m., Owen still had not shown up. Jeff went back into the lodge and to the ski-school office to ask where the beginner lessons ended. The woman at the desk told him they were taught and ended at West Village.

Damn. How'd I miss that? Copper Resort has three villages: East Village, Center Village, and West Village. If he had stuck around the lesson area that morning, he would have seen the snowmobile pulling a twelve-person sled to transport the beginner students to West Village after the upper classes left.

The lesson would be over, so he headed to the Edge, where he knew the ski-school locker room was located from his previous visit. He sat down in the lobby and tried to see if he could spot Owen, but without uniforms and helmets everyone looked different. He was about to give up when several people walked by, and he heard Owen's name. He quietly followed them out of the building. It took a moment, but he was able to determine which one was Owen and confirmed it was the instructor from the morning lineup. He heard them say they were headed to Endo's for a beer or two.

Jeff headed in a different direction. He killed some time walking around the village and then went to Endo's. Owen was sitting with several others whom Jeff figured were also instructors. He ordered a beer and a snack and patiently waited. A couple of hours passed before the group broke up and left the bar. A surprise snowstorm had blown in, and it was coming down hard. Owen and a friend split from the group and headed toward the bus stop. Jeff discreetly followed.

Copper Resort has two large free parking lots a short ride away from the ski hill. A free bus service runs late into the night, allowing guests to travel between the base areas and the parking lot. Owen and the other instructor seemed to enjoy the snow while they waited for the bus. Jeff waited quietly off to the side with some other people. He was also pleased about the snow; it would limit visibility.

When the bus arrived, Jeff boarded through the back side door with other passengers while Owen and his friend entered via the front. The bus was mostly empty, and Jeff took a seat by himself toward the rear, several rows behind other passengers. He spent most of his time looking down or out the window to avoid contact with anyone. At the parking lot, Owen and his friend said their good-byes and went in different directions toward their cars.

It was dark, and most skiers had left for the day. Even so, a fair number of cars were still in the lot. Jeff scoped out the scene. Owen was walking in the opposite direction from the other bus passengers and appeared to have parked a good distance away from them. Instructors had to arrive much earlier than the general public, so they usually parked toward the front of the lot. Owen's friend must have arrived late and parked farther back. Jeff decided the time was right.

He followed Owen, stopping for a moment to pretend he didn't remember where his car was. When he heard the beep from Owen's remote unlocking the door, he quickened his pace. He took off his gloves, pulled out his revolver, and fastened the silencer. Just as Owen was about to pull out, Jeff knocked on his window.

Owen lowered his window. "Can I help—?" The bullet pierced his left eye before he finished the sentence.

Jeff looked around. No one had heard the nearly silent pop in the wind. He put his gloves back on, opened the door, moved the seat lever to slide the seat back, and pushed Owen as close to the floor as possible. The job was finished.

CHAPTER 10

That same evening, Senator Benn was working late. The official 2015 legislative session for the Senate was a paltry 188 days—where the average American works 240 days—but most members of Congress work seventy hours per week. The actual legislative sessions are just a small portion of what lawmakers do.[17] The balance of their work is for constituent services: being accessible and responsive to the voting public. Thus, the work of members of Congress is never really done. Senator Benn, however, spent most of his time scheming to increase his personal power and wealth—the general public be damned.

He was tired and thinking of leaving his office to have a nice dinner when his phone rang.

"Senator Benn," he said.

"Have you talked with Jill…um…dammit. What's her last name?" VP Andrea Locker asked without announcing herself.

"Hill," Benn responded.

---

17 A legislative session is when members of Congress convene to conduct the business of lawmaking. Congressional elections are held every two years, creating a new Congress. Each new Congress sits for two sessions of one year each.

"Oh yeah. Who the hell would ever name their child Jill Hill? Anyway, have you contacted her and John Moore, the representative from Virginia?"

"Yes. Everyone is mourning the death of Gregory, at least politically, if you know what I mean. That's probably why things are moving slowly."

Locker was working late as well. She hadn't seen any news reports, nor even an in-house report, about their ruse. "And what about the claim that the murder was revenge or a terror attack? I haven't seen or heard any such rumor."

"Damn. In the mess-up over the witness, I forgot to ask Jeff about that, but I'm sure he handled it correctly," Benn said.

Although it was Locker who held the key to Jeff's black-mailed life, Benn was working out the finer details. Locker, without telling the whole story, let Benn know just enough about Catson to fit him into their plans without giving up any of her control.

"Well, I'm not sure," Locker said. "Please double-check with him. Our ruse better have worked."

Benn knew that when the VP used the word *please*, she was not being polite. That was an order to "do it or else."

"Yes, Madam Vice-President." The words left a bitter taste in his mouth. He hated being belittled, especially after helping her obtain her position. He hung up and called Jeff Catson.

Catson was sound asleep in his hotel room at Copper Mountain when his cell phone rang. He pulled himself together when he saw the caller ID.

"Yes, Bill, what do you want?"

"Did you scalp Welsh and leave the note?"

"Yes, of course."

"Then why hasn't the press reported it?"

"I don't know. Probably the FBI convinced all involved to keep quiet about it until they can piece together more of the details. But I'm also surprised it hasn't leaked anyway. I'd give it a couple more days. A lot of people were involved in getting him off the hill and to the hospital," Catson replied. "Someone is bound to leak it."

"All right, all right." Benn hesitated before saying, "I'm being pressured about it. If it doesn't hit the papers in a couple of days, I'm going to leak it myself—anonymously, of course. How's the other operation going?"

"It's taken care of. The witness said good night."

"Good to hear. Now end your so-called vacation, get back to work, and report to me when you can," Benn barked before hanging up.

"And good-bye to you too," Catson said sarcastically to the dead line.

The "ruse," as Andrea Locker called it, was to put the blame on an American Indian organization that called itself Native Rights in America. It was a radical Native American group that had been implicated in damaging police cars, mining vehicles, and other equipment its members claimed should not have been on Indian land. Though, the group's involvement in the destruction had never been proved. It was based out of Oklahoma, but it had been seen across the country wherever it felt Native American rights were being violated. The group frequently went by the acronym NRA. The feds thought it must be some kind of inside joke, although the National Rifle Association wasn't laughing.

In New Mexico, a large oil and gas company had approached a tribe for drilling rights on its reservation. They offered 5 percent of the profits from the drilling in exchange for those rights; it was an unprecedented amount. The tribe had held a half-dozen meetings, and the proposal was narrowly approved. The tribe, like most others, could use the money. Although the drilling was approved, the tribal chief was concerned about the precedent it could set. A tribal reservation is technically private land, but it maintains a close relationship with the federal government. It was this relationship that weighed heavily on the chief's mind.

For the past year, the tribe served as a pretest area for Senator Welsh's Meissner study bill. In his personal life, Senator Welsh was a spiritual person. He was not religious but felt there was more to life. In his quiet search, he stumbled upon research claiming to produce a field effect that created positivity in the environment. The effect was produced by a specific meditation technique in the Vedic tradition.[18]

This intrigued Gregory Welsh, and he had learned the technique. Soon afterward, he had discovered #HGTechnique on Twitter and become a frequent follower. Although the HGT method of meditation was not his, the information he acquired from @HGTGuide and the experience of his own meditation convinced him that the techniques could be one and the same,

---

18 *Veda* means "knowledge." In ancient times, rishis or seers, sitting in deep meditation and experiencing pure consciousness, "heard" the sounds of creation manifesting. They had sung out these sounds, which became known as the Veda. Within the structure of these sounds is the understanding of the laws of nature, the structure of creation itself. There are forty branches of the Veda that cover all areas of life.

just using different names. The knowledge he learned from @ HGTGuide further convinced him that the field-effect study was legitimate.

He decided a larger study was needed. Using his influence as a senator, he raised enough money and volunteers from the original research to conduct a more conclusive study. The New Mexico tribe was chosen as the best candidate, and the positive results they received inspired him to move forward with his Meissner study bill.

During the study, Senator Welsh developed a close relationship with the tribal chief. The chief was now hoping to use that to his advantage. Though the specifics of the drilling negotiations were private, he felt that an official government statement sanctioning the drilling would be beneficial. So he approached Senator Welsh. The senator was not thrilled about the idea. It took some convincing from both the chief and the CEO of the oil and gas company to change Welsh's mind.

He drove a bill through Congress, giving official approval for the drilling on the reservation. The bill passed with a lot of elegant legislative divination about how beneficial this would be for all parties, and everyone except the NRA was happy. The land happened to be near sacred burial grounds, and the roads that had to be built, the traffic, and the environmental impact were simply too much for the NRA. The group went against the tribe and caused major headaches.

Would the NRA commit murder to get its point across? Senator Benn and VP Locker decided to make it look like they did. They told Agent Catson to scalp Welsh and pin a note to the scalp reading, "Get off our land!" The note would be unsigned, but the implication would be clear.

That was why Jeff did not go after the witness immediately after the murder. It did not take him long to remove a small section of Gregory's scalp, but he had to be careful not to get any blood on himself. He took one of Gregory's ski poles and jammed it through both the scalp and the note and then into the snow. Why it hadn't been mentioned in the press was incomprehensible, a problem he and his accomplices had not anticipated.

CHAPTER 11

Also that same evening, Kevin was at Sheely's birthday party for Paul. It was a small gathering. Besides Paul's girlfriend, other guests included Steve Lewis, the youngest of the group at twenty-two, and Pete Ferrell, the bartender from Endo's. Pete was once a ski instructor but found he made more money from bartending. It made for long nights, yet most of his days were free for skiing. A few other instructors Kevin recognized were at the party, but he couldn't remember their names. In uniform, everyone wore name tags.

Kevin had a quiet personality and just a few close friends. He had a lot to keep to himself. The HGT tradition was private, and this caused some heartache while Kevin was growing up. Though his life had never been a struggle, it was frequently misunderstood. Fortunately, his grandfather was always there for him as his consciousness grew. After high school, he spent an uneventful four years at the University of Colorado, skipping classes more than he would like to admit to go skiing. In his third year, he was hired at Copper Mountain Resort and started instructing part time on weekends.

He spent too much time, according to his grandfather and mother, studying and practicing for his skiing certification exams and not enough time studying for his classes. By the end of the ski season during his senior year, he had passed both the level-one and level-two PSIA certifications. Somehow, he also managed to graduate with a bachelor's degree in business. He knew graduate school was in his future, but skiing called. He figured a couple of years off would do no harm. During his second season of full-time instructing, he passed the PSIA level-three exam and became fully certified. Four years to level three is a fast path, but Kevin had talent. Now, as a twenty-six-year-old in his sixth year of skiing instruction, he didn't know when he would get around to graduate school.

Even with his challenges, Kevin had always been happy. But witnessing a murder caused a deep uneasiness, which he hid as best he could. It was easiest when he was teaching because he adopted the personality of a ski coach. Outside of teaching, his worry was harder to hide. Sheely sensed this. Her intuition,[19] as

---

19 Intuition is known to be a refined level of thought. There are different levels of thought. Talking out loud is the most gross level, thinking quietly to oneself using words without speaking is more refined, and thinking using images is still more refined. Emotions are commonly called feelings. They are actually thoughts, but on a highly refined level. The finest level of thought most people experience is intuition. This is also called a feeling, but it is more of a knowingness: one just knows.

Thought is a wave form—a form of energy. This is in an energy-based universe. All creation is merely an excited state of the unified field, which is at the base of creation. Layers of energy lie one upon another, from the gross, immensely diverse levels of creation everyone is familiar with to the molecular levels and down through the more unified quantum levels, all the way to the unified field itself.

Levels of thought energy mirror levels of energy in creation. Intuition, being at a highly refined level, is thus closest to the unified field. Since the finest levels of creation are more coherent and more powerful and contain a deeper level of intelligence, one's intuition mirrors these characteristics.

Kevin was soon to find out, was truly unbounded. Besides this change in Kevin, she knew there was more to him.

Sheely, like Kevin, was taking a break. She didn't know what she wanted to do after graduating from the University of Utah. She started skiing as a child and loved it. Her first visit to Copper Mountain was during a ski vacation in Colorado. She liked her hometown resort, where she taught part-time while in school, but teaching skiing at Copper felt like the logical next step—a chance to live somewhere else and meet new people.

Sheely quickly made a group of friends within the ski school, and hosting a birthday party was her quiet way of saying thank you. The party was also a strategy for getting closer to Kevin.

They were gathered in her small living room with some overflow into her kitchen. Like many other young adults, she lived in a one-bedroom rental apartment. The kitchen appliances were functional but showed their age. The carpet and furniture had worn spots. Still, it was comfortable. She had hung some of her favorite posters to give it a homier feel.

Early that morning before work, and hurriedly after skiing, she cleaned her living room, kitchen, and bathroom. She wasn't a slob, but she didn't find it all that necessary to be neat while living alone. She didn't feel like cleaning her bedroom, so she kept the door closed. No one seemed to notice, and the conversations flowed easily.

"Hey, Kevin, how'd your private lesson go the other day?" Steve asked.

"Fine," Kevin said. "It was a bit of a struggle in the morning. Typical students, they think they're listening to you but nothing changes. The guy had pretty good technique, but the wife was sitting back. I did the old ski-maps-in-the-boot trick, and it worked. The mind-body coordination kicked in, and she finally heard what I was teaching and made the connection. So, all in all, it turned out well."

"Did you get a nice tip?"

"Reasonably good," Kevin said, "but they'll be coming back, so at least I got two more students as clients."

Sheely walked in with the birthday cake, and the singing began. Paul made his wish and blew out the candles. He got a kiss and hug from his girlfriend and Sheely. The women started passing out the cake. While filling their mouths, the friends shared stories about teaching and made the usual complaints about the supervisors. Steve and Sheely were planning to go for their next level PSIA exam and got a lot of suggestions and encouragement from the others.

Since Kevin had already passed all three exams, his advice was eagerly sought. The exams take place over three days. Day one is typically about movement analysis. In the morning, the candidates watch a video and decide what the skier is doing right and wrong. They then create a lesson plan to make improvements. In the afternoon, they do the same thing but with real skiers on the hill. On day two, the candidates must ski various maneuvers and terrain and are judged on their ability. The final day is mock teaching. The candidates are randomly assigned a task, such as teaching moguls. The candidate gets one run to go through a teaching progression using the other candidates in the group as the students.

The examiners coach the students through the level-one exam, if necessary. They want everyone to pass. Sheely, like

Kevin, passed her level-one exam at her local resort while in school. Level two was significantly harder, and not everyone passed. The level-three exam was impossible for many of the candidates. A level-three instructor would be qualified to teach anyone at any level, anywhere on the mountain.

As the party wound down, Kevin found himself sitting off to one side chatting with Sheely. He didn't pay much attention to her over the few months he had known her, but he did take silent notice of her looks. Tonight, however, he was sensing her warm affection and her special personality—her mind had a unique feel to it that he hadn't noticed before.

"OK, Kevin. I know there's something on your mind. You've been different these past few days," Sheely asserted. "What's up with you?"

Kevin fell silent. He wanted to tell her. Hell, he wanted to tell someone—anyone—but how? He was even beginning to doubt what he had seen. How could it be possible? A double-crossing police officer shooting a senator?

"Kevin, you can trust me," Sheely coaxed.

Kevin remained silent. Sheely bent in and kissed his cheek, and then she got up and walked away. Kevin, awakened from his internal confusion by the kiss, got up and followed her.

"Sheely, I need some time," he said. "I promise I'll tell you. I need a few more days."

CHAPTER 12

It wasn't until late afternoon the next day that Owen's body was discovered. It was Saturday, Valentine's Day. The overnight snow prevented people parked next to his car from seeing through the windows, even if they had the notion of doing so. After the day warmed up and the snow melted, a skier walking back to his car that afternoon passed Owen's car and noticed a body bent over in the front seat. That seemed odd. The skier stopped to see if the person in the car was all right and then saw what appeared to be blood splattered on the seat.

It took only a few minutes for Copper Mountain security to arrive after the skier's 911 call and about fifteen minutes for the Frisco police to arrive. But it wasn't until the next morning that the ski-school instructors heard the news.

"Morning, everyone." Sheely beamed at the small crowd in the lounge area of the locker room. No one seemed pleased by her enthusiasm. "What? Didn't you guys have a nice Valentine's Day?"

"You haven't heard?" one of the instructors asked.

"Heard what?"

"Owen was shot in the parking lot yesterday."

"You're serious?" Sheely gasped.

"Dead serious, shot dead. Not a nice Valentine's Day present."

No one felt like working, and there was a tense silence at the lesson lineup. No one knew what to say. Sheely wanted to talk to Kevin, but he had left on a private lesson. Steve finally broke the silence.

"I can't believe it. This is horrible."

"I know," Paul said. "Do you think…God, I hope not."

"What?" Sheely asked.

"What if his killing was because he saw the murder of Senator Benn and went to the police?"

"Do you really think that's possible?" Sheely asked anxiously.

"How could the killer possibly know that?" Steve wondered.

"Well, Owen wasn't exactly quiet about it. He didn't tell us exactly what he saw, but he told everyone that he saw something. So who knows who else he told?" Paul said.

The association of the two killings didn't come together for Kevin until the end of the day. Back in the locker room, Robert approached.

"Hey, Kevin, would you look at this video I took the other day? There was a lady in my class whose skiing I could never get to change."

"Sure," Kevin said, "let me see it." While watching the video of the skiers, he saw that one was wearing a light-colored jacket with red stripes on the sleeves. He paused the video, staring. "Is that the guy who kept bouncing between instructors that all of you were talking about? Who is that guy?"

"I think his name was Joe or John. I'd have to look at my class list to be sure," Robert said. "He said he was some sort of cop and investigated murders."

The word "cop" was what brought it together for Kevin. "Did you ever talk about the senator being shot?"

"Yeah, we all got into a conversation about it at lunch. They wanted to ski on the run where he was killed. Sick, if you ask me," Robert said.

"Did Owen's name ever come up?"

"I can't remember, but the cop guy was curious about the murder. He wanted to know if we had heard any rumors."

"What did you tell him?"

"Well, I did mention that an instructor saw something, but I don't think I mentioned Owen by name. Why?"

"Oh, just curious about how the public is reacting here at Copper," said Kevin, not wanting to reveal his intentions. "Can you send me that video, and I'll look at it tonight and get back to you tomorrow?"

"Sure. You don't want to do it now?" Robert asked, surprised.

"Sorry, Robert, I really have to go. Send me the video. I promise I'll look at it." Kevin strode out of the locker room and into the supervisors' room.

"Mary, I'd like to look at my class list from the other day. I can't find my copy, and I want to write down the names," Kevin said.

"Sure, the lists are over there."

Kevin went through the lists one by one until he found Robert's. *Nope, not this one*, he thought. *Here...here's the right one. Joe. Joe Smith from Texas. That's surely a fake name and of course no phone number. Shit, I bet that's the guy.*

That evening, Kevin pulled up his e-mail account and downloaded the video Robert had sent him. He viewed it several times before pausing the video and cropping out the best image of "Joe Smith" from Texas. "Yep, that's him," he said out loud. It was definitely the guy he'd seen in the lobby of the Edge. He was skiing in sunglasses, so his face was not as hidden as it would have been if he were wearing goggles. He also wasn't wearing a helmet or even a hat, which would have made recognition even harder.

This might give someone a decent chance of recognizing him. But who? The police could probably find out, but he wasn't sure he could trust going to them after what had happened to Owen. He didn't want to be another casualty. Kevin closed his eyes and retreated into silence. From the inner experience of the Holy Grail, he knew the right answer would come.

CHAPTER 13

Senator Benn's cell phone rang. "Hello, this is Bill."

"Hello, Senator Benn."

Benn went silent.

"You know who I am, yes?"

"Yes," said Benn.

"Then you know what I want."

"Yes."

"Get it done soon, or you will be joining your colleague, Senator Welsh. Understood?"

"Yes," Benn managed.

"Good. Oh, and by the way, good job with Welsh."

The phone line went dead.

A long time before William Benn became a senator, but while he was rising in the ranks of public service, he was heavily involved in gambling—and not the legal type. Over time, he owed a lot of money.

Benn grew up in the rough Vinegar Hill neighborhood of Brooklyn. Vinegar Hill is known to have one of the highest violent crime rates of all five New York City boroughs. He avoided gang activity but was by no means an honorable citizen. He used his street smarts to work his way through local politics. Unfortunately, he had a hidden gambling habit that came close to destroying his political ambitions and perhaps even his life, but luck had intervened.

He was approached by the underground boss of an influential criminal organization that controlled much of the East Coast. They made him an offer he couldn't refuse. The FBI called this group the East Coast Criminals for lack of a better name, or ECC for short. The ECC had more than one politician in its control and had been watching William Benn. Benn was a brash, natural leader who usually managed to get his way. This had not gone unnoticed, and the ECC felt Benn's financial status gave them the green light to approach him.

"We want to make you a US congressman," the boss explained. "Your job will be to pass any bills we ask you to, and in exchange, we will forgive your debt...and let you live."

With the organization's funds and influence, Benn won the next state election and became the Republican representative from his district. Benn proved to be successful in getting legislation that benefited his secret boss passed at the state level. Eventually, he ran for the US House of Representatives and won easily with the clandestine backing of the ECC. It took time to gain influence as a congressman, but over the years, Benn had managed to get bills passed that seemed honest on the surface but put money into the ECC's pockets. After three terms in the House, he won his state's Senate seat, again with the backing of the ECC, but this time through a super PAC that it controlled.[20] He soon became one of the more influential US senators.

Of course, Benn's so-called debt was never really forgiven, but it took him years to realize it. He was given commissions on financial gains that the ECC reaped from legislation he was able to pass, so life was comfortable. But now, he was getting tired of the pressure.

He had been asked to use his influence as a senior senator to pass a bill that would fund the development of a laser weapon. Benn knew of only one company that could develop such a weapon, and he knew the owners had ECC connections. That wasn't the problem. He had no scruples when it came to corruption and murder to get what he wanted for himself and his country, but he did not like the idea of US weapons getting into the hands of enemy foreign states. That, he felt, was exactly what would happen if this bill went through Congress with the ECC involvement, so he was stalling.

Senator Benn hung up the phone, opened his cabinet, and poured a stiff drink.

Byron Pierce was having a drink as well, in celebration. He was a reporter for the *Summit Dispatch*, a local newspaper for Summit County, and had just uncovered the year's best story.

---

20 Political action committees (PACs) are organizations that pool together contributions and donate use of those funds to campaign for or against a candidate. They are allowed to raise unlimited funds but cannot work directly with a party or candidate.

Owen's body was brought to the hospital at the Summit Medical Center in Frisco. A nurse at the hospital was a friend of Owen's and was so upset that she called her friend Byron the next morning. She needed to talk to someone. During the conversation about Owen, the nurse also told him about the scalping of Senator Welsh.

"You saw it?" Byron asked. As a reporter, he wanted confirmation.

"Yes. I work in the emergency room, as you know. When the body was brought in, it was covered. When it was uncovered to start the examination, well…you should have seen everyone's faces."

"Wow!"

"The FBI asked us not to talk about it, but I think people need to know what happened. It's scary."

After the nurse calmed down enough for Byron to end the conversation, he hurried to his computer to write the lead article for the paper. He had put two and two together and now believed the murders were connected. And the scalping—well, that was icing on the cake.

What was that about? he wondered. He picked up his cell phone and called his PI friend, Russell Kelly, in Boston.

"Russell Investigations, how can I help you?"

"Hey, Russell, it's Byron."

"Byron, hi! Nice surprise, hearing from you. How's that mountain life of yours? Oh, and by the way, do you have any news on Senator Welsh's murder? That happened in your neck of the woods, right?"

"Well, as a matter of fact, that's why I'm calling."

"Cool! Give me the scoop."

"OK, you probably didn't hear this, but a local ski instructor was murdered a couple days ago," Byron said.

"No kidding."

"No kidding. A nurse friend of mine at the hospital called me all upset because she knew the guy. She also told me she was there when the senator was brought in. He had not only been shot twice, but also was scalped."

"Scalped?"

"Yes, scalped. She said the FBI told everyone not to mention it, but she's scared. This is a small town. She felt people needed to know." Byron paused. "Anyway, as you probably know, there was an unidentified witness to the shooting. I'm wondering if the murdered ski instructor was that witness. I'm going to do some snooping around at the mountain, but, more important, do you have any thoughts on the scalping? I mean, he was a senator after all. There has to be some connection, some political statement or something attached to that. Don't you think?"

"I wouldn't be surprised," Russell said.

"You're much more connected than I am. I'm just a small-town local reporter," said Byron, feigning humility. "Can you use your investigative skills and contacts to piece together something? Confidentially, of course, and let me know?"

"You bet I will. Give me a few days."

Byron went back to his computer to continue writing his story. He got a good start but put it on hold until he heard back from Russell. He also wanted to do his own research on Senator Welsh. He wanted all his facts in a row before presenting the story to his editor.

CHAPTER 14

S heely's kiss awakened Kevin's instincts, and he decided to ask her out. That was a new feeling for him. He was happy and busy with his life and had just never got around to dating. Yet, there was just something about Sheely. He knew they both had Tuesday off from teaching, so he asked her, casually, if she'd like to ski with him that day.

It had been an eventful three-day weekend. On Friday, Owen was killed, Saturday was Valentine's Day, Sunday was when everyone learned about Owen's death, and Monday was President's Day. Just a week earlier, a senator was killed in front of Kevin's eyes. They deserved some free skiing time.

Kevin offered to help Sheely prepare for her level-two PSIA exam. To him, it would seem more of a friendly get-together than a formal date. Sheely, on the other hand, took it as a Fat Tuesday date. Kevin showed up in the locker room with Mardi Gras beads around his neck. He wanted to give some to Sheely, but she showed up with beads too. They both smiled and exchanged a few strands. Wearing beads outside their jackets was a Fat Tuesday tradition among instructors.

As they skied the morning together, Kevin occasionally gave Sheely a tip or demonstrated what the PSIA examiners wanted to see. Sheely was a good skier and quick learner, but Kevin sensed when she had had enough.

"Come, follow me. I'm going to show you a trail few people know about," Kevin said.

They headed to the black-diamond run named Far East. About fifty yards down, Kevin ducked into the woods on the right.

"What are you doing?" Sheely asked.

"Follow me."

She hesitated but followed him down a narrow path through the trees. And there it was.

"What's that?" she asked.

"That's a smoke shack."

"A what?"

"It's where people sneak away to smoke a joint or two."

Sheely pushed forward and ducked her head inside to take a look. It was the remains of what might have been a cabin at one time but was now mostly an open-air hangout.

"Yuck, creepy."

"Yep."

Kevin let Sheely check out the site and then said, "We'll ski down this way." He pointed down a narrow trail.

"You're kidding."

"It was cut for a power line or something, but it's quite skiable."

"Isn't this out of bounds?"

"We don't want to get caught."

"How'd you know about this?"

"Another instructor showed me a couple of years ago. Come on, follow me. We go a hundred yards or so and then cut back to Far East."

It was a little tricky for Sheely, but she made it. They skied to the bottom of Far East and rode the Alpine lift back up, cut across to the Excelerator lift, and headed to do some bumps on the Mine Dump trail. Sheely decided it was her time to show off a little. She took off from the top side of one mogul and landed on the down side of another about eight moguls away with a little extra height of air in between.

Kevin stared. He wasn't sure exactly how many moguls she cleared because he couldn't believe what he just saw.

"That's not possible," Kevin said, though he'd done it many times. It defied the known laws of gravity to go that far and that high, given the physics of that jump, unless...

"How'd you do that?" Kevin asked at the bottom of the run.

"Do what?" Sheely responded innocently.

"You know what I'm talking about."

Sheely smiled and said, "You know how I did it."

There was a long pause while they studied each other's eyes through their goggles.

"No way," Kevin said.

"Yes way," Sheely teased.

Kevin lifted his goggles off his face to get a better view. Sheely did the same. Again, they silently studied each other.

"I know who you are," Sheely said. Her strong intuition had kicked in. "You can perform some of Patanjali's yoga sutras."[21]

---

21 Patanjali was an Indian seer who lived circa 400 CE, although there is controversy about that. Other documentation shows that he could have lived circa the fourth century BCE. He is famous for his yoga sutras, which are 196 sutras or aphorisms in four chapters, which describe the essence of his eight limbs of yoga. They describe the experience of unity (yoga), which is the complete settling of the mind, and the special abilities that can come with it. Kevin knew the same experience through the Holy Grail technique.

"Who's Patanjali?" Kevin asked.

That startled Sheely. "You don't know who Patanjali is?"

"No, should I?"

Sheely shook her head in disbelief.

"OK, do you know what the Holy Grail is?" Kevin countered.

That cinched it for Sheely, "You know the Holy Grail technique, but you don't know Patanjali? That's sad." She laughed but then became serious. "Kevin, I'm from that line, the Knights Templar Holy Grail line. Just like you."

Kevin took a deep breath. His eyes became moist as they locked on to hers. Sheely smiled broadly.

"I always knew there had to be others," Kevin quietly responded, and they hugged.

It was a little early for lunch, but the moment was right to take a break. They skied to Solitude Station, the cafeteria restaurant at the top of the American Eagle lift. Since the long weekend was over, plenty of tables were available. They took one in the back corner of the lower level and removed their helmets, coats, and gloves before getting some water. They had agreed ahead of time to pack a lunch.

They ate quietly, occasionally looked at each other and smiled, and sometimes laughed. Kevin finally said, "I have something I need some help with."

Sheely looked up.

"You know the murder of that senator?"

Sheely nodded. "Yes."

"Well, I was the witness."

"What about Owen?"

"I don't know. He may have seen something, or maybe he made it up, but no one else was there at the time except for the killer and the senator," Kevin said. "After I saw what happened, the killer pointed his gun at me, and I immediately skied into the woods and became invisible."[22]

"You can become invisible?"

---

22 Chapter 3 of Patanjali's yoga sutras (titled *Vibhūti-Pāda*) contains fifty-six sutras that describe special abilities.

Sutra 21 states, "Through saṃyama on the form of the body and preventing manifestation through the eyes, invisibility is gained." This explains how Kevin was able to disappear.

Sutra 43 states, "Through saṃyama on the relationship between the body and the ether and the contemplation of the lightness of cotton fiber one can move through the air." Sheely had just demonstrated that with her brief levitation in the moguls.

Modern physics has proved that the laws of nature are not absolute. They are statistical laws, "approximate laws [that] depend on the probable occurrence of many microscopic events" according to a Kilby-award-winning physicist. If one can alter the "microscopic events" at the Planck scale of life, the level of the unified field, one could affect the outcome at the surface level of life.

Consider gravity. Beyond Newton's and Einstein's understandings of gravity is quantum gravity. At this level of life, which is ten million, million, million times smaller than the nucleus of an atom (Planck scale), a small variation can have a dramatic effect on the surface level of life.

One who can experience pure consciousness (which is the unified field) and introduce an intention or desire at this level (which is the source of all the laws of nature) can statistically change the shape of the gravitational field at that quantum mechanical level and produce a new, coherent direction that allows gravity at the surface level of life to produce an upward pull.

Historically, more than four hundred individuals have been credited with the ability to levitate, including Milarepa (eleventh century) from Tibet, Hu San Gong (c. 156–140 BCE) from Asia, "clever men" from Australia, Saint Joseph of Cupertino (1603–1663) from Europe, Rabi'a al-Adawiyya al-Qaysiyya (c. 717–801 CE) from the Middle East, native North Americans, and Indian sages.

Modern physics has demonstrated levitation through the use of superconductors and the Meissner effect. Andrew Z. Jones, "What is Quantum Levitation (and How Does It Work)?," *About Education*, accessed November 20, 2016, http://physics.about.com/od/quantumphysics/f/QuantumLevitation.htm.

"Yes. You can't?"

"Apparently my ancestors could, but the knowledge got lost somewhere along the line. Anyway, you were lucky to get away." Sheely paused. "I knew something else was going on with you."

"I'm really worried about going to the police because of what happened to Owen. I believe the guy who killed Owen also killed the senator. He killed Owen because he thought Owen was me, the witness," Kevin speculated. "Do you remember that guy who kept taking lessons a few days ago with different instructors?"

"Yeah, I think I remember him," Sheely said.

"Well, he told Robert he was a detective. Robert took a video of his class, and he gave it to me."

"So…" Sheely was somewhat confused.

"Oh, sorry, I'm getting ahead of myself," Kevin said. "Let me back up. After I managed to get away safely, I went back to the locker room. I saw you there, if you remember. Anyway, after putting everything away, I went into the lobby, and there was a large commotion. Were you there?"

"No, I left through the locker room's back door."

"There were several police officers talking to Tom, our director, some ski patrollers, and I think some FBI agents, or at least I heard FBI mentioned. Then this guy showed up wearing a jacket that matched the one I saw on the guy who shot the senator. It was a light-colored jacket with red stripes on the sleeves. There was also heavy, dark energy about him. I'm almost a hundred percent sure he's the killer. He walked by me and up to the group and showed a badge. He was a cop."

"A cop!" Sheely was shocked.

"Apparently," Kevin said. They sat in silence for a moment before Kevin continued. "Robert had asked me for some advice on a student he was having some difficulty with. He had taken a video of the class and showed it to me. In the video, I saw there was a guy wearing that same jacket with the red stripes. It looked like the same guy I saw in the lobby. I asked him to send me the video, and I'd get back to him. At home, when I was able to take a closer look, it definitely was him.

"I had been teaching privates all week, so I was never at lineup when he was there, or I would have noticed him. I think Robert innocently told him about Owen when they had a discussion about the murder at lunch. This guy must have assumed Owen was me—that is, the witness he saw."

"That's horrible." Sheely barely got the words out. "Why do you think I can help?"

"I don't know. But now that I know who you really are," Kevin replied with a big smile, "maybe we can come up with something together."

"Can I see the video?" Sheely asked.

"I actually cropped out his picture, so I can e-mail it to you. Why?" Kevin asked.

"Well, I know a guy who might be able to help. He lives in Washington, DC, and I have this feeling he has connections."

"But how do you know him? I'm very leery about telling anyone."

"I used to date him," Sheely said shyly.

"So you had a boyfriend?" Kevin joked.

"Ha-ha. Yes, he was my boyfriend. Anyway, his dad was the head of Homeland Security a few years back."

"You're kidding!"

"No, seriously, his father was the secretary of the Department of Homeland Security."

"Wow, I'm impressed. So this ex-boyfriend of yours does what?"

"We've stayed in touch. He usually calls me on my birthday, and I get a Christmas card when he remembers," Sheely said.

"And?"

"And, he's told me that he handles investments, but I think he does something else."

"What? Like CIA? Did he follow in his father's footsteps?"

"Like, I don't know. I just sense something and, anyway, because of his dad, he probably has connections or connections to connections. So I think he may be able to help."

"You think he may somehow be able to find out who this guy is from the picture?" Kevin asked hopefully.

"I don't know, but it's worth a shot," Sheely said. "I'll make up some story, so he'll have no idea of our real reason for asking."

They finished eating, cleaned up their table, and went back to skiing. In the locker room at the end of the day, Kevin went to find Robert. After skiing the other day, he had pointed out a few ski and body-performance issues with Robert's student and given him some suggestions. Skiing with Sheely today gave Kevin some additional ideas that he wanted to pass on to him.

CHAPTER 15

That evening, Kevin sent Sheely the photo of the suspected killer and paced around his small condo for a few minutes.

"I've got to get my mind off this," he said to no one in particular. He went back to his computer and logged into his Twitter account. Kevin felt his knowledge of the Holy Grail was so valuable that he had to tell people about it. The few times he had attempted to explain the knowledge to his friends—in a general way—he was surprised at how little interest it generated. Nevertheless, spreading this knowledge was important to him, so he started an anonymous Twitter account using the hashtag #HGTechnique. Of course, he did so unbeknownst to his grandfather. This knowledge, after all, was not to be given out to just anyone, according to the tradition,[23] and many times his grandfather had to remind him of this. He would quote Jesus from Matthew 13:11–13: "The reason I speak to them

---

23 This was also true of the Vedic knowledge of Patanjali. The knowledge of pure consciousness was kept in the deep forests and mountains of India; it was passed down only through generations of master-disciple relationships. It wasn't until the late twentieth century that the correct understanding of how to experience pure consciousness was made available to the general public.

in parables is that 'seeing they do not perceive, and hearing they do not listen, nor do they understand.' " Then he would explain to Kevin, "Even the parables were misunderstood, and they are still misunderstood today. It's useless and potentially dangerous to discuss this knowledge."

Kevin understood that, especially when it came to the special abilities. Some could think those were the work of the devil, but surely not meditation. He believed meditation and the knowledge of pure consciousness could benefit everyone. His research showed him that even other traditions believed true meditation was important. He had stumbled upon the following quotes in the Jewish tradition:

> You should know that many great, famous saints said that they only reached their high level through this practice of meditation. If you have wisdom, you will understand the importance of this practice.[24]

> The root of everything is meditation. It is a very great and lofty principle making a person worthy.[25]

What fascinated him, even more, was discovering that Native Americans also knew of the benefits of pure consciousness and understood they were universal. He loved this quote:

> The first peace, which is most important, is that which comes from within the souls of people when they realize

---

24 Rabbi Nachman (1772–1810).
25 Rabbi Chaim Yosef David Azzuli (1724–1806).

their relationship, their oneness with the universe and all its powers, and when they realize that at the center of the universe dwells the great spirit, and that this center is really everywhere—it is within each of us.[26]

Kevin would keep trying to teach it. At last count, @HGTGuide had 137 followers on Twitter. Kevin wanted to be as incognito as possible. He would give out points of knowledge about consciousness, which his followers apparently found intriguing. Though he was pretty sure most did not understand the significance of his tweets, he was happy to have any followers. He read a response:

Phil M @pjsxk108 · 5h
@HGTGuide Enjoyed your last tweet #HGTechnique!

He tweeted Phil back:

Holy Grail Technique @HGTGuide · now @
pjsxk108 Guess what? I found another highly skilled practitioner. A beautiful female.

He also had set up a Facebook page for friends and family, but he didn't do much with it. He preferred Twitter; he could reach more people, and he didn't have to use his name. Phil sent another message:

Phil M @pjsxk108 · 2m
Kissed her yet? #HGTechnique @HGTGuide

---

26 Black Elk, Sioux holy man (1863–1950).

Ha-ha. That was fast, Kevin thought. He read some more:

Ken Paul @KenMD51 · 2h
RT @SagesScientists @HGTGuide
Our daily inspiration! #Consciousness

He figured Ken must be a doctor, but he had never tried to find out what kind. A notification came:

Jill Spencer @jillspencer108 · 3m
I'm jealous! @HGTGuide #HGTechnique

Jill Spencer was an avid tweeter and, from time to time, indicated a romantic interest in @HGTGuide. Kevin never responded to her comments, but he found it interesting that she and several others of his followers used *108* in their user names.[27] *Were they HGT practitioners?*

Kevin was surprised by the people who started following him. #Consciousness brought in several new followers every few months when curious users saw his tweets. Kevin was hoping to see a tweet from @SenW1937. There was nothing, so he sent a message:

Holy Grail Technique @HGTGuide · now
@SenW1937 Missing your tweets.

---

27 The number 108 is considered sacred by several Eastern religions, including Hinduism, Buddhism, and Jainism, and also in yoga- and dharma-based practices. In the HGT tradition, it represented the number of Knights Templar who escaped the persecution of the king of France.

Kevin had tweeted "Missing your tweets" more than once. @ SenW1937 always had interesting points of view on how consciousness research could help government. @SenW1937 also often asked probing questions about consciousness, which Kevin enjoyed answering.

He got retweets from #Consciousness and #Meditation that his followers would tweet about, but Kevin never followed these hashtags with any real interest. He already knew the technique. Even so, he was frequently asked to comment on them, and occasionally he did. He read some more messages.

Joe Celler @jceller108 · 4h
RT How do I learn #HGTechnique? @HGTGuide #Meditation

Pam Anners @pamanners · 6h
@jceller108 I don't know about #HGTechnique but contact @TMmeditation #Consciousness

"Enough." There were more tweets, but he had something else on his mind. He typed *Patanjali* into the search field, but Twitter did not have much to offer—just some rantings and product offerings. He logged off Twitter and typed the name into the browser search field. Google produced a list of results, and he clicked on the Wikipedia entry.

He didn't get much information from that either, other than the fact that there could have been multiple people by that name, but there were several mentions of the Yoga Sutras. He clicked on one of those links.

Ah, considered to be the foundation of yoga. Kevin finally understood. He skimmed through it and took notice of a couple of statements. He read this one several times:

> Samādhi is oneness with the subject of meditation. There is no distinction, during the eighth limb of yoga, between the actor of meditation, the act of meditation, and the subject of meditation. Samādhi is that spiritual state when one's mind is so absorbed in whatever it is contemplating on, that the mind loses the sense of its own identity. The thinker, the thought process, and the thought fuse with the subject of thought. There is only oneness, *samādhi.*[28]

Kevin felt *samādhi* must be the experience of pure consciousness—what he experienced. He continued reading:

> Vibhuti Pada (56 sutras). Vibhuti is the Sanskrit word for "power" or "manifestation." "Supra-normal powers" (Sanskrit: *siddhi*) are acquired by the practice of yoga. Combined simultaneous practice of Dhāraṇā, Dhyana, and Samādhi is referred to as Saṃyama and is considered a tool of achieving various perfections, or Siddhis. The temptation of these powers should be avoided, and the attention should be fixed only on liberation. The purpose of using Samādhi is not to gain siddhis but to achieve Kaivalya. Siddhis are but distractions from Kaivalya and are to be discouraged. Siddhis are but maya, or illusion.[29]

---

28 See *Wikipedia*, "Yoga Sutras of Patanjali," last modified November 27, 2016, https://en.wikipedia.org/wiki/Yoga_Sutras_of_Patanjali, sections 2–2.9.
29 Ibid., 2–2.0.

Further on, kaivalya was defined as emancipation or liberation from the relative aspects of life. Kevin took this to mean the experience of HGT, and again, he immediately recognized this practice. He didn't understand the terminology used, but the result was unmistakable. Siddhis seemed to be what he knew as special abilities. He knew that these abilities were used primarily to enhance and further develop the state of HGT. He knew this from his own experience and from his grandfather's teachings, but he disagreed that they were distractions. They were fun!

Meanwhile, Sheely was on her computer as well. She was stalling. She was debating how to tell her friend Todd about the photo she had received from Kevin. It was definitely the guy she remembered from morning-lesson lineups. The picture wasn't the best for a facial-recognition program, which was what she hoped Todd would be able to use, but it was all they had. She had yet to tell Kevin, but through the ancestral Holy Grail technique, she had developed the advanced ability to gain knowledge of another's mind.[30] In her family history, it was mainly the women who possessed nervous systems refined enough to live the Holy Grail and pass on its secrets. Her dad had been an exception, and when he died her aunt became her mentor.

Auntie was what Sheely called her. She wanted to call her *Auntie Blue* or *Auntie Bright* or *Auntie Eyes*, but none of those did her justice, and they also sounded sort of silly, so she just called her *Auntie*. Auntie was a rare, enlightened being. Sheely

---

30 Patanjali described this ability in his aphorism 19.

loved to look into her clear, bright blue eyes. It was like looking into the universe.

Auntie had the ancient knowledge of the special abilities that the inner group of Knights Templar had kept so closely guarded. Unfortunately, over time, many of the techniques to develop those abilities had either been lost or distorted. It is also believed that these distant keepers of the knowledge deliberately promoted misunderstandings and wrong techniques to further hide the truth from the undeserving.

Auntie was taught the essence of many of those techniques by her mother, but only a few of them had worked. What Auntie did was make the connection to the ancient Vedic knowledge of India, and in particular, the knowledge Patanjali had so beautifully articulated in his aphorisms. With her background, knowledge, and experience, she was able to grasp what Patanjali meant by the technique of saṃyama. That understanding corrected the distortions that history had inserted into some of the original techniques of the Knights Templar.

Using this insight, Auntie mastered several special abilities from her tradition and passed those on to her niece. One of them was the ability to gain knowledge of another's mind. That was how Sheely knew there was more to Kevin than he let on; she sensed something special about his mind. It was also how she knew, beyond the obvious changes in his behavior, something was bothering him. This ability did not allow her to know the content of a person's mind, only the feeling of it. Her ex-boyfriend's mind had a mysterious, clandestine, adventurous feel, and also a darkness. That led her to believe he was, in her words, "some sort of secret agent spy guy."

It took Sheely a while to find Todd's phone number. She had his e-mail address, but his phone number was not in her contacts folder. She finally found it in her snail-mail address book, which was buried at the bottom of one of the storage boxes piled up in her closet.

Her one-bedroom apartment had limited space. Most non-essential things were packed away in boxes. Like Kevin, she needed to have a place to herself to keep her advanced Holy Grail practices secret. The expense stretched her budget, but her family helped out when necessary. Over the years, all the HGT families gained the support of nature,[31] and financial needs were always met.

She called Todd's number. She was a little nervous and was halfway hoping he wouldn't answer, but he did.

"Hello."

---

31 Jesus's Sermon on the Mount sums up the meaning of "support of nature: "Therefore I say unto you, take no thought for your life, what ye shall eat, or what ye shall drink; nor yet for your body, what ye shall put on. Is not the life more than meat, and the body than raiment? Behold the fowls of the air: for they sow not, neither do they reap, nor gather into barns; yet your heavenly Father feedeth them. Are ye not much better than they? Which of you by taking thought can add one cubit unto his stature?

"And why take ye thought for raiment? Consider the lilies of the field, how they grow; they toil not, neither do they spin: And yet I say unto you, that even Solomon in all his glory was not arrayed like one of these. Wherefore, if God so clothe the grass of the field, which today is, and tomorrow is cast into the oven, shall he not much more clothe you, O ye of little faith? Therefore take no thought, saying, 'What shall we eat?' or, 'What shall we drink?' or, 'Wherewithal shall we be clothed?' (For after all these things do the Gentiles seek:) for your heavenly Father knoweth that ye have need of all these things. But seek ye first the kingdom of God, and his righteousness; and all these things shall be added unto you."—Matthew 6:25–33, King James Bible.

Kevin knew the kingdom of God is the inner HGT experience of pure consciousness. Once that is established, support of nature is spontaneous.

"Hi, Todd. It's Sheely Shannon."

"Sheely! What a surprise! How are you? Aren't you in Colorado now? Still teaching skiing?"

"Yes, yes, and I'm good," Sheely said. "How are things in DC?"

"Same as always. Busy and full of political intrigue and nonsense, which makes the financial markets go crazy and in turn makes me go crazy," Todd said with a laugh.

"Todd, I have a favor to ask," Sheely said cautiously.

"Shoot."

"A friend of mine has a picture of a guy he believes to be a cop of some sort. He wouldn't give me details, but he said it was very important to find out who this guy is."

"What can I do?"

"Todd, I know that you say you're some sort of financial analyst, but I think you do more than that, and even if you don't, you know people with connections."

Todd remained silent for a moment. "Sheely, I'm just an analyst."

"Todd, this is really important. I promised my friend I wouldn't say anything, but…it has to do with something that has been going on out here."

"Welsh's murder?"

"I'm…I'm, um…Todd, if you can do anything to help…"

Todd was silent.

"Todd?" Sheely said softly.

"Send me the photo, but I can't promise anything," Todd said.

"Thank you," Sheely said. "I'll e-mail it to you right away. And thank you again."

"I'll call or e-mail you if I'm able to help," Todd said reluctantly.

"Thank you, Todd. Take care."

"You too."

Sheely let out a long breath of air.

CHAPTER 16

Private investigator Russell Kelly's career was not without its problems. He started his career with the Boston police. The captain he reported to invited him into his office one day when he had been with the department for three years.

"Officer Kelly, have a seat."

The captain looked at him closely for a few moments to decide how to say what he needed to say. He was firing Russell.

"Officer Kelly."

"Yes sir."

"Officer Kelly...I'm recommending you to the FBI."

"Sir?"

Russell didn't try to be a troublemaker; he just wasn't good at following orders. He had an unconventional way of solving problems. One might say he stretched the law from time to time when he felt it was morally justifiable. More than once, unexplainable events had led to a conclusion—a positive one—that baffled his department. Those events always pointed back to Russell. He denied everything but secretly enjoyed the bewildered looks of his coworkers.

In this way, he was like Sherlock Holmes, who used strategic lies that would eventually lead to a brilliant but baffling conclusion to a case. But Russell would rather take flak for not doing what he was told than step forward with an explanation they would not understand.

His captain, on the spur of the moment, couldn't fire him. He liked Russell. Cases got solved when Russell put his nose into places it wasn't supposed to be. Perhaps the FBI could tame him. At least he would be someone else's problem.

Russell moved to DC and worked out of the FBI office for nearly ten years before his supervisor politely asked him to resign. His supervisor did not want to fire him; like the Boston captain, he liked Russell. But circumstances beyond his control and above his pay grade dictated that Russell had to go. Russell understood and left quietly. He moved back to Boston.

He wasn't about to give up on his profession, so he opened a private investigation firm. In Massachusetts, the state police license private detectives, and there are prerequisites to being licensed. Russell now had thirteen years of experience as an officer of the law. He had a bachelor of science degree in criminal justice from Boston University. He had no felony convictions or violations of any kind, so he had no problem getting a Massachusetts firearm safety certificate. What gave him trouble was a clause in the Authorization for Release of Information form:

> It is my specific intent to provide full access to and disclosure of information and records relating to me... employment and preemployment records, including background reports, efficiency ratings, complaints, or grievances filed by or against me.

This caused a considerable delay in obtaining his PI license. It took the current superintendent of the police bureau where Russell used to work, who also happened to be his former captain, to sway the decision-making process.

Russell Investigative Services consisted of two small rooms. Being in the right place at the right time, he was able to secure office space near the Beacon Hill area, a prime but expensive location. Two years ago, Russell's friend Byron Pierce laughed at the size of the office when he came to visit.

Byron and Russell both grew up in the Boston area, and Russell was the older brother Byron never had. They met in grammar school and became fast friends. Their paths diverged in college when Byron pursued journalism and Russell majored in criminal justice, but they kept in touch.

Some would say it was a coincidence or just plain luck, but nothing in the universe happens by chance. Russell's interest in the murder of Senator Welsh was not driven just by Byron's call. He had been working on an investigation that led him to Senator Welsh and his involvement with a New Mexico Indian tribe.

Cetanwakuwa (known as "Hawk"), the president of Native Rights in America, was concerned that his only daughter, Luyu, was getting involved with the wrong crowd. She had rejected her Indian ways and moved away from her home and family in Oklahoma to Boston. She had all but disowned her family, but she did keep in touch with some of her tribal friends. Thus, rumors were passed up to her dad, causing him to worry.

Although prejudice against Native Americans generally does not make the news, it still exists. They suffer from the same economic and social problems as other ethnic minorities.

There are 2.5 million Native Americans living on 310 reservations, and one in four lives in poverty. It was no wonder Luyu—whose name means "wild dove"—wanted to leave the reservation. Hawk didn't fault her for that, but what concerned him was that she was a single young female minority in a large city. He needed to know what she was getting herself into. An Internet search for private investigators led him to Russell.

Russell accepted the job. As a black man, he was familiar with the problems of racial minorities. He had overcome most of them through a strong will, a good education, and an innate ability to solve problems. He felt Cetanwakuwa had a similar personality and sympathized with him, so he accepted the job.

He knew little about the NRA and thought researching them might be a good place to start. It could give him some clues about the daughter's behavior. As he researched the organization, he wondered if accepting the job had been a good decision. He didn't realize just how many demonstrations were blamed on the group. It wasn't the demonstrations that concerned him but the criminal activities associated with them. *Was Cetanwakuwa a criminal?*

Although it wasn't national news, Russell discovered that the NRA was causing a major headache for a large oil and gas company over drilling rights in New Mexico. Several expensive pieces of equipment had been destroyed, and the NRA was suspected to be responsible because the drilling was taking place on tribal Indian land. The tribal police chief had called in the state police to help. Russell, at that point, called the NRA president.

"First of all, please call me Hawk," Cetanwakuwa said. "I understand your concern, Mr. Kelly. It's my concern as well. I don't condone such actions by the NRA. Unfortunately, there's an outside radical group that causes these issues, and we get blamed. I haven't been able to contain them, and frankly, I'm at a loss as to what to do."

"Thank you for your honesty," Russell said.

They discussed the New Mexico protest and other incidents for several minutes. Russell was satisfied that the NRA president, although perhaps not the most ethical citizen, at least wasn't a criminal.

"I'll let you know when I have some information on your daughter," he said.

Hawk thanked him.

Afterward, Russell dug further into the controversy and discovered Senator Welsh's congressional bill that gave approval to the drilling deal with the tribe. Out of curiosity, he called the chief of the New Mexico tribe. He learned about the senator's involvement with the tribe in a study using the "Consciousness Generated Field Effect." He thought that was interesting.

Then Byron called.

"This just got *more* interesting," Russell said to himself after hanging up with Byron. Given the circumstances he had uncovered, he wondered if the NRA was involved with the scalping. After a few more calls to the NRA president to discuss the scalping and to pass on some information about his daughter, he believed the group wasn't involved, at least not directly. *So then why was the senator killed?*

He called Byron back.

"Byron, it's Russell. I've got some news for you."

"Great," Byron said.

"Do you know the NRA?"

"The National Rifle Association," Byron answered.

"That's what most people would say, but in this case, it stands for the Native Rights in America group."

"Who are they?"

"They're described as a radical Indian group that champions Indian rights. They're based out of Oklahoma and have been implicated in several crimes but never indicted. I've discovered that they're mostly misrepresented by the press. Anyway, as it turns out, Senator Welsh was responsible for pushing a bill through Congress that gave an official OK to drill for oil on Indian land. The media interpreted the bill as the government using eminent domain to steal land that belonged to the Indians and then giving it to the oil and gas industry."

"So what you're saying is that the senator was killed and scalped by this NRA group as some kind of retribution? To make a point? To bring attention to it?"

"On the surface, that's what it appears to be, but it doesn't fit in my mind. It doesn't match the research I've done."

"What do you mean?"

"It's too obvious, and the NRA isn't that radical. The stuff they've been accused of might get them some jail time if they were ever convicted, but murder and scalping? I don't think so. But that's just my opinion."

"Interesting," Byron mused.

"I think there's something else involved here, but I haven't been able to put my finger on it."

"So it was a setup?"

"Maybe. Anyway, when you print your story and get your big promotion—"

"Like that will ever happen."

"Well, when you decide to move up to the big time, I have connections here," Russell said.

"Thanks, Russell. I owe you."

After talking with Russell, Byron went to his computer to modify his story based on this new information. He also added the information he had obtained from his own research on Senator Welsh. He had contacted a couple of Copper instructors he knew to ask if Owen was indeed the witness. One of them said it was common knowledge that Owen had seen something and had gone to the cops. Byron added that to the article as well.

He ran the story by his editor, who grilled him about the content, offered a few suggestions, and approved the story. It was too late to get the article in for the next day, but the day after that, the *Summit Dispatch* paper edition and website broke the story.

SUMMIT DISPATCH

SENATOR GREGORY WELSH SCALPED
By Byron Pierce, Senior Staff Reporter

Thursday, February 19, 2015—Senator Gregory Welsh (D-MT) was shot twice and killed on February 6 while skiing at Copper Mountain Resort. *Summit Dispatch* has learned, through an anonymous source, that he was also scalped. Senator Welsh was responsible for pushing a bill through Congress that authorized the drilling for oil on a Native American reservation in New

Mexico. The Native Rights in America (NRA) organization, a protest group, has been boycotting the drilling site. There is speculation that the NRA may have been responsible for the scalping. Also, Owen Baker, the witness to the shooting, may have been killed to prevent his deposition.

The article continued with a brief description about the life of Senator Welsh, the NRA, and Owen Baker. In no time at all, dozens of phone calls poured in. Summit County has four ski areas, and three others within a short driving distance. It's a high-volume recreational destination both in winter and summer, and many influential people could be vacationing in the county on any given day. As it so happened, several editors, reporters, and executives were vacationing there, and articles appeared the next day in major newspapers across the country. By evening, it was the lead story on all the TV news channels.

The FBI showed up at the *Summit Dispatch* office the next day. The interrogation lasted for some time, but Byron refused to divulge the name of his source on the scalping. That didn't go over well, but there was little the FBI could do. Byron did admit that the connection between the senator's death and Owen's was conjecture, as was the connection to the NRA. For the FBI, it wasn't just a guess.

It also wasn't a guess for VP Locker. In fact, she was thrilled that the news had gone national and called Senator Benn on her secure line.

"Congratulations, Bill. Your agent pulled it off."

"My agent? You mean your agent."

"Whatever. With the blame on the NRA, we should be able to get a few more of the bills on our agenda passed."

"I'll start working on my fellow senators."

"I'll work on the president," Locker said. "Have you killed the Meissner study, Bill? Pun intended."

"Ha-ha. It's being done as we speak."

PART 2

The Washington Gazette

WASHINGTON, DC, SATURDAY, FEBRUARY 21, 2015

SENATOR WELSH WAS SCALPED
By Abe Southerly

An anonymous source within the FBI has verified that the murder of Senator Gregory Welsh (D-MT) while skiing at Copper Mountain, Colorado, may have been an act of retribution. A portion of the senator's scalp was removed and attached to a note reading, "Get off our land." The FBI is investigating a possible connection to the Native Rights in America organization.

The FBI is also investigating the murder of Owen Baker, a ski instructor at Copper Mountain. Mr. Baker has been identified as a possible witness to Senator Welsh's murder.

CHAPTER 17

IN DECEMBER 2014, Congress passed H.R. 3979 the
National Defense Authorization Act. An eleventh-hour
rider was added by two Republican senators that authorized
the trade of 2,422 acres of Arizona land for 5,344 acres that
had belonged to a copper-mining consortium. Within the
swapped land was the Tonto National Forest, and within that
forest was tribal land that was considered sacred: the Oak Flat
Campground. The deal was driven by strong outside influ-
ences, and it outraged the Arizona Native Americans.

In 1978, the American Indian Religious Freedom Act was
passed. It authorized the federal government to preserve the
religious rights of all Native Americans and declared sacred
lands protected. This latest Oak Flat trade agreement was a
clear violation of the 1978 act and a 1955 decree by President
Dwight Eisenhower closing national forest land to mining.

Although the mining consortium gave assurances that it
would protect the site, the tribe was skeptical. Despite protests
and Democratic legislators' outcries, little progress was made
in removing the rider. Based on these developments, the FBI
believed the agreement Senator Welsh had advanced through
Congress sanctifying drilling on the New Mexico tribal land

had pushed the NRA too far, and they were at the top of its suspect list for Welsh's murder.

"Mr. Cetanwakuwa," the FBI agent said, mispronouncing his name as he continued his interrogation. Hawk was sitting in the Oklahoma City FBI office. He had been on Fox News and CNN disclaiming any association with the murder of Senator Welsh. "We fight for Indian rights. We do not kill for Indian rights" was his mantra. Nevertheless, the FBI spent several hours questioning him.

All the FBI had was a male unsub, an unknown subject, who was a good skier and who had a jacket possibly with some red on it and green-colored boots, matching bullets from Senator Welsh's and Owen Baker's bodies, a scalp, and a note implicating the NRA. No fingerprints were found on any of the evidence. Since the bullets from both bodies matched, the FBI suspected the same person killed the senator and the ski instructor.

On the night of Owen's death, the security cameras in the Copper parking lot had produced only a fuzzy image of someone walking up to and away from Owen's car. The person's size suggested it was a man, but the snowstorm blocked any distinguishing features. The person headed toward the main Copper road and disappeared.

The FBI figured the killer was most likely an out-of-towner. Checking all rentals out of Denver International Airport took days. Through hours of questioning, the FBI was able to determine who had gone skiing and who had gone to Copper Mountain. One of those people was Jeff Catson.

The agent following that lead was embarrassed to follow up with the Secret Service agent and apologized ahead of time for the questions he had to ask. Jeff said he was on vacation at Copper Mountain Resort and took several ski lessons. He said he did not know about the instructor's death until he read about it in the paper. The agent also questioned him about the death of Senator Welsh, since it was well known that he was at Copper Mountain the day of the murder. Jeff had an alibi for that as well.

VP Locker had planned a policy speech in Denver. Colorado had recently approved the legalization of marijuana, and she would be speaking about the federal government's position. It was sure to bring a large crowd. Jeff was sent ahead to manage security.

"I was on a security detail for the vice-president's upcoming trip," Jeff explained. He told the agent that he had taken a side trip to Copper one day to check it out. He explained that he had skied at several other areas in Colorado but never Copper. When he heard about the shooting and that the victim was Senator Welsh, he offered assistance. He didn't mention that he was actually trying to find the ski-instructor witness.

Jeff said the vice-president canceled her trip after the senator's murder, which gave him free time. He felt he needed a vacation and decided to go back to Colorado to ski at Copper. The investigating agent spent another couple of days verifying Jeff's statements. He checked with the Denver police, who were involved with helping to set up the vice-president's security. The police said Jeff was professional and helpful. Investigators also checked sources at Copper Mountain and in DC and eventually removed Jeff from the suspect list.

That left the NRA as a prime suspect. During the interrogation, Hawk admitted to nothing other than what the FBI already knew about the group. He did not mention that he had received knowledge about the scalping from PI Russell Kelly. That revelation drove him to do his own internal investigation, which found nothing, and he did tell the FBI about that.

Notwithstanding, the FBI continued to question Hawk about any and all connections to Senator Welsh and every other suspicious activity of the NRA. Hawk adamantly denied every theory and accusation except the well-publicized demonstrations his organization was known to have been involved. Finally, the FBI had to let him go.

Hawk was furious, but there was little he could do. The only positive out of the day was that the FBI had not brought up his daughter. She wasn't used as some form of leverage to get him to talk, and it meant she wasn't in any serious trouble. That also confirmed what PI Russell had passed on to him. His daughter was involved with a crowd smoking marijuana. That was the negative, but it was not unusual for a young adult and not likely to get her into trouble. The positive was that she was taking night classes at the local community college. That thought warmed Hawk's heart, and the fury inside him subsided as he got into his car.

The FBI didn't know it, but there was more to come.

CHAPTER 18

In the locker room after a long day of teaching, Sheely finally got a chance to check her messages. One message told her the forest service was doing a controlled burn, and please don't call 911 if you see smoke. She deleted it.

In Colorado, the mountain pine beetle, a type of bark beetle, has killed more than 1.2 million lodgepole pine trees on more than 264,000 acres, one of the largest deforestations in the country. The forest service clears areas filled with dead trees that are close to residential areas. The dead trees are piled up and burned during the winter months.

The second message was from her friend Todd:

Got some info 4 U. Sending via email.

Great. She had been patiently waiting to hear from Todd for nearly a week. She decided to wait until she got home to read the e-mail. She had not seen Kevin all day and was not sure whether he was on the slopes or not, so she texted him:

Come over tonight. Have information.

She also wanted to tell him she had finally gotten her silver medal in NASTAR.[32] Normally, she was assigned full-day lessons, and with a full-day lesson, instructors are required to eat with their students. Today, she was assigned a half-day private in the morning and then a half-day group lesson in the afternoon, which enabled her to tuck in a race during the lunch break. A silver medal was one of the prereqs for attending the PSIA level-two exam. It gave some measure of proof of the skier's ability.

While driving home and munching on a protein bar to dull the hunger pain from missing lunch, her phone beeped: a message. She waited until she was home to read it. It was from Kevin.

Will do. 🐝 there about 8.

She laughed out loud at the use of the bee emoji. Then she signed into her computer and checked her e-mail. There was Todd's:

Information You Asked For   2/23/15
Todd Harris
To: Sheely Shannon
Sheely,

---

32 NASTAR stands for National Standard Race. It is a recreational snow sports race program in which skiers and snowboarders can compete against others across the country. All ages and abilities compete using a handicap system based on age. The par handicap of zero is set by a member of the US ski team or former champion. Most ski areas have a NASTAR course set up for the public to use.

I was able to get you the following:

There were 4 matches with sufficient probability. Photos attached. The first, Jose Lopez, has been in prison for 3 years. The second, Patrick Moore, is a police officer in Philly. The third, Keith Anderson, is a retired naval officer. And the fourth, Jeff Catson, is a Secret Service agent assigned to the vice-president.

I hope this helps. Take care,
Todd

Sheely let out a sigh and laid her head on the desk. She recognized the man in the fourth photo right away; it was clearly the closest match. The Secret Service agent was definitely the guy who kept taking lessons with different instructors, the same guy in the photo that Kevin had given her. She printed out the e-mail, sent Todd a thank-you message, and got up to take a shower, eat dinner, and wait for Kevin.

When Kevin knocked, she opened the door and gave him a long hug.

"It's cold. I think we should go in and close the door," Kevin whispered.

Once Kevin took off his coat and hat and sat down on her couch, Sheely handed him the e-mail and photos from Todd. Pointing at the fourth one, she said, "That's him. It's that guy you saw at the Edge. It's the ski-lesson guy. He's a Secret Service agent."

"A Secret Service agent? Do you trust your friend on this?"
"Yes."

Kevin read the e-mail and checked out the photos. A few moments passed before he spoke. "I agree it's him, but I have no real proof other than what I saw. Who's going to believe me compared with a Secret Service agent? And if this guy finds out I'm the real witness, he could go after me. I'm afraid to tell anyone."

"I know," Sheely said. "I've thought about this. I think my aunt can help."

"You mean your auntie?" Kevin kidded.

"Very funny. And how do you know I call her that?"

"You mentioned her once at morning-lesson lineups. I thought it was cute that you called her that."

"I did? I don't remember. Oh! Before I forget, I got my NASTAR silver medal today."

"Sheely, that's great. Now you're all set to take the exam, right? Oh, you still have to take one more clinic."

"Yes, but I have that scheduled."

"I'm really proud of you."

"Thanks."

"OK, what were we talking about? Oh, so what can your auntie do to help?" Kevin asked.

"She's always hinted that she knows other HGT guides," Sheely revealed with a smile.

"Wait!" Kevin knew she was in the Holy Grail tradition, but calling it HGT? He was the only one he knew who did that. Then he put it together. "You're on my Twitter account? I mean, you follow me?"

"Yes, I'm Jill."

"Jill…um…*S* something," Kevin sputtered.

"Spencer," @jillspencer108 confessed.

"Jill Spencer. You?"

"The one and only. Like you, I wanted to be anonymous because of our tradition."

Kevin stared at her, and she smiled in return.

"Then how'd you know it was me?"

"I didn't at first. I just knew whoever it was knew about our tradition. Then, when we discovered each other"—her smile got bigger—"I put two and two together and guessed."

"I almost blocked you. You kept flirting with me, sometimes implying even more." This time, Sheely smiled inside. "But you had some insightful comments at times, so I let you follow me."

"Thank you for not blocking me." Sheely wanted to ask him about the "implying even more" comment @jillspencer108 had tweeted about, but wasn't the right time. *At least Kevin is here and trusting me.*

They fell silent.

"Can I get you something to drink?" Sheely finally asked.

"No thank you. Maybe later. Tell me about your aunt."

"You mean my auntie?"

"OK, OK. I won't make fun of what you call her."

"It's OK. I sometimes laugh at myself for still calling her that." Sheely paused. "She taught me everything. I feel blessed to have her in my life. She's one of us. Actually, I should put that the other way: we're part of her heritage."

"I understand," Kevin said. "My grandfather taught me. What about your parents?"

"I love my parents. My father died when I was young."

"Same with me," Kevin said.

"I'm sorry. I didn't know."

"No, no. It's OK. I didn't know about your dad either. Wasn't your mom able to teach you?"

"My mom practices but only transcends in meditation. She can explain theory but not actual experience. My father's sister, my auntie, filled in all the gaps, so to speak."

"My mom's the same." He paused. "Transcending.[33] You used that term a lot in your tweets. I've come to believe it's what we do in the Holy Grail technique. Also, I did some research on Patanjali, since you laughed at me for not knowing about him, and I came to the conclusion that his siddhis are the same as our abilities."

"They're one and the same," Sheely said. "You don't know much about other forms of meditation, do you?"

"I've done research on Western traditions, but I've never really looked at Eastern ones. My grandfather always told me not to get involved with other practices. It seems sort of silly now that I didn't at least read up on them. My grandfather often quoted Jesus: 'Seek ye first the kingdom of God, and his righteousness; and all these things shall be added unto you.'[34] Then he'd explain that the kingdom of God was the inner experience of pure consciousness, which scientists have discovered as the unified field,[35] that area of life beyond the finest level of creation."

---

33 Transcending is going beyond the normal limits of experience—in this case, to go beyond the experience of thought to the source of thought and experience pure consciousness.

34 Sermon on the Mount, Matthew 6:3, King James Bible. Jesus and Patanjali understood the power of acting from the kingdom of God—the level of pure consciousness. When acting from that level all desires are fulfilled. (Also see footnote 31, chapter 15.)

35 The unified field is at the basis of all creation and is the source of all creation. It is mathematically explained via superstring theories. (There are

"Yes, the kingdom of God is within," Sheely said.[36]

"You know?"

"Of course, Kevin. I'm just like you." She explained that transcending was what all the great teachers taught. "It's what we do," she said. She briefly talked about other meditation techniques and explained that although they produced some benefits, they were not transcending techniques.

"There is a distinct, measurable difference between them," she said, and she explained why. She knew of only one other tradition that taught a technique like theirs—a Vedic tradition. She said her auntie did a lot of research, looking for information that would clear up some questions she had about their practice, and discovered the Vedic tradition. Her auntie, she said, understood right away that it was the same but was in the language and time of a different culture.

"In fact, there has always been this rumor that the HGT, as you call it"—she tilted her head and smiled in such a cute

---

seven classic superstring theories, which are different limits of a single, underlying theory, M-theory.) Its characteristics of unboundedness, having all intelligence, unlimited potential, and complete dynamic silence match perfectly the ancient Vedic description of pure consciousness. (Also see footnote 22, chapter 14.)

36 "The kingdom of God does not come from observation...For indeed, the kingdom of God is within you," Luke 17:20–21, New King James Bible. According to modern physics, the unified field, at the basis of all life, is omniscient, omnipotent, and omnipresent. Thus, in religious terms it is the home of God. The experience of pure consciousness is the experience of the unified field. In the language, culture, and understanding of the time, more than two thousand years ago, this experience was described as "the kingdom of God." (Other translations use the term "the kingdom of heaven.")

way that it touched Kevin's heart—"had an ancient connection to India."

"My grandfather has mentioned that as well. OK, you can tell me more about that later. You said your auntie can help, and she knows others in our tradition?"

"Yes, I'd like to tell her about this. Would that be OK?"

"My grandfather always felt there were others like us, and I felt the same way, but we had no idea who or where they could be. Then I met you," he said with a smile. "Would it be all right if my grandfather and your auntie met? Maybe we could all get together and decide what's best."

"I agree. Let's do it."

CHAPTER 19

It was time to get the elders involved. Kevin and Sheely decided they should meet at Kevin's grandfather's home in Boulder. His grandfather was in his seventies. Sheely's aunt was in her fifties. It made sense to persuade Auntie, who lived in Utah, to travel to Boulder.

Making time for the meeting was easier said than done. For three weeks in March, when families and college kids on spring break migrate to the slopes in droves, instructors are encouraged to work as many days as possible. Sheely's and Kevin's supervisors were not happy about shifting their work schedules around. They had to agree to make up the days at a later time but got the changes they needed.

Kevin's mom lived in Centennial, a suburb of Denver. She practiced HGT, but her nervous system was not as evolved as Kevin's or her father-in-law's. She, like Sheely's mom, knew the knowledge and the tradition from marriage, but her experience was limited. Kevin decided she did not need to be included in the meeting because she would only worry about his safety.

Kevin showered and dressed after a day of work and left his condo in Frisco for the nearly two-hour drive to his grandfather's home. He was welcome to drop by at any time. He'd usually call first, but not tonight. There was too much on his mind.

As Kevin turned off Interstate 70 onto US Route 6, he was glad it was a clear night. US Route 6 descends through Clear Creek Canyon—a two-lane, winding road with sixty-six curves and many sheer rock faces. It's a scary drive in a snowstorm. The road was finished in 1952 with six tunnels through rock cliffs. Tunnel four was closed when the new intersection to Colorado State Highway 119 was built, and that was where Kevin ran into traffic from the popular casinos in Black Hawk and Central City seven miles north of the intersection. Anyone unlucky enough to get behind a line of casino tourist buses and slow cars was stuck for the eleven miles into Golden, the home of the Coors brewery and a gateway into the Denver area. Luck was not with Kevin this night.

From Golden, Kevin took State Highway 93 north toward Boulder. At his grandfather's home, he parked in the short driveway, grabbed his overnight bag, and knocked on the side entrance.

"Hi, Granddad," Kevin said as his grandfather answered the door.

"Hey there, Kevin. What brings you here tonight?"

"I need to talk to you about something."

"OK. Have you eaten?"

"No. How about we order some pizza?"

"Done."

Kevin grabbed a glass of water and settled on the living-room couch while his grandfather called in an order. Grandfather then settled into a chair next to Kevin. "So, what's up?"

"This is a bit hard for me to talk about because it's almost unbelievable. You heard about the senator being shot at Copper?"

"And supposedly the witness as well," Grandfather said. "Did you know the instructor who was killed?"

"I did. Owen was a colleague, but he wasn't the witness. I was."

Grandfather straightened up, wide-eyed. "Oh."

"That's not the half of it," Kevin continued. "The guy who shot the senator, and probably Owen, is a Secret Service agent assigned to Vice-President Locker."

"OK, you've got my attention. How do you know that?"

Kevin explained how he saw it happen and disappeared to get away. He described how he saw the same man with the red-striped jacket pull out a badge as he was talking to some police officers and the ski patrol.

"How could you tell it was the same man?"

"Besides the same jacket, he just had this sense about him. You know, how you taught me to recognize the nature of one's mind and energy."

"But you haven't mastered that yet."

"True, but I'm good enough at it, especially when I put my attention on it. Anyway, I sensed darkness in him." Kevin explained how he obtained a photo of the suspected killer. How his friend, Sheely, whom he said he'd talk more about in a moment, was able to find out through a friend of hers that the man's name was Jeff Catson, and he was a Secret Service agent assigned to the vice-president.

"That's quite a tale." Grandfather looked straight at Kevin. "I'm assuming you haven't gone to the police about this."

"No, I'm afraid. Who's going to believe me? And after what happened to Owen, I'm even more afraid."

"Ah, I see." Grandfather sighed. "Well, let's think about this."

"That's why I'm here, but there's more I need to tell you."

"I'm listening."

"You know how you've always told me there had to be other keepers of our knowledge, and I've always believed that as well?"

Grandfather nodded.

"Well, my friend Sheely, the one I just told you about? She's one of us."

"You're kidding!"

"No, it's true. I never knew until I saw her pull off a little levitation, which I believe she did on purpose to test me, or maybe tease me, and then it all came out."

Silence overtook Grandfather, and then a big smile broke out. "I just knew it. I've been hoping to meet others my entire life. Can I meet her?"

"Granddad, that's why I'm here. She and I want us all to meet. Sheely is inviting her aunt as well. She calls her Auntie, so you can't make fun of that. Anyway, her aunt is her teacher, just like you are mine."

Kevin's grandfather gave him a loving look. "You've been a good student—well, most of the time—but you've always been a great grandson. Our tradition would be very proud of you." He paused and thought for a moment. "This situation you're in concerns me a lot. I'm glad we'll be getting together. When are they coming?"

"Sheely's going to tell her aunt all about this, and she's sure her aunt will come. As soon as she calls me, I'll know better. We want all of us to sit down together and figure out what to do."

"I think that's a great idea."

Jennifer Shannon, Sheely's father's sister, had never married. She noticed Sheely's special aptitude at an early age, and after her brother's untimely death, she took over Sheely's training. Jennifer never regretted not marrying. As an enlightened woman,[37] she was always fulfilled. Nevertheless, her curiosity kept her searching for answers and for deeper meanings to the understandings that her tradition, the HGT, had ingrained in her from her parents and grandparents. These understandings she passed on to her niece, who easily absorbed the knowledge, but more than anything else, they just enjoyed being together.

---

37 Enlightenment, which is the development of consciousness to its full potential—pure consciousness, is now known via scientific verification of brain waves and blood chemistry to be a higher state of consciousness. It is a powerful state of alpha1 coherence throughout the brain, especially in the prefrontal cortex, along with a strong contingent negative variation preparatory response, concurrent with beta activity.

In addition, blood chemistry reveals a steady state of ojas, an advanced chemical that is produced by a body with a stress-free nervous system and is the material aspect of soma. Soma has historically been said to be produced from a plant, but that is a misunderstanding. It is spontaneously produced in the body of an enlightened person. Together, soma and ojas refine the senses to enable one to experience the finer aspects of creation.

As a young adult, Kevin was always trying to learn more as well. He would frequently try to improve on his teachings and, as a result, got lectures from his grandfather.[38]

"Let go, let God." That concept took time for Kevin to understand, but Sheely never had that issue. She innocently followed her aunt's instructions. She allowed the natural tendency of the mind—driven by the force of evolution to seek more: more joy, more knowledge, and more fulfillment—to work for her. The ultimate fulfillment for the mind is the experience of pure consciousness, the Holy Grail of life. As such, it acts like gravity, naturally drawing the mind inward. Sheely's naturalness allowed her consciousness and special abilities to grow quickly and strongly.

Sheely wasn't sure how to approach the subject with her aunt. Through several e-mails, she arranged a time to Skype. They talked for about an hour. Sheely loved looking at her aunt, even through a computer screen. After some girl talk, Sheely explained why she had called. Her aunt listened quietly and intently. When Sheely finished, Auntie didn't hesitate.

"I am behind you one hundred percent. Let's find the source behind these horrific acts and allow justice to take its course. When do you want me in Denver?"

---

38 Effort of any type directs the mind—that is, it tells the mind to perform some action. Whether it is a form of focus, concentration, dispassionate awareness, maintaining an orientation of nonjudgmental observation of thoughts or breath, or maintaining a sense of presence, it doesn't matter. Any interference by the ego will keep the mind on the surface level and prevent it from seeking its own direction, which is transcending and experiencing pure consciousness.

CHAPTER 20

Sarah Chapman, the chairman of the House Budget Committee, had left a phone message for VP Locker: "John Moore is going forward to obtain funding for the Meissner study, even though Jill Hill has technically canceled it."

"What?" Locker cursed and immediately called Senator Benn. "Call me on my secure line as soon as you get this message."

Benn was in a meeting. By the time he was able to get back to her a few hours later, she was fuming.

"What's up?" Benn asked.

"What's up? Are you ignorant?" she barked into the phone.

"Excuse me?"

"Funding for the Meissner study is still being pushed through."

"That's not possible. Representative Jill Hill, the chairperson of the Committee on Science, Technology, and Infrastr—"

"I know who she is, you idiot."

Benn took a deep breath. "She told me she would kill it. We had an agreement."

"Well, John Moore is apparently still pushing it."

"Are you sure? I haven't heard—"

"Yes, I'm sure. Sarah from the House Budget Committee informed me."

"OK, OK. I'll check into it." Senator Benn abruptly hung up. Hanging up on the VP was definitely not a sign of respect. He'd get flak from her, but he didn't care. He wasn't about to take her insults.

Benn asked his assistant to get Representative Hill on the phone. A few minutes later, the assistant reported, "She's not in her office at the moment, but her assistant said she'd get back to you as soon as she can."

"Bullshit," Benn said under his breath, but he would have to wait.

It wasn't until the next day that Jill called him back. She too had heard from Sarah that the funding proposal was still in play. She was stunned, but she had to put it out of her mind. She had too many other pressing issues that needed her attention.

That was yesterday. Today, sitting in her office, she knew she had to address the funding proposal, and she wasn't looking forward to it. She and John were on the same team, and she didn't understand how he could have done such a thing behind her back. She was hating the game of politics more and more. She had given in to Senator Benn against her better judgment, and now she felt betrayed. She needed to confront John before calling Benn.

She took a deep breath and rose from her desk.

"I expect to be back shortly," she told her assistant before she headed toward Representative Moore's office. She ran into him in the hallway.

"We need to talk," Jill said politely.

"I'm on my way to a meeting."

"We need to talk *now*." Jill was no longer polite.

John stopped, stepped backward, and raised his hands in defeat. "OK, in my office."

When the door was closed, Jill demanded, "What are you doing?"

"You're talking about the Meissner study?"

"Yes, of course, I'm talking about that."

"Look, Jill, that study could change the direction of our country for the better. I know you killed it in committee, but with some slight revisions, I was able to reintroduce it on my own."

"I didn't want to kill it, but as I explained to you in private, I was forced to do so, and now you're jeopardizing projects I have worked very hard for."

"I'm sorry, Jill, but I can't let that bill die."

Jill shook her head and stared at him in disbelief. "I'm sorry too. Don't expect my support in the future." She left his office.

Back in her office, she called Senator Benn.

"This is Jill," she said when Benn answered his phone.

"You *know* why I called," Benn said. It wasn't a question.

"I did what we agreed to. I killed the bill, but I can't always control what other congressional members want to do. John Moore has revised it and is reintroducing it as his own bill. I have nothing to leverage him with."

"Well, you'd better find something."

"Senator—" The line went dead.

After hanging up, Senator Benn mumbled, "Damn women; they can't get anything done." He paused a moment and then called Jeff Catson.

CHAPTER 21

Representative John Moore was sitting in his office. Nearly a week had gone by since his encounter with Jill. He still couldn't believe she had given in to political pressure, especially from William Benn. He admitted that the National Park System was important, but the health of the nation surpassed everything else. It hadn't taken much effort to sufficiently modify the Meissner bill so it could be reintroduced. He was proud of himself and disappointed in his colleague at the same time. He also had his family to think of, an angle he was sure Jill, a single lady—*Did she even date?*—wouldn't understand.

He thought of his three-year-old daughter, Katie. She was so cute this morning when she wouldn't let go. "Daddy, please stay. Cutsie wants to have tea with you." Cutsie was her doll, and John was an experienced tea partier, a skill he'd learned from his five-year-old daughter, Korie. He told Katie they could have the party when he got home from work. John's innate ability to relate to his daughters was just one of the characteristics his wife, Katherine, admired about him. God, he loved his family.

He knew it would be tough getting the bill through the maze of Congress. Nevertheless, he was confident he could do it. He had several terms of experience over Jill. What pissed him off even more than Jill's defection was the theft of his car. It was stolen several days ago while he was shopping. He had to call his wife to pick him up.

When the police finally found his car, they told him it was "slightly damaged." That slight damage turned out to be a twelve-hundred-dollar repair, and he had a five-hundred-dollar deductible on his insurance policy, so the balance would have to come out of his pocket. The police had swabbed for fingerprints but found only his and his family's. Still, he was glad to have his Jeep Cherokee back, even with the damage.

"Well, that should do it for today," Moore said with a sigh. He was relieved that the day had come to an end, and he was looking forward to getting home and having a tea party. He packed up his briefcase, said good evening to his staff, and headed to his Cherokee.

John lived in Tysons Corner, Virginia. As he drove through DC, he was pleased that the traffic wasn't too bad. He quickly turned onto Interstate 66. He entered the two cordoned-off HOV lanes in the five-lane road. Among the special privileges of being a congressman was having a special license plate to drive in HOV lanes, even when alone.

As soon as his car hit sixty miles per hour, he noticed a little jerk. It passed, and he didn't pay any more attention to it. *Some bump in the road.* He continued accelerating, approaching seventy miles per hour. Nobody obeyed the speed limit. He closed in on a van in front of him, moved over to the left HOV lane, and accelerated to pass it. Moving back into the right HOV lane, he stepped on the brake to slow down. His foot went to the floor. The car continued to accelerate. He panicked, reached to the center console, and pulled up the electronic parking brake switch. Nothing.

The car was now approaching eighty-five miles per hour. In the cordoned-off HOV lanes, there was nowhere to turn off—not that it would have done any good. He was fast approaching traffic ahead of him in both HOV lanes. He leaned on the horn, hoping the cars would get out of his way, but there was nowhere for them to go. At over ninety miles per hour, he struck the side barrier in an attempt to miss the car in front of him, but all that did was bounce him into the car. The car he hit twisted sideways, striking the barrier. John's car nosedived, twisted, and rolled, just missing a second car, and bounced over the right barrier into the non-HOV lanes. An oncoming eighteen-wheeler hit the brakes but smashed into the Cherokee. The driver of the car hit in the HOV lane was badly injured but survived. The truck driver walked away cleanly, but Representative John Moore, Democrat from Virginia, was pronounced dead at the scene.

CHAPTER 22

O n that same day, Sheely was waiting patiently at the exit area of the underground tram in the main terminal at Denver International Airport. Auntie Jennifer Shannon was arriving on Southwest Flight 374 at 5:10 p.m. Several waves of passengers passed through before her aunt appeared.

"Welcome to Denver!" Sheely gave her aunt a big hug and kiss.

"Hi, sweetie." Auntie's eyes twinkled. She had a carry-on bag and no checked luggage, so they skipped the baggage claim and went directly to Sheely's car. While driving back to Frisco, they managed to catch up on each other's lives. At Sheely's home, they continued chatting as they both pitched in to fix dinner. They finally sat down.

"So, how are you *really* feeling?" asked Auntie.

"I'm worried about Kevin."

"You like him, don't you?"

Sheely blushed in response, and Auntie smiled.

"OK, when are we meeting?"

"Tomorrow evening at Kevin's grandfather's house in Boulder."

"Good. Now tell me all about your boyfriend, Kevin."

"Auntie! He's not my boyfriend."

"But…"

"OK, I really, really like him. As you've already figured out."

Over dinner, Sheely talked more about Kevin, and Jennifer told Sheely about her latest research connecting HGT to ancient philosophical and religious traditions, especially the Vedic tradition of India. She had discovered there were seven separate and distinct levels of consciousness.[39] These seven states, she said, correspond with elements of other traditions, such as those of the ancient Incas. The Incas defined these states as progressions of awareness, and the shamanic tradition called them progress toward self-realization—different names, but the same fundamental understandings.

Surprisingly, this fascinated Sheely. "Please tell me more." She was normally not interested in such details, but having her auntie here was such a joy, she couldn't help herself.

Auntie went on to explain how science was now verifying the existence of pure consciousness. She told Sheely about research she read in the journal *Consciousness and Cognition* documenting the existence of alpha1 brain waves during a meditation technique that produced transcending. She felt this must be what happens in their HGT meditations.

They moved to Sheely's computer. Auntie brought up research from the journal *Sleep* showing that this alpha1 state exists between the normal states of consciousness: waking, sleeping, and dreaming. The research called this the junction point, the gap between the states of consciousness.

---

39 The seven Vedic states are *sushupti* or sleep state; *swapn* or dream state; *jāgrat* or waking state; *turīya* or the temporary experience of pure consciousness known as *samādhi*; *turīyātīt*, a permanent state of *samādhi*; *bhagavad* or celestial state; and *brāhmī* or unity state.

"Most people do not experience this gap. If they think about it at all, they probably believe there is a gradual transition between consciousness states," Auntie said. "Actually, there isn't. There is no gray area. One state of consciousness completely stops, then there is a gap, and the next state begins. The gap is the experience of pure consciousness—that is, consciousness by itself, that alpha1 experience.

"You and I, through our Holy Grail practice, have refined our nervous systems to be able to experience this. We call it witnessing." She went on to describe how researchers also explain the witnessing experience during sleep. Unlike most people, advanced practitioners of HGT, like Auntie and Sheely, "watch" themselves sleep. The body is asleep—that is, all the senses are asleep. One can't hear, feel, see, taste, or smell, but consciousness is awake with the brain experiencing alpha1 waves.

"Thoreau wrote about this," she said.

"The poet?" Sheely asked.

"Well, he was more of an author. Let me find it for you." She searched Google. "Here it is." She brought up *The Blog of Henry David Thoreau* dated March 18, 2008, titled, "In the Infinite Mind, Thoreau's Journal: 17-Mar-1852":

> I am conscious of having, in my sleep, transcended the limits of individual…As if in sleep our individual fell into the infinite mind, and at the moment of awakening we found ourselves on the confines of the latter. On awakening we resume our enterprises, take up our bodies, and become limited mind again.

"Wow! Do you think he was one of us?" Sheely asked.

"There are rumors to that effect." Auntie also told Sheely about research that found that people who naturally have a higher level of alpha1 coherence during the waking state are also more successful in life.[40]

"That would make sense," Sheely said.

Her aunt went on for some time. She explained that leading scientists such as Max Planck and Erwin Schrödinger believed consciousness was primary and matter was secondary. That is that consciousness gave rise to matter.

"What does that mean?" asked Sheely.

"It means that our consciousness exists regardless of our physical body. It is immortal, unbounded. You know this. It's what you experience every day. In scientific terms, the experience of pure consciousness is the experience of the unified field, the source of all creation. Matter is merely vibrating consciousness."

"Oh yeah, I guess. I'm just not into the science end of all this," Sheely said. "But it's fascinating, Auntie, really. Can we go to bed now before my head explodes?"

Auntie laughed. "Of course, dear."

Sheely let her aunt sleep in the bedroom, and she tucked herself in on her living-room couch. She was small enough that she didn't have to open it for the sleeper bed; besides, the sleeper bed wasn't that comfortable. She just grabbed her sleeping bag and a pillow, and she was set.

Auntie loves that research stuff, she marveled silently before closing her eyes. Tomorrow would be a long day.

---

40 H. S. Harung and F. Travis, "Higher Mind-Brain Development in Successful Leaders: Testing a Unified Theory of Performance," *Cognitive Processing* 13, no. 2 (2012): 171–81, doi:10.1007/s10339-011-0432-x.

CHAPTER 23

"What we need is a Kinsey Millhone," Auntie said in all seriousness. They had gathered at Kevin's grandfather's home.

"Who?" Kevin asked.

"Kinsey would be great, Auntie," Sheely said. "I didn't know you knew about her."

"Oh yeah, we're great friends."

"Who's Kinsey?" Kevin asked again.

"She's one of the best private investigators you'll ever find," Sheely said.

"Are you talking about who I think you are?" Grandfather chimed in with a wink.

"Absolutely," said Auntie, acknowledging the wink.

"Great, I'll go get her right now," Grandfather said.

"She's here?" Kevin asked, completely confused.

"Well, she usually hangs out in my bedroom, but I'll have to check," Grandfather said.

"What?" Kevin was startled.

"Keith, how could you?" Auntie said, laughing.

Kevin stood with his mouth open. His grandfather disappeared into the bedroom and returned with a book. Kevin shook his head in confusion. Everyone burst out laughing.

"Kevin, Kevin," Sheely finally managed between laughs. "Kinsey is a fictional character."

"What?" Kevin was still confused.

"She's a character in books."

Kevin grabbed the book from his grandfather. "Sue Grafton, *T Is for Trespass*," he read.

"Yes, Sue Grafton is the author of the alphabet series, whose main character is private detective Kinsey Millhone," Auntie explained.

Kevin looked at his grandfather, then Auntie Jennifer, and finally Sheely, whose sparkling eyes were full of joy, laughter, and love. He smiled back. "You got me."

Sheely hugged him. "Sorry, I guess we just couldn't resist."

They all met about two hours earlier. Keith, Kevin's grandfather, fixed a wonderful dinner. They exchanged family stories and HGT tales. There was such a wonderful feeling about finally meeting others of their kind that the Kinsey Millhone joke just spilled out.

"OK, in all seriousness, I believe we do need someone like Kinsey Millhone to help us. We have lots of abilities and skills, but we aren't detectives," Auntie said.

"I agree," Grandfather Keith said. "Do you have anyone in mind?" He already knew the answer. The vibrations were clear. Intentions could be read between the elder HGT guides.

"Sheely, I've never told you before, but you have another cousin. Technically, he's a third cousin. You and he have the same great-great-grandfather," Auntie said.

"Auntie!"

"I was always going to tell you. I was just waiting for the right time. It's the right time."

"Well?"

"His name is Bradley Grant. He lives in DC and works for the CIA."

"He's a spy?"

"Yes and no. He was a spy in the field, but now he's an analyst. He's also one of us." She paused. "He's from the Holy Grail tradition and has special abilities like we do."

"Wow. It's just too bad we didn't know ahead of time. I would have invited him," Kevin said, as he thought about the advice he had recently received at lunch from the California couple: find a friend in another law-enforcement agency.

"Well, I sort of did that for you," Auntie said. "He's available by Skype."

"You're serious?" Kevin said.

"I called him shortly after Sheely told me all that happened. He's agreed to help."

"Where's your computer, Keith? I can't wait to meet him," Sheely said.

They phoned Brad to set up the Skype call. After introductions and pleasantries, they got down to business.

"Well, you know that karma eventually takes care of everything," Bradley Grant said.[41]

"Brad's right. Did you know that modern science has validated the effects of karma?"

---

41 "Karma means action, work or deed; it also refers to the principle of causality where intent and actions of an individual influence the future of that individual. Good intent and good deed contribute to good karma and future happiness, while bad intent and bad deed contribute to bad karma and future suffering." See *Wikipedia*, "Karma," last modified November 23, 2016, https://en.wikipedia.org/wiki/Karma.

"Auntie, please, we don't need one of your scientific lectures," Sheely blurted.

"Hey, coz, I've never heard this," Brad said. "Please, Aunt Jen, continue."

Sheely fell silent.

"It's well known that how you think and act comes back to you. That is, good brings you good and negativity brings you, well, things you don't want," Aunt Jennifer began and continued. "The Christian Bible describes it like this: 'As ye sow, so shall ye reap.'" She explained that they all had experienced this through their own consciousness and that it was the basis for the Golden Rule.

Seeing the confused looks, she added that the ancient masters in all cultures intimately knew this relationship with nature and expressed it in their teachings. She brought up several examples:

"In the Bible, Matthew chapter seven says, 'So always treat others as you would like them to treat you.' The Talmud says, 'What is hurtful to yourself do not to your fellow man.' And Buddhism says, 'Hurt not others with that which pains yourself.'"

"Enough, Auntie," Sheely pleaded.

"No, no, no. This is great stuff, Aunt Jen. How do you know all this?" Brad asked.

"It's sort of her hobby," Sheely said before Auntie could speak.

"May I continue?" Auntie asked. "Today, science has validated the ancient understanding of karma. In classical physics, it was Isaac Newton who said, 'For every action, there is an equal and opposite reaction.' Meaning that for every action, there is a reaction equal to the first but in the opposite direction. And modern physics, through quantum theory, has proposed the boson effect.[42] Bosons are known to attract like bosons, and it is believed that thought energy is made of bosons."

"OK," Brad said, trying to soak it all in.

Aunt Jennifer continued. "New Age philosophy calls it the law of attraction.[43] What you desire comes back to you, but there's a catch."

"What do you mean, 'a catch'?"

"The clarity of that fulfillment depends upon the strength of the thought. A desire from the surface, everyday level of one's mind will come back, but it will be so diluted that the connection is rarely, if ever, made. A desire with more heart

---

42 Bosons are one of two primary particles that make up all creation. Fermions are the other type. Neither is actually a particle but rather a wave function (i.e., energy). Bosons of the same species attract one another; they can occupy the same space. Fermions repel each other and cannot occupy the same space. Fermions are considered the constituents of matter, while bosons are the interactions. Bosons are also considered the glue that holds matter together.

Some believe thoughts are a form of bosonic energy and therefore attract their like-energy forms. This is known as the boson effect, which gives rise to the law of attraction, or karma at the surface level of life.

43 Law of attraction: In physics, this is known as field particle exchange (bosons/fermions) and the bonding that occurs from it. In New Age thought, this term has been around since 1891. In 1904, Thomas Troward claimed that thought proceeds physical form, and William Atkinson used the phrase in his book, *Thought Vibration or The Law of Attraction in the Thought World* (Chicago, IL: The Library Shelf, 1908). In 2006, Rhonda Byrne, the author of the book *The Secret* (New York: Atria Books, 2006) and executive producer of the movie by the same name (DVD, directed by Drew Heriot, Melbourne, Australia, 2006), brought widespread attention to the concept. But it is the work of Abraham-Hicks, who have held multiple seminars and written multiple books on the subject, that has probably generated the most attention to this concept in Western life.

to it—one that is clearer and stronger from a deeper, more refined level of thought—generally comes back as what one calls a coincidence.

"Even at this level, most people don't get the connection." But, she said, if that intention came from the level of the Holy Grail, which is the level of pure consciousness, then that desire was fulfilled virtually instantaneously.

"How is that possible?" Brad asked.

"Finer levels of creation are more powerful." She reminded them about the atom bomb, how it was far more powerful than TNT, a surface chemical reaction. She also reminded them that thoughts were forms of energy. Thoughts that come from deeper, quieter levels of the mind are more powerful than thoughts that generate from the surface level.

"It's simple. Finer levels of thought correspond to finer levels of creation. And finer levels of creation are more powerful."

"Ah, now I understand. It's how our abilities work." Brad was thinking about his own experience.

"Exactly. Through our practice, we have developed the ability to think from a very fine, profound level of the mind, which in turn quickly attracts the corresponding positive or negative results, based on the quality of our thought. You're exactly right—it's how our special abilities work. When our thoughts are generated from the level of pure consciousness, they are instantaneously fulfilled."

"I never thought of it that way before."

"OK, OK. We all understand karma. Can we get back to why we are all here?" Sheely begged.

"Not here and now," Brad said. "When Aunt Jen called me and started to tell the story, I asked her to keep the details at a general level. As you know, the electronic eavesdropping by NSA listens in on almost all calls, even Skype calls. We don't want to trigger an investigation that involves us. Trust me; I'm aware of such things." Brad let that dangle. "Did you know that another congressman died here in DC?"

"A car accident, wasn't it?" Grandfather Keith asked.

"Yes, it's a sad time here," Brad said.

"I'm sorry to hear that," Kevin said, "but we could really use your help."

"I wanted to meet everyone tonight, but we really need to physically get together. I have some vacation time coming, and I'd love to have a ski vacation. Sheely, any chance I can get some ski lessons?"

"Are you kidding me? Of course you can. I'd love to ski with you."

PART 3

The Washington Gazette

WASHINGTON, DC, WEDNESDAY, MARCH 4, 2015

REPRESENTATIVE JOHN MOORE KILLED
By Abe Southerly

Late Monday afternoon, House Representative, John Moore (D-VA) was killed in an automobile accident while driving home. The early report from the Virginia State Police indicates it was due to mechanical failure. They are checking with Chrysler, the manufacturer of the Jeep Cherokee he was driving, to determine if any defects were known with that vehicle. An updated report is expected within the week.

CHAPTER 24

The media reported John Moore's death as an accident, and Congress scheduled another funeral. The vehicle inspection conducted by the FBI was not reported; only the local and state police reports were issued. Since this was the death of a congressman and it happened shortly after the death of a senator, the FBI quickly got involved. Their inspection, like the police report, showed that the braking system had failed. It was too difficult to tell if anything else might have contributed to the accident because of the damage to the vehicle, but the FBI technician who examined the automobile said its computer showed nothing that would have indicated anything but an accident.

But even the FBI can make mistakes. It took a convicted computer hacker to redirect the investigators' search. The hacker agreed to work undercover for the FBI in exchange for immunity from prosecution. She was always carefully watched and proved true to her word. She knew that modern car computers could be hacked and completely controlled. She reminded them of the CBS *60 Minutes* report in which the Defense Advanced Research Projects Agency (DARPA) demonstrated it.[44] She

---

44 February 8, 2015.

suspected that was what had happened to the congressman's car and couldn't believe the FBI missed it, but it gave her great satisfaction.

The initial blame on mechanical failure turned out to be a deliberate ploy. It was difficult to prove because the car was so damaged, but an FBI computer technician's reexamination made it clear that the car's computer had been hacked, and a virus had been inserted that took control of the car's electronics. They figured it had happened when his car was stolen.

The accident was triggered by the odometer reading. If Representative John Moore were alive, he would have sworn it happened when he reached sixty miles per hour when he felt that little jerk, but the virus was set to take control at an exact mileage, which was wirelessly transmitted the day of the accident.

The FBI figured the person who planted the bug had shadowed John's driving habits, and that is exactly what happened. The "mechanic" saw that John was consistent in his drive home, always taking the same route. That made it easy to choose the location for the "accident." Even so, it was still an approximation, due to factors he couldn't control, such as any side trips. Yet the cordoned-off location was sufficiently long enough to allow for some variation. It was even a gamble that Moore would die, but the mechanic had success in the past with the same approach. Thus, his car was stolen and the virus inserted. It was also purposely damaged to give the impression it was simply stolen for a joyride.

The mechanic had wanted to trigger the "accident" via GPS, but John's car didn't have one. He considered attaching a GPS device, but a close inspection would find it. Thus, he used his tried-and-true, old-fashion mileage method. He was confident that the brake-failure strategy would be considered an accident. Thus, he figured triggering the "accident" based on mileage would get the congressman close enough to where the road was cordoned-off on either side by concrete barriers to produce success.

This new information set the anxious FBI on a whole different path. A dozen agents were now working the Welsh and Moore cases. Half of them were assigned to find out who murdered Moore and also tasked with determining if there was any connection to the Welsh case. Those agents figured the tampering had to have been done by someone who was exceptionally skilled, so they searched their internal databases for suspects. They were able to narrow down their search to six people and eight locations where those suspects could be at any given time. Only three suspects lived in the DC area, but the others who could have handled the mechanics and electronics involved could have traveled into the area to carry out the job.

Investigators hit all repair shops that were known to have any connection, quietly or openly, to criminal activity or suspected chop shops. After several days, all angles seemed to point back to the ECC, but there was no concrete evidence. Without any strong leads, all they could do was continue to keep up the pressure.

The half assigned to investigate Senator Welsh's murder was not making any progress either. Was there a connection between the ECC and the NRA? If so, what was that relationship? Were they missing something? Two members of Congress and a witness killed: there had to be a connection.

But what it was, they still didn't know, though suspicions were starting to rise.

Part of the FBI's investigation was talking to members of Congress to gather whatever historical background they could. Piecing together that information led to the Meissner bill. Was this the driving force behind those murders? The FBI was determined not to make any additional errors and returned to further question members of Congress who were associated with the Meissner bill.

They learned from Senator Benn that Representative Jill Hill was especially upset with Representative Moore for reintroducing the bill after she had killed it. That raised the suspicion on Hill, and she was approached.

"What!" Jill couldn't believe what she was hearing. She was about to swear and throw the two FBI agents out of her office, but stopped. She took a deep breath and politely answered their questions. After they left her office, she was so upset that she grabbed her coat and left.

She figured she had paced around the Capitol Building for nearly an hour before returning to her desk. She had an idea.

"Mr. Kelly?" Russell had just answered the call with his typical response: "Russell Investigations, how can I help you?"

"Yes ma'am, that's me."

"Hi, I'm Representative Hill from Utah. Do you remember me?"

Russell thought for a moment. The name sounded familiar. Then it came to him, "Jill Hill. You were on that special investigative committee?"

"Yes."

"What can I help you with Ms. Hill?"

"You aren't the easiest guy to find. Don't you have a website?"

"Yeah, I guess I should have one. One of these days. You can still find me if you google for PIs in Boston."

"Well, I'm glad I found you. I was impressed by the work you did uncovering that corruption. Though, I have to admit you spooked several members of Congress with your uncanny methods. I remember one member thinking you were some sort of alien." They both chuckled at that.

"By the way, when did you leave the FBI?"

"It was a while ago. I always wanted to have my own investigative business," Russell said wanting to hide the actual details.

"You've heard of the murders of Senator Welsh and Representative Moore?"

"Of course."

"The FBI has been snooping around Congress gathering background information. They talked to Senator Benn. Do you know him?"

"I know of him."

"He's not my favorited Senator. We've had confrontations in the past. Anyway, the FBI just visited me and implied that I was a suspect in Moore's murder. I barely kept it together. I had nothing to do with that. It's insane they even thought it. I believe Senator Benn purposely pointed the FBI in my direction. I don't have proof of that. It's just a strong feeling I have—something is not right."

Russell remained quiet.

"I'd like to hire you to look into this."

"I don't understand."

"I don't know how you do it, but you have good instincts—scary good instincts." She paused. "There were several here in Congress who were against Senator Welsh's bill. It's almost like it was a conspiracy."

"The Meissner bill?"

"Yes, that's correct. You know it?"

"I came across it recently."

"Senator Benn was one of those who opposed it. As much as I dislike him, I don't believe he would implicate me in a murder unless something else is going on. It bothers me a lot that this happened. I'd like you to quietly dig around to see if my suspicion is true or not."

As strange as this request was coming from a congress-woman, it further sparked Russell's interest because of what he already knew. He accepted the challenge.

CHAPTER 25

Agent Catson initially rejected Senator Benn's order to eliminate Representative Moore. Benn was not the VP and did not know Catson's background. Thus, Catson knew he could not be blackmailed. He was tired of being ordered around and just simply refused. But Benn had to get this done for more than one reason; he softened his approach. The "order" became a "request," and Catson finally said he could facilitate the request, but it would be expensive. Benn said, "Whatever, get it done, but make it look like an accident."

Catson knew what to do. Yet, as skilled as he was, he knew little about cars, but he did know where to look for someone who did. As a federal agent, he had access to information that the general public didn't. Contacts he could get from internal federal databases were well documented but couldn't be searched without leaving a trail. He knew he could also search the Internet and possibly find the type of skilled auto mechanic he needed, but it would be a gamble. So he took a different approach.

Catson's youth far from pristine. He grew up in Englewood, one of Chicago's seventy-seven official communities. Englewood was by all measurements the most dangerous neighborhood in Chicago, with a poverty rate of 46.6 percent. On top of that, being a white boy growing up in a neighborhood that was 97 percent black didn't help his situation. Though as a youth, he received positive behavioral influence as a member of the inner-city ski league, he still became involved in a gang.

Chicago is known for its colorful history of corruption, from its mayors to its abundant street gangs. Thus as a teenager, Catson found it virtually impossible to avoid gang involvement. Catson belonged to the Five-Sided Devils, also known as the 5SD. The five sides were east, west, north, south, and in your face, meaning they were everywhere and not to be messed with. He learned many skills from his association with the gang, and these skills served him well in his adult life.

Catson grew up an orphan. He knew his family history only from stories he heard on the street. Apparently, his dad was killed in a gang war, and his mother left him on the steps of an orphanage at age two. He had a vague memory of his mom saying she'd be right back. All he remembered was that he woke up in a bed, and from there, he spent years in and out of foster homes and orphanages.

He managed to graduate from Englewood High School—which eventually closed—but his last years of school were a struggle. He lived with his foster gang mom who was anything but encouraging about education. He had no problem getting good grades, but he became less involved with school and more involved with the gang. That was when he became aware of the red band—the sign of 5SD membership, which years later inspired him to purchase his ski jacket.

After graduation there was no clear path to college, so he became even more involved with 5SD. He quietly worked his way up. Eventually, he was asked to kill off an offending member of another gang to prove his loyalty. That earned him the red band, and he was very proud of this badge of honor. Outside of official 5SD business, he wore it under his shirt on the right arm. When acting as a 5SD representative, he always wore it outside.

When he was twenty-two years old, he pulled off a bold move. Catson had something that most of his colleagues didn't: intelligence. Quietly, he had paid attention to the workings of the gang. He didn't care much about who did what and where, but rather was interested in how the money flowed. He became a runner for deposits into so-called legitimate bank accounts and investments and quickly pieced together 5SD's underground financial network. Most gang members were not technically savvy, and a slip here and there allowed Catson to learn passwords. He already had account numbers, so the rest was easy. Though proud of his red band, he wasn't above putting himself first.

Over time, he was able to siphon $297,345.33 of the millions the gang was making into his own secret bank account. Where the thirty-three cents came from, he wasn't quite sure, but he didn't care. Eventually, the gang accountants recognized the loss of funds. Catson was still too far down in the gang hierarchy to be an immediate suspect. One day, word got around that Joey, who handled some of the larger sums of money, was missing. Around that same time, Catson noticed a finger or two missing from others who handled the gang's finances. He decided it was time to leave, and he quietly slipped away and joined the army.

Catson was eventually accepted into the Special Forces and went through training at Fort Benning, Georgia. Special

Forces training consisted of eighteen months of rigorous preparation, assessment, and selection. Catson struggled with some of the physical training but excelled in the psychological and cognitive training. He was asked several times to attend officer-candidate school, but he always turned down the opportunity. His gang training taught him that being in the background and quietly observing required less work and produced a greater payoff.

This attitude almost worked for him on his second tour in Iraq. He learned of a wealthy family trapped behind enemy lines. It was his job to pass any intelligence up the chain of command; this time, he didn't. He knew the area well from reconnaissance missions and aerial mapping. Plus, his gang involvement had taught him a thing or two about clandestine activities. One evening, he sneaked off the makeshift command post and, with luck and skill, managed to bring the entire family into a safe zone.

He anticipated a nice financial thank-you from the wealthy family. Unfortunately, all he got was a handshake from the father and a strong reprimand from his commanding officer. Nevertheless, word of his exploit got around, and a positive news article was written in the *Army Times* about the event. He appreciated the recognition but would have preferred money.

Back home, he did get a payoff: a $3.5 million one. Catson spent twenty years in the army, including one tour in Afghanistan and two tours in Iraq. He spent his final years in the service at Fort Carson, Colorado. Also stationed there was an MP who was a former 5SD gang member. It was pure coincidence that they bumped into each other; recognition of their past connection was immediate and silent. Later, they met in a bar to discuss the old days, and they developed a friendship over time. The MP worked on a detail that provided security for the base's money handling. Through him, Catson slowly learned of the comings and goings of the base's finances.

He developed a plan to steal some of this money and asked his MP friend, hypothetically, whether someone could pull this off.

"Hypothetically?" His friend laughed. "Hypothetically, you would need someone on the inside." They stared at each other for a moment.

"Look, before I left 5SD, it was rumored it was probably you who stole their money."

Jeff said nothing.

"So it was you."

Jeff still didn't respond.

"OK, OK. I'll pretend I know nothing about that, but if you're seriously thinking about robbing the base, I'm in. I've thought about this myself and have some ideas."

His friend gave valuable feedback, and together they developed what they felt was a foolproof plan: foolproof for Catson, anyway. For his friend, it was a death sentence. Catson couldn't allow any connection to his past, and during the robbery, he eliminated his friend and the MP who was with him.

Catson knew of a legitimate financial planner who had been blackmailed and threatened into handling 5SD's money. His name was Lee Colby. Catson believed that trusting him was a better approach than trying to launder the money himself. He knew that Lee did not manage the gang's money willingly. He did not know the reasons, but he figured Lee might enjoy a little revenge. Catson told Lee the truth about what happened to the missing gang money many years ago. The amount, now over $300,000, was sitting unattended in a Chicago bank account. Lee had a good laugh over that.

"I will pay you one hundred thousand dollars if you will set up a Cayman account for me. I have three and a half million dollars in paper money that needs to be moved into it," Catson told him. Lee accepted. Catson took some leave time and personally delivered the money, being careful to avoid any 5SD contacts.

Over time, Lee had been forced into developing a well-defined underground financial network. One of his connections was a law firm out of Panama. Its modus operandi mirrored that of Mossack Fonseca.[45] Though this firm was not as connected as Mossack Fonseca, it still had company offices around the world, including the United States, and managed thousands of shell companies worldwide.

Working with his established contacts in the Panama law firm and trusted, paid couriers, Lee was able to get $3.4 million of the heisted money into a new Cayman account. He claimed the process took an additional $100,000 in payoffs. That seemed high to Catson, who figured Lee had helped himself to a little more than the agreed amount. But he had what he needed, so he let it go. He also transferred the balance of his Chicago account into his new Cayman account and then resumed his military life.

---

45 Luke Harding, "Mossack Fonseca: Inside the Firm That Helps the Super-Rich Hide Their Money," *The Guardian*, April 8, 2016, accessed May 3, 2016, https://www.theguardian.com/news/2016/apr/08/mossack-fonseca-law-firm-hide-money-panama-papers.

He had two more years on his enlistment contract, which he completed in an honorable fashion, and was quickly accepted into the Secret Service. After three years of exemplary service as an agent, and with the history of his military experience, he was chosen to head up security for the vice-president.

Now, at age forty-six, he again contacted Lee, asking another favor in exchange for $50,000. Lee was hesitant but agreed. He thoroughly enjoyed the irony behind his last transaction with Catson, as well as the financial compensation. This time, Catson wanted to know a contact in the underground automotive repair business who could handle advanced "repairs." He didn't want to go directly to any 5SD members because he didn't want any of them to know his whereabouts or even that he was alive. He knew Lee probably wouldn't know of anyone offhand, but he was confident that Lee could get a name.

It took Lee a couple of days of placing calls and mostly leaving messages to a chain of faceless gang members he knew by name only. "Look, I've been handling your affairs for years, and I've never asked for anything. All I'm asking for is a contact name," Lee would say over and over. The evening of the second day, he answered his phone and heard a single name before the line went dead. With a little more digging, he was able to get the phone number and passed this information on to Catson.

Using a burner phone, Catson called the contact and explained what he wanted. The cost: $500,000, wired in advance. Catson didn't care about the details, only that the work would be done professionally and in a way that couldn't be traced. The mechanic said the contract could be accomplished, but due to the high profile of the target, the money needed to be deposited up front.

In these kinds of deals, one never knew who could be trusted. Catson felt a half-million dollars was a lot, but since it wasn't his money, he agreed to the terms without negotiation. Catson relayed the information to Senator Benn, who wired the money—including Lee's payment—the next day. Catson didn't know how Benn was able to put together such a quick financial transaction and told himself he would find out one day.

CHAPTER 26

Unrelated to the congressional murders, another branch of the FBI was reviewing Asian Progressive Banking Corporation (APBC) documents leaked by one of its employees. APBC was one of the largest international banks. Once these documents became public, APBC had no choice and admitted hiding clients' finances so taxes could be dodged. Records of thousands of clients with accounts in 134 countries showed that the bank actively helped wealthy customers conceal millions of dollars of assets through tax-avoidance strategies. The impact of this disclosure was felt throughout the international banking community.[46]

The FBI's copies of these documents disclosed that dozens of US clients were involved, among them known criminals and one William Benn, who turned out to be *the* Senator William Benn. Due to the prominent positions of some of these individuals, the

---

46 This disclosure of APBC's client banking records was similar to the well-publicized theft by Hervé Falciani of client bank records of the Swiss subsidiary of HSBC Holdings, possibly the world's second-largest bank. For details of the impact of that disclosure, see Bill Whitaker, "The Swiss Leaks," *CBS News*, July 12, 2015, accessed November 15, 2015, http://www.cbsnews.com/news/hsbc-swiss-leaks-investigation-60-minutes-2.

FBI requested additional transaction information from APBC in the follow-up years. APBC was not a willing partner, but given the fines, sanctions, and other punitive actions Congress had considered taking against the bank, as well as similar threats from other countries, the bank had no choice.

As a result, several quiet internal investigations were conducted, including one on the senator. One of the recent transactions that raised a red flag was $500,000 transferred to a Chicago bank account that the FBI was already investigating. That account was known to handle illegal-fund transactions. Why Senator Benn would transfer money to it was a mystery.

The Welsh and Moore murders were also a mystery. Although the FBI was struggling to find answers, the head of the ECC was not. It didn't take long for word to get around about the FBI's investigation and its conclusion that the ECC had to be involved. That word quickly worked itself up the criminal chain of command. Though the FBI never directly mentioned why it was investigating repair and chop shops, it didn't take much to connect the dots.

Such high-profile contract assassinations are kept quiet, but for the head of the ECC, information flows a little easier, particularly when brutal interrogation techniques are used to induce confessions. One of the shop mechanics who was present during the hack finally offered up what he knew.

The mechanic who performed the job had flown in from Chicago. He was an independent contractor. The ECC knew of his reputation and had great respect for this man. Nevertheless, the ECC interrogator who was sent to see him began speaking in a manner that the mechanic quickly caught on to: answer or else. Thus, the mechanic told the interrogator what he knew about his contract, which was very little. The call had come from a blocked phone number and was probably a throwaway phone. He confirmed that he had been paid up front, but he did not disclose, nor was he asked—as a professional courtesy—how much. But he did disclose that the payment was made via a transfer from an international bank.

The ECC interrogator did not travel alone; backup security of two bodyguards was always present. This entourage was easily noticed, and its activity was eventually reported up the chain of command of the 5SD gang. Along the way, it reached the gang member who gave the mechanic's name to Lee Colby. He got an idea. Perhaps he could make a smart career move by providing a favor to the ECC in the form of information. It was worth a try.

He took a vacation under the guise of visiting family members in Maryland. He didn't want 5SD to know his real intentions. Once in Maryland, it took a few quietly placed calls to locate an ECC member of sufficient placement. The meeting took place in a small café in DC, where the 5SD snitch told the ECC contact about the men who went to see the mechanic. He knew they were also ECC. He went on to explain that rumors were swirling around making a strong connection between the mechanic and Representative Moore's accident.

"If the rumors are true," the snitch concluded, "I know who hired the mechanic."

"And what do you want for that information?" the ECC lieutenant asked, getting straight to the point.

"Do you know who I am?"

"Of course. I wouldn't have come without that knowledge. You're Tony Sanchez. You're what I would call a midlevel 5SD captain," the lieutenant answered.

"Close enough. I would like to move up in my career. All I ask is that if an opportunity arises, I'd like to be considered for a position within your organization."

"I see," responded the ECC lieutenant. "I can arrange that."

"Thank you." Tony paused. "I gave the mechanic's name to Lee Colby. He does financial transactions for us. Here's his phone number and address." He handed over a piece of paper. "I trust that you will contact Colby confidentially. I'd like to remain around, if you get my drift, for my new career move."

"Of course."

CHAPTER 27

On the day after the "accident," Catson walked into Senator Benn's office carrying several containers of food. Benn had asked him to pick up some dinner on the way. He was pleased with the way Catson made the John Moore problem go away.

"What'd ya get?" Benn asked, looking at the paper bag.

"Chinese," Jeff said.

"Excellent!"

They pulled a side table and two chairs together and sat down to eat.

"Congratulations on a job well done—and quickly too," Benn said, smiling.

"Oh, you mean Moore?"

"Yes."

There was a pause, and then the conversation turned serious.

"Now I have another job for you, and I'll pay you handsomely for it."

"I don't need the money." Besides his salary, he had his offshore bank account and his military pension for twenty years of service.

"Well, if you say so, but I want you to be committed to what I'm asking."

Jeff sighed.

"I have some old history I need to deal with."

Jeff continued eating.

"There is a group I owe a debt to, and I was promised that debt would be forgiven if I did certain things for this organization. That was years ago, and they have yet to honor their agreement."

"Somehow, that doesn't surprise me."

"Well, I want to convince them that the deal is over."

"Who is this group?"

"As far as I know, they don't have a name, but they control most of the East Coast, if not all of it. I met someone I think was the leader years ago. I never learned his name."

"Alfonso Cesare, known as Caesar," Jeff said.

"You know this organization?"

"Well, yes. If it's the one I think you're talking about, which it most likely is. We've kept tabs on them for years. Any group that could threaten the president is continually watched. We don't consider them much of a real threat, but they're on our list anyway. They control most of the criminal activity up and down the East Coast, as you said. No one knows what they call themselves. In law enforcement, we call them the ECC, for East Coast Criminals. Not very creative, but it works. How the hell did you ever get mixed up with them?"

"It's a long story, but that sounds like the correct group," Benn said. "I want you to find the head of this organization and assess whether you can take him out."

"Whoa...you're asking me to kill Caesar?" Jeff nearly spit out his food.

CHAPTER 28

Jeff was hesitant to accept the senator's offer, but after reflection, he felt that finding the head of ECC would probably benefit his Secret Service career. It might be better to bring him in rather than kill him, however. Or…he pondered a more interesting alternative.

The Secret Service and the FBI had been investigating the ECC for years. They attained many convictions over those years and were confident that they knew most of the leadership. As Jeff had told Senator Benn, the head of the organization was believed to be Alfonso Cesare, known as Caesar. No undercover agent had come close enough, nor had any informant or confession been trusted enough, for the agencies to be certain Caesar was who they thought he was. But there were plenty of leads, which gave Jeff an idea.

One of these leads, though only indirectly associated with the ECC, had produced an investigation into a threat to the president that had dead-ended. The investigation was now on inactive status. Jeff told his boss, the director of the Secret Service, that he was intrigued by the broken pieces of the investigation. He asked if he could follow up on it—on his own time, of course. The director warned that he'd be wasting his time but said, "Sure, what the hell, go ahead." That enabled Jeff to use Secret Service and FBI resources without suspicion.

Jeff started his ECC hunt officially as a Secret Service agent, introducing himself and using his badge when asking questions. After several days with no progress, he went undercover. His background, both inside and outside law enforcement, taught him how to blend in with the underground criminal population. Days passed quickly for Jeff since he was now working two jobs: one protecting the VP and the other as a private detective for Senator Benn.

One exhausting evening, as he was leaving a downtown bar and walking toward his car, a GM Suburban with blacked-out windows pulled up next to him. He thought it was a government car and wondered who it was and how they found him. Two men jumped out.

"Mr. Catson, please come with us," one said politely while pointing a silenced Glock 17 nine millimeter at Jeff.

Not government, Jeff thought, as he recognized the gun immediately and knew that most agencies used a Glock 22. He considered resisting. He had the skill and would probably survive, but it was a risk. He got into the car.

"Where are we going?" Jeff asked.

"Never mind that. I'm afraid we're going to have to blindfold you," the other man said.

"Why am I not surprised," Jeff mumbled under his breath.

CHAPTER 29

Caesar had sent a representative to meet with Lee Colby. It quickly became clear to the representative that Lee was just a middleman, and it quickly became clear to Lee who was asking. He volunteered Catson's name without hesitation. So Caesar knew someone named Jeff Catson had probably ordered the hit on Representative Moore. Then, since Jeff started his investigation using his official Secret Service title, it didn't take long for the ECC organization and Caesar to make the connection.

Caesar came from a family of gangsters. His grandfather, Alfonso Demetrio Cesare, was a Mafioso boss in the Sicily Cosa Nostra at the relatively young age of thirty-one, after the untimely death of his father. It was 1926, smack between the end of World War I and the beginning of World War II. Alfonso Demetrio had a flair for organizing, and he excelled in finance. He had been well schooled by his father in their business and was equipped to manage the large fortune—at least by early twentieth-century standards—that his father managed to accumulate. Even though he was young when he took over the business, he had earned the respect of the family. This respect, coupled with his keen intellect, enabled him to unite several *coschi* (families) into a single organization. This was unique at the time.

Benito Mussolini, who became Italy's prime minister in 1922, set out to destroy the Sicilian Mafia in 1925 to boost his strength as a leader. His *carabinieri* (militiamen) arrested and imprisoned thousands of suspects, and Mafia families were falling apart under Mussolini's siege. Alfonso's *cosca* went further underground. This was when his skill as a modern-day CEO came into play. Many members of other families were left stranded as their leadership crumbled. Alfonso offered leadership and money; thus, many willingly accepted him as their new boss. Nevertheless, it was a struggle to keep the organization intact.

Mussolini's campaign ended in 1929, the same year Alfonso Demetrio's son, Enrico Cesare, was born. Still, it wasn't until 1945, the end of World War II, that Mafia families started to regain strength and growth. The changing economic landscape caused by the war produced much infighting among the *coschi*. It was a time of notorious upheaval. Although it was unusual for Mafioso to leave Italy, many did. Carlo Gambino and Joseph Bonanno went to New York City and restarted careers there. Alfonso was getting tired of the scene and feared for the safety of his family and his only son, Enrico. He secretly arranged for several key members of his organization and his son to leave Sicily and immigrate to Colombia, South America.

Life was hard for the immigrants. New customs, new language, and new food all presented a challenge, but at least they were safe. Communication back to the homeland was also a problem—not impossible, but not very efficient. They soon realized they had skills and ways of doing business that were new to the Colombian gangs. Enrico did not have his father's skills, but he was a good, young man and respected. However, it was other members of the family who played important roles in getting things started in Colombia.

Drug use was not part of the business for Alfonso in Italy. He was heavily into smuggling, manipulating politicians, and rigging the bidding of contracts for companies in his control. He was aware, simply by association, of the heroin trade coming out of China, the Golden Triangle area of Southeast Asia, and the Middle East. Yet in general, the Italians avoided narcotics.

The United States, at that time, was steadily increasing its demand for drugs. In 1949, the Communists took control of China, and the whole network of organized crime in the country fell apart, nearly killing the narcotics trade. This disruption caused a stir in the worldwide narcotics underground network and caught Alfonso's attention.

In Colombia, drug usage at the time—marijuana and coca—was limited and existed mainly as part of the lifestyle of indigenous tribes. Alfonso's family members began to describe the drug-manufacturing process, and Alfonso listened. Eventually, he saw an opportunity and instructed his Colombia family to develop the connections necessary to manufacture and transport narcotics back to Sicily, where he could use the existing smuggling operation to distribute it. Just as the first shipment was about to go out to Italy, word came that Alfonso had died.

The Colombian family was never able to find out how he died, and the resulting chaos in Italy prevented any further progress on the plans. Still, the family thought the idea was good, if not great. Instead of smuggling drugs to Italy, they would ship directly to the United States, where demand was continuing to grow.

Enrico married a local woman, and in 1952 they had a baby boy whom they named Alfonso Cesare, after Enrico's father. Some believe the dark skin tone of the Sicilians was inherited from the Islamics, who ruled southern Italy for nearly two centuries prior to 1100 CE, but it was the complexion of Enrico's native wife that produced a child with a handsome, multicultural appearance. Like his father, the young Alfonso grew up in the family business, but unlike his father, young Alfonso had his grandfather's natural gift for organization and financial insight. Even as a lad, his reputation grew, and he gained respect among the leaders.

In the late 1960s and 1970s, as the demand for drugs grew in the United States and elsewhere, competition developed in Colombia in the form of cartels. Enrico's clan merged with the Medellin cartel, headed by Pablo Escobar. Alfonso, now in his early twenties, had finished college and held a master's degree in finance from New York's Columbia University. When he returned home, he became what the Mafia called a consigliere to the Medellin cartel and helped manage its finances. While Alfonso was growing his career, his dad, Enrico, was fading out of the business and enjoying life with his wife.

As the drug trade grew in the United States, the political action against the cartels also grew. In 1973, the Drug Enforcement Administration was formed by an executive order of President Nixon, and the formal war on drugs began. Life in the cartels began to get more dangerous. They needed a better way to launder their money, so the Medellin and Cali cartels formed the First InterAmericas Bank in Panama. Even though Alfonso was a trusted Medellin financier, he wasn't above secretly siphoning off money for himself. In the confusion of the times, he easily hid millions of dollars from both cartels. There was some suspicion inside the organizations, but pressure from the Colombian government and the DEA kept the cartels too busy to investigate the missing money.

By 1995, the war on drugs dismantled the Medellin and Cali cartels. Many years before, the unmarried and now very wealthy Alfonso immigrated to Washington, DC. They say opposites attract, but in reality—in nature—like attracts like. Now, as fate would have it, Alfonso Cesare was about to meet Jeff Catson.

CHAPTER 30

Still blindfolded, Jeff figured they had traveled for about a half hour in the car. There had been a lot of stops, so he was probably still within the city limits. After exiting the car, he was brought up some stairs into a building and then into an elevator. After a short ride of maybe two or three floors, Jeff thought, and going in and out of several doors, his hooded blindfold was removed.

Jeff was standing in what he thought was an office or library. It was a large wood-paneled room with six dark-wood bookcases mostly filled, several oriental rugs partially covering a hardwood floor, and a large, carved wooden desk. He also noticed half-dozen large wooden candlesticks. *This guy likes wood*, Jeff thought.

"I understand you have been looking for me," the man in the wooden room announced.

"Alfonso Cesare, known as Caesar," Jeff presumed.

Caesar dipped his head slightly in confirmation.

Jeff stepped forward and held out his hand. "Delighted to meet you."

The two goons behind him moved forward, but they stopped when they saw Jeff was just offering a handshake.

Caesar was unmoved and smiled. "Please sit," he said, without shaking Jeff's hand.

"Thank you," Jeff said.

"Let me come straight to the point," Caesar said. "You are Jeff Catson. Former 5SD member, former Army Special Forces, and current Secret Service agent assigned to Vice-President Locker. You also had Lee Colby get you the name of a mechanic who arranged the hit on Representative John Moore." He paused and looked hard at Jeff. "Do you like my biography so far?"

Jeff remained silent.

"I have no problem with your activities. In fact, I'm quite impressed. I also know that various government agencies have been looking into our activities for a long time. You call us the ECC, the East Coast Criminals gang, yes?"

Jeff nodded his head.

"We're more of an East Coast corporation, but that's beside the point. What I want to know is why you're specifically looking for me. I mean, other than the obvious. There seems to be something personal about it."

Jeff surveyed his predicament. The wooden room was conservatively decorated and dimly lit with closed curtains, so he couldn't see out the windows. The two goons were hanging quietly in the darkened background. Caesar got up and walked over to a panel in the wall. He was about Jeff's height, with a stocky build and dark complexion. Jeff noticed a slight Latin accent, but he looked like he could be Middle Eastern or even Italian. He wore a closely cut goatee and had an impressive, commanding presence.

Caesar opened the panel and removed two beers from a small refrigerator. He offered one to Jeff. Jeff nodded and accepted the beer. Caesar sat back down, and they quietly sipped their beers for a few minutes before Jeff spoke.

"I've been hired to kill you."

"Oh, and who hired you?"

Jeff hesitated before answering. "Actually, I wasn't going to go through with the contract. I was looking for you so we could negotiate."

"Negotiate for my life?" Caesar laughed.

"No, for information."

They looked at each other closely before Caesar said, "I'm listening."

"You know, as you first mentioned, we have detailed records of your organization's activities. We've made several convictions over the years, as you are also probably well aware. We believe your corporation—may I call it that?"

Caesar nodded.

"Your corporation, we believe but can't prove, among other obvious things, financially benefits from congressional bills that have hidden backings from PACs and lobbyists. There is a lot of what you might call finger-pointing."

Caesar gave no confirmation one way or the other.

"Anyway, the information I have to offer you, I believe, can benefit you financially. Maybe not immediately, but I'm sure you will be able to find a way to use it."

"Continue," Caesar said.

"I'm going to need protection. I'm deeply involved in activities that can put my life in a permanently restricted state, if you get my drift." Jeff was carefully considering his words.

"What sort of protection?"

"I'm not exactly sure. It depends on how this all plays out, but being exonerated would be nice." Jeff smiled. "Realistically, though, maybe hidden deep within your organization, if things get out of hand…"

Again, silence.

"The hit on Congressman Moore was ordered and paid for by Senator William Benn," Jeff said.

"Interesting," Caesar mused. "Is he also the one who wants me dead?"

"Yes."

Caesar leaned back in his chair. "Do you know why he wants me dead?"

"He indicated that you are holding some sort of debt over his head."

"Hmm." Caesar took a long sip from his beer. He got up and paced around the room, apparently in deep thought. Finally, he said, "Were you involved with that senator's murder at that ski area?"

"Yes, that was me."

"I see. Was that also ordered by Senator Benn?"

"Yes, but I'm also being blackmailed by the vice-president."

"Andrea Locker?"

"Yes," Jeff affirmed. "There is some sort of relationship between her and the senator, and I'm being used as their henchman."

Jeff detailed everything that had occurred. Caesar reciprocated by explaining that Senator Benn had been a valuable asset.

"His influence in Congress has increased our financial positions considerably, and he is rewarded in kind. But lately, he has become less productive."

Ah, Jeff thought as he made the connection to the hit payment.

"So, given the current circumstances..." Caesar paused. "This actually is a negotiation for *your* life. Why shouldn't I have you killed right now?"

"First of all, I'm skilled at what I do. Second, I have great respect for what you have accomplished. Law-enforcement agencies, of course, see it differently, but I was always struck by the sophistication of your operations." He paused to let that sink in and then continued, "You can always use a highly placed asset in my official position, and I'm sure we can negotiate compensation for future transactions."

Caesar and Jeff spent another silent moment staring at each other, trying to discover any hidden agenda. Finally, Caesar went back to his desk, picked up a card with his contact number on it, and handed it to Jeff. Then Caesar picked up his beer and held it out for an impromptu toast. "Welcome to the family."

PART 4

The Washington Gazette

WASHINGTON, DC, THURSDAY, MARCH 12, 2015

REPRESENTATIVE JOHN MOORE'S DEATH MAY NOT HAVE BEEN AN ACCIDENT
By Abe Southerly

The Washington Gazette has learned through an anonymous source that the auto accident that killed Representative John Moore (D-VA) may have been caused by an intentional act. The congressman's car was reported stolen several days before the accident. It is now believed the car may have been tampered with during that time. When asked to comment on this information, the FBI only confirmed that the accident is under investigation and gave no further details.

CHAPTER 31

"I'm getting tired of your screw-ups," Vice-President Locker managed to say into the phone without yelling. You told me this *accident* was never going to attract any suspicion."

"The job was done by the best in the field. I have no idea how the FBI figured it out. In fact, I'm impressed by their capability," Senator Benn admitted.

Locker shook her head. "I hope they can't connect all the dots."

"I don't believe they are that capable," Benn said. "Jeff arranged it through his previous connections. No names were exchanged, and the transfer of money was confidential. The mechanic who bugged the car is not even known by the authorities. I'm not worried."

"Well, we need to be extra careful. I would normally be informed about an investigation of this caliber. It concerns me that I wasn't. Keep your eyes and ears open."

"Will do."

CHAPTER 32

It took several days for Brad to arrange his vacation. His girlfriend, Kathy, was not happy that he was going skiing in Colorado without her. She was a good skier and had skied in Utah but never Colorado. They had been dating for two years and had a good relationship. The only sticking point in Brad's mind was that she didn't seem to be interested in meditation, at least not yet. He had also mentioned, in a roundabout way, special abilities such as levitation and mind reading. She just laughed at that. Thus, having her come with him to Colorado didn't seem like a good idea. Regardless, she had a wonderful heart, was an all-around good person, and in Brad's eyes, was beautiful as well.

As a journalist, Kathy was naturally skeptical yet curious at the same time. She was hesitant to start meditation, but Brad sensed a hidden curiosity, which was good, because he had definitely fallen for her. He wanted her to understand not only meditation, but also the special abilities that can be developed through it. He had to be careful, though. The HGT tradition was private and secretive; not just anyone could be brought in. If she started meditation and liked it, then Brad felt he could take the next step.

While Brad was making his plans, Aunt Jennifer stayed at Grandfather Keith's home and enjoyed the Boulder scene. She and Keith had some wonderful discussions. They shared information about their tradition and other traditions they knew of, and of course spent a lot of time talking about their families. They also talked about the situation the kids were in and came up with some ideas. Jennifer's only regret was that she hadn't brought more clothes.

Kevin and Sheely were busy teaching skiing during the spring-break season. It was exceptionally busy due to the early season promotion. Still, they occasionally found time to get together with their ski instructor friends to discuss the day and relax. Kevin was growing closer to Sheely by the day. One evening Kevin took her out to dinner. It was a special evening for him. When he brought her home and walked her to her door, Sheely leaned in and gave him a kiss. They had exchanged some hugs and cheek kisses, but this was their first real kiss. It lasted for several seconds. What really touched Kevin's heart was that it was initiated by her.

Kevin also spent time on his Twitter account, where he enjoyed giving out pearls of wisdom. He reviewed a couple of recent ones.

Holy Grail Technique @HGTGuide · Mar 12
Spontaneous right action is the natural product of being in the state of HGT #HGTechnique

Holy Grail Technique @HGTGuide · Mar 13
#HGTechnique #Consciousness Mental direction of any kind prevents HGT

That last tidbit was something his grandfather had instilled in him. "Other forms of meditation," his grandfather would say, "have misunderstood the characteristics of the goal—that is, the experience of pure consciousness—to be the path to it."

Kevin reminisced and recalled what his grandfather meant was that "remaining unattached," "eliminating desires," trying to "silence the mind," maintaining a sense of "presence," and other forms of control were misunderstood to be paths to pure consciousness. In reality, enlightened individuals appear withdrawn only because they are not affected by outside experiences. Pure consciousness is never overshadowed by any activity. Such a person is in a state of complete fulfillment and thus needs nothing—possessions or desires—for fulfillment. Also, an enlightened person is "silence in motion" and ever "present."

Kevin sat for a moment, smiling at the memory of his grandfather's depth of wisdom, and then went back to his computer. He was still concerned about not hearing from @SenW1937, so he tweeted,

> **Holy Grail Technique** @HGTGuide · now
> @jillspencer108 Have you heard from @SenW1937?

He was expecting her to tweet back, but some time later she called. "Hi, Kevin."

"Hi, Jillspencer108," Kevin said jokingly.

"Kevin, you don't know who SenW1937 is, do you?"

"No. Remember, I didn't even know who you were."

"Are you sitting down?"

"Yeah, I'm at my desk. Why?"

"Kevin, SenW1937 is, or I should say was, Senator Gregory Welsh."

"What? Are you sure? How do you know that?"

"Well, the *S-E-N* moniker generally refers to a senator."

"Really?"

"And his profile says his name is Greg Welsh."

"Oh yeah. I never paid any attention to that."

"Kevin, you're really a wonderful guy, but I'm always amazed at your innocence."

"But I'm innocent in a nice way, yes?"

"Yes, you are innocent in a nice way." Sheely smiled. "I was curious, and I guessed that the 1937 part referred to a birth year. So I looked up the birth dates of senators. Several were born that year, including Senator Welsh, and since he frequently tweeted about government—"

"And he hasn't tweeted for a while…you believe it must be him," Kevin said.

"Yes."

"Damn. I feel stupid."

"You're not stupid, Kevin. You just prefer to stay in the background. Your quiet personality radiates inner strength, and you have a wonderful, pure aura. It's what initially attracted me to you. I find the purity of your innocence charming."

Kevin didn't know what to say. Sheely remained silent. Kevin started to speak but couldn't find his words. He finally got out, "You know…I'm falling for you."

CHAPTER 33

Bradley Grant arrived in Denver and was met by his cousin, Sheely. They exchanged a warm hug.

"How was your flight?" Sheely asked.

"More important, how's the snow?" countered Brad.

Sheely laughed. "It's good. How's your ski legs?"

"I work out regularly, so I should be OK."

"Good, 'cause I'm going to challenge you."

"Sounds like a threat."

They both laughed. It was good to see each other in person. Brad was thirty-six, with quite a lot of life experience because of his job. He was fit, but to twenty-four-year-old Sheely, he seemed old. At home over dinner, Sheely brought Brad up to date on all that had happened. After dinner, they watched TV for a short while and then headed to bed. Brad spent the night on her sleeper sofa.

"That's not the most comfortable bed you have there," Brad said the following morning.

"Sorry. Did you get any sleep?"

"I woke up early because of the time change, but I feel rested enough to ski your legs off."

"Oh, now you're threatening me!"

After a good breakfast, they headed to Copper. Kevin wanted to join them because it was his day off as well, but a former client requested him for a private lesson. During the day, Sheely brought Brad down some of Copper's more difficult terrain. He struggled a bit but managed. She praised him.

"I told you I could do it," Brad said after one of the more challenging trails.

"Yes, you did, and you did pretty well. Can I give you some tips?"

"Of course."

She explained to Brad in some detail the technical aspects of skiing. Since he was a CIA analyst, she figured he could handle the subtleties of the sport, at least in the areas she knew. She also did a little levitation over some moguls just to tease him. That evening after dinner, Kevin came over.

"How'd Brad do skiing?" Kevin asked.

"I did fantastic," Brad said before Sheely could answer.

"You're a good skier," Sheely said.

"Thanks. It's too bad you couldn't join us, Kevin."

"I would have, but I couldn't turn down a request private. I taught this family last year, and it was nice to have them back."

"Did they learn anything new?" Brad asked.

"I hope so," Kevin said with a laugh. They chatted about the day and eventually got down to business.

"Changing the subject, has Sheely filled you in on everything that's happened?" Kevin asked.

"Yeah, I believe I'm up to date."

"Any questions?"

"Have you guys given any thought as to what you want to do?"

"We need evidence. Even if law enforcement believed my story, there's no proof. The guy's a Secret Service agent, after all. Why would they ever believe me?"

"I've thought about that," Brad said. "It may help if we could tap his desk phone, but it's not likely he uses it much. So, I don't think it would be worth the effort."

"Can we tap his cell phone?" Sheely asked.

"We'd need NSA capabilities for that," Brad said. "I can get my hands on advanced recording bugs that we could place somewhere, but recording cell phones is a different story."

"Isn't that illegal without a warrant or something?" Kevin asked.

"Yes, we'd definitely have to do it without getting caught, which I'm sure we could, given our special abilities."

"Well before we bug anything, shouldn't we first alert the vice-president about our suspicions? Wouldn't she want to know about her Secret Service man?" Sheely asked.

"I can probably arrange that."

"That sounds like a good idea," Kevin said. "But how do we keep ourselves out of it?"

"That won't be a problem. I may be an analyst now, but I learned a thing or two in my nine years as a field agent," Brad said.

"Well, let's talk about it tomorrow evening when we get together with my grandfather and Sheely's auntie," Kevin suggested.

"Auntie." Brad chuckled. "That's right. I remember you called her that the other day."

"I know, I know. I guess I just never grew out of it," Sheely confessed.

"That's so cute," Brad and Kevin said in unison.

"Can we just please forget it?"

Like that will ever happen, the guys thought.

After Kevin left and Sheely and Brad were about to settle in for the night, Aunt Jennifer called.

"Hi, Auntie," Sheely said.

"Hi, sweetie. I've got some bad news. Well, it's not really that bad. But I have to go home tomorrow."

"Why? What happened?"

"My neighbor saw water coming out of my back door—the one where my kitchen is."

"Oh no!"

"She has a key to my house, so she ran over and found the master valve and shut off the water. Apparently, there's a leak or broken water pipe somewhere."

"Is there much damage?"

"Mostly in the kitchen."

"Do you know how it happened?"

"They had some very cold weather while I've been here, down to twenty-five below. When I'm home, I generally turn the heat up as insurance against anything freezing, but I wasn't home. So I guess that's what happened."

"I'm so sorry, Auntie," Sheely said.

"It's OK, dear. I have insurance, but I need to leave right away. My neighbor called me just a couple of hours ago. So I won't be able to meet with all of you tomorrow."

"Don't worry, Auntie. We've come up with a possible first step. Brad believes he can contact the vice-president and warn her about her agent. We were going to discuss it tomorrow, but maybe we should go forward with it."

"Keith and I thought about that as well and came up with the same idea. Can Brad do it without getting us all involved?"

"Yes. He said that wouldn't be a problem."

"Great. Well, I'm off early in the morning."

"You take care, Auntie. And please update me on your home. I love you."

"I love you too. Bye." Auntie hung up.

"That was your aunt?" Brad asked.

"Yes, a water pipe broke in her home, and she has to go back tomorrow."

"Bummer. So I guess we aren't meeting tomorrow evening."

"Well, the four of us could meet, but I think you warning the vice-president is a good first step. I'll call Kevin in the morning. I'm sure he'll agree," Sheely said. "Let's see how your meeting with the VP goes and then follow up from there."

"Sounds like a plan," Brad said.

CHAPTER 34

Bradley Grant skied a couple of more days by himself because Sheely had to teach. He then spent a day with Grandfather Keith in Boulder before taking a red-eye flight back to Maryland. When he arrived home, he left a text message for Kathy and headed to bed for a couple of hours. While having breakfast, he saw Kathy's text welcoming him home:

I'll call tonight, xoxo.

She always ended her notes and e-mails with *xoxo*, which made Brad smile.

He was about to leave for work when he remembered that the forecast called for rain. It was mid-March, and the weather in DC was warming up. He grabbed his umbrella and headed to his car for his commute to Langley, Virginia.

Brad joined the CIA out of college. The agency had always intrigued him, and secrecy was part of his heritage. During his training, he was spotted as a good candidate for fieldwork. He was five feet, eight inches, slim, and average looking. On the surface, there was nothing special about him, and people on the street would completely overlook him. Yet he had quiet inner strength and a keen intellect that did not go unnoticed. Those qualities made him an excellent candidate. He was approached and accepted the position as a field agent. He spent nine years in the field and generally enjoyed the work, but he eventually decided it was too risky and took a job as an analyst.

At his desk, he spent the morning catching up on his regular work. He also researched the vice-president's schedule. No public appearances were listed for the next several days. That could be good news, but he couldn't be certain. Brad wanted to check further, but he had to be careful not to attract attention. Everything employees did at "the Company" was monitored.[47] Even his quick check of the VP's schedule online was a small risk.

The CIA constantly tracked the activities of the major heads of state, including the president and vice-president, so it was not unusual for their whereabouts to come up in conversation. At lunch, Brad was able to manipulate a conversation thread in the direction of the VP and discovered that she was in DC and probably working from her office. He decided to visit her during his lunch break the following day.

The rest of the day was uneventful, and he didn't need his umbrella after all. He shook his head, *Another "accurate" weather report*. Kathy called him at home that evening.

"Did you enjoy skiing?"

"Very much so, and I really enjoyed meeting my cousin Sheely. She's a ski instructor at Copper Mountain and taught me a lot."

---

47 This nickname was popularized by Philip Agee in his book *Inside the Company: CIA Diary* (London: Penguin Books, 1975).

"So, you think you can keep up with me?"

"Is that a challenge?"

Kathy laughed. "No, just teasing you. Hey, I went to some of those websites you told me about."

"The ones on meditation?"

"Yes, silly, the ones on meditation."

"And…"

"Well, it's interesting and all—"

"But you're still not convinced."

"Hey, I'm a journalist. I'm skeptical about everything."

"Don't I know."

"But you love me anyway, right?"

"Yes, I love you and miss you. When can we get together?"

He always enjoyed talking with Kathy but found it hard to be present. There was a lot on his mind.

The vice-president has a small office in the West Wing of the White House, known as the Executive Office Building. The VP also has an office in the Eisenhower Executive Office Building on Seventeenth Street Northwest, just west of the White House. It has a formal feel with ornamental decorations on its ceiling and walls; its chandeliers are replicas of old-fashioned gas lamps. The patterned wood floor is made of cherry, maple, and mahogany, while the two fireplaces gleam from Belgian black marble. The desk in the office was used by several early presidents and has been used by every vice-president since Lyndon B. Johnson. The inside of the top drawer has been signed by its users since the 1940s.

Brad figured the personality of Andrea Locker fit the Eisenhower office more than the West Wing office and took a chance that she would be there. Parking would be the bigger issue.

He drove his Ford Mustang to DC. The first garage he approached was full, but he lucked out on the second at 1701 Pennsylvania Avenue, about two blocks away from the Eisenhower building. He paid the twenty-dollar rate and headed toward the VP's office. On the way, he went over his plan in his head. Brad, like his cousin Sheely and her boyfriend, Kevin, had special abilities derived from their HGT tradition. As all the HGT practitioners knew, not all these abilities survived the passage of time.

Those that did survive, whether misinterpreted or not, were practiced and handed down through the centuries. As family connections were lost, so was some of the knowledge, and not all families knew of all the abilities. Brad's family tradition had kept the purity of mind transfer.

Brad knew of his family's connection to Aunt Jen and her family, but other than the occasional cards among the elders, no formal contact had been made until the recent get-together. During Brad's stay with Sheely, they had talked about their HGT understandings. Sheely was very open, and since she had teased Brad with a little levitation when they were skiing, she helped Brad gain the proper execution of it. It had never worked for him before because of his family's misinterpretation. One's consciousness has to be developed enough to experience any of the abilities, but proper usage is also required. The first time he used the method Sheely taught him, he burst out laughing at the exhilaration.

But Brad did not share much from his side of the family. *Something about guys and their sharing*, Sheely thought. She didn't push it, although if Auntie were present, she would have dug every last ounce of knowledge out of Brad. Aunt Jennifer would have recognized Brad's mind transfer technique as similar to Patanjali's sutras 39 and 44, in which one could enter another person's body or mind. Brad had developed the ability to project his thought patterns outside his body and into the mind of another.

The keepers of the HGT knowledge are highly evolved, and negative thoughts or tendencies rarely appear in their minds. Brad, as a young man, was sometimes playful with his mind transfer ability. Once, when he was an adolescent in school, his teacher was trying to explain how simple a subject was. "It's as simple as two plus two equals four" was what she intended to say, but because of Brad's interference, what came out was, "It's as simple as two plus two equals five." It caused a lot of laughter in the classroom.

Such playfulness caused no real harm, but he quickly learned through his parents that using his abilities that way was wrong. It was, however, a great skill to have as a spy and helped him move up the CIA ranks. Today, that skill would help him again.

At the entry guard station, Brad was asked his purpose for being there.

"I have an appointment with the vice-president," he announced, silently hoping she was there.

"I believe she's in today. Let me check for your appointment." As the guard looked at his monitor, Brad transferred the thought *Ah, yes, I remember. Please walk through the scanner.* The guard said the words out loud and gave him a visitor pass.

Brad had never been in the building, so it took him a few minutes to find the VP's office: room 246. He entered and said confidently, "I'm here for my appointment with the vice-president."

"I didn't know she had an appointment. She's not busy at the moment, but let me check," the assistant said. As she turned to her computer, she had a thought and said, "Oh yes, I remember. She's expecting you. Please go right in."

Brad entered the VP's office. Andrea Locker looked up, surprised, and was about to speak, but Brad beat her to it.

"Madam Vice-President, I'm very sorry to bother you, but I have information you need."

"Who are you?"

"More important is the information I have about your Secret Service agent Jeff Catson and Senator Welsh," Brad said, wondering why he had not seen Jeff anywhere.

"What?"

The assistant appeared at the door. "Madam, the president is on the line."

Andrea was momentarily confused, but she gathered her thoughts and asked her assistant, "Would you please have this gentleman wait for me in the reception area?" Brad was escorted out, but he had "heard" and sensed enough. Once in the reception area, he asked where the men's room was and quickly left the office, not to return.

Security cameras were everywhere. These did not concern Brad, since it would be difficult to discover his identity. Even though he now had a desk job, his former position as a field spy kept his picture and other identifying information highly classified and unavailable to any outside law-enforcement databases.

Even within the CIA, it was virtually inaccessible. What did concern him was what he had just found out. One of the easier special abilities was knowing the nature of another person's mind. Sheely and Kevin were both accomplished at that, but Brad had taken this skill to the next level. If the other person's thought pattern was strong enough, he could not only "see" the nature of that person's mind but also "hear" its contents.

So much had transferred from Andrea's mind in the instant he had mentioned Catson's and Welsh's names that Brad had to take a step backward to regain his balance. Although the details were fuzzy, it was clear that the VP knew of Jeff's involvement and that a senator named Benn was also involved. Brad had not expected that. The wave of images passed through his mind so quickly that he was overwhelmed. He needed no further time with the VP.

CHAPTER 35

Brad spent the next couple of days quietly doing some research on Senator Benn. He knew from the instantaneous transmission he had received in the VP's office that Benn was involved somehow, but why? What was Benn's connection to all of it? Most of the research he did at home, but he also gathered as much as he could at work without raising any suspicion. He learned that the senator was sixty-eight years old. He grew up in New York City and rose quickly through the political ranks. He was able to raise large sums for several of his campaigns, which appeared to come from a super PAC group. He was chairman of the Senate Finance Committee and was considered one of the more influential lawmakers on Capitol Hill.

But why him? Brad was stumped, and it showed. He and Kathy went out to dinner one evening and spent the night at her home. They met for lunch the next day. Midway through lunch, she asked, "What's up with you?"

"What do you mean?"

"You haven't been yourself since you came back from your skiing trip."

"I know. I'm sorry."

"It's OK. I know you get wrapped up in your job at times, and you can't tell me what's going on. I get that. It's just that when you're like this, I feel like I'm in the way. I'd much rather let you be and have you text me from time to time that you're OK."

"You're never in the way."

"You know what I mean."

They looked silently at each other for a few moments.

"This one may take a while," Brad said.

"It's OK. Honestly, it's OK. I'll spend my spare time reading about meditation." She smiled.

Brad laughed.

That evening, Kathy spent the night at Brad's home. She wanted as much of him as she could get before he left for "a while." After she left in the morning, Brad admitted to himself that he felt more at ease. Besides being distracted, he also felt guilty about not telling Kathy what was really going on. He was happy that Kathy had no problem expressing her feelings and understanding his. This gave him a more relaxed state of mind, and he decided to take a different direction with his research. He would look into the background of Senator Welsh. *Maybe I can find the reason he was killed.*

He learned that the senator had left a successful law practice to run for Congress. All evidence pointed to the fact that he was well respected in his home state of Montana and in Congress. *Why would someone want him dead?*

A Google search on Welsh revealed that his wife had died two years earlier. He had three sons and four grandkids. Brad also discovered that the senator had graduated from Harvard.

A smart guy. Browsing through various Google suggestions, Brad stumbled upon a reference to an article Welsh had written for the *American Economic Review.* The article was picked up by the *Annual Review of Financial Economics.*

Brad found an online review of the article. The review was highly critical. It said Welsh had twisted the facts, giving a misleading impression about "perhaps the most important institution ever created," according to the author. That further piqued Brad's curiosity. *Why's the Fed the most important institution?* He found a link to the article online but had to pay to download and read it. It was only five dollars, so he went for it.

The article was long. After reading it, Brad understood how someone in the establishment could be critical. Yet if the information presented was true, would someone kill over it? It didn't make sense to Brad.

He expanded his search to reviewing the online news channels: CNN, Fox, and MSNBC. Over several days, he was becoming an expert on the activities of Congress but not making any progress as to why someone would have wanted to kill Welsh. One evening, he was about to give up when he came across a news article.

It was a short article on the death of the Meissner study. A bill, it said, Senator Welsh had sponsored. Brad didn't know what that was. The article proposed, or rather insinuated, that the study seemed to have come to a quick end because of the deaths of Senator Welsh and Congressman Moore. That caught Brad's attention.

He learned that after the death of Senator Welsh, Jill Hill, who was chairwoman of the Committee on Science, Technology, and Infrastructure and originally a strong proponent of the

Meissner study bill, had suddenly reversed her position and canceled it. Yet John Moore, who was also on the committee, reintroduced it. Then he died in an automobile accident that may not have been an accident, and all activity on the bill died with him.

Finally, the article suggested that Senator William Benn was probably privately smiling and toasting in his office because he was a strong opponent of the bill. The article implied questions that Brad was about to ask himself. *Did someone not want that bill passed? Was Senator Benn responsible for Welsh's death?*

Brad searched for Bill S. 362, the Meissner study. The study claimed it could increase coherence in society via a meditation technique. This hit home with Brad. Although he had never heard about this bill or this concept, it made complete sense to him. The bill also referenced a preliminary study conducted on an Indian reservation in New Mexico, which reminded him that the FBI was investigating the Native Rights in America group. That led him to read about the NRA protests over drilling rights on the tribe's land, which in turn led him to Senator Welsh's bill that gave Federal approval of the drilling. All this suggested a connection to the senator's scalping, but it was so bizarre that Brad had a hard time wrapping his mind around it.

"Wow!" Brad let out a long breath of air.

CHAPTER 36

The monetary policy of a country controls the supply of money and interest rates, both of which affect the inflation rate. The fiscal policy of a country controls the flow of the revenue via taxation and government spending. Monetary policy together with fiscal policy is used to affect macroeconomic variables in the attempt to promote stability and growth in the nation's GDP.[48]

This concept was well understood by Senator Gregory Welsh. Though he was a lawyer before becoming a member of Congress, he had a strong background in economics from his university days, which he kept alive. It was a hobby of his, and now and then he wrote an article about it that managed to get published.

---

[48] "Gross domestic product (GDP) is the monetary value of all the finished goods and services produced within a country's borders in a specific time period." See *Investopedia*, "Gross Domestic Product—GDP," accessed November 20, 2016, http://www.investopedia.com/terms/g/gdp.asp. The term was first used in a congressional report in 1934 and came into common use in 1944. Today, some economists believe it is a poor measure of the nation's prosperity, though it continues to be used.

He knew that in November 1910, a secret meeting was held at the estate of J. P. Morgan on Jekyll Island, Georgia. The seven plutocrat attendees of that meeting, representing several major banks, Congress, and the Treasury, conceived of the Federal Reserve System. On December 23, 1913, President Woodrow Wilson signed the Federal Reserve Act into law, and the Federal Reserve System was formed as the country's central banking system. Though its name contains the word "federal," it is completely independent of the government.

The Federal Reserve Bank, also known as the Fed, manages the monetary policy, and Congress manages the fiscal policy. It is composed of twelve regional Federal Reserve Banks in major cities throughout the country. The lead bank is the Federal Reserve Bank of New York, which is controlled by its chairman.

The Fed does not receive funding from the government, nor does it need approval from any government branch or agency for its monetary decisions. Senator Welsh had personally heard Alan Greenspan, chairman of the Federal Reserve (1987–2006), say on PBS, "There is no other agency of government which can overrule actions that we take."[49] The Fed has no oversight committee and by law cannot be fully audited. It is owned by stockholders; in other words, it is a private corporation. The stockholders are US banks. Which banks? Welsh had discovered that was a closely held secret, which irritated the hell out of him.

---

49 Abe Day, "Greenspan Admits Fed Is Not Beholden to Any Government Agency," *Prison Planet*, September 21, 2007, accessed November 26, 2016, http://www.prisonplanet.com/articles/september2007/210907Beholden.htm.

He did learn that the banks that were fortunate enough to hold these stocks earned an annual dividend of 6 percent on that investment. He once explained how it worked to one of his colleagues: "The US Treasury borrows currency by issuing bonds, which are nothing more than IOUs, in order to pay for the government's spending. The bonds are bought by banks, which in turn sell them to the Federal Reserve for a profit. The Fed buys those bonds with a check, essentially an IOU, against money it does not have.

"Remember, the Fed is not funded by any institution. It has no money. The banks deposit those checks and use that new currency to buy more bonds at the next Treasury auction. Thus, this exchange of IOUs between the Treasury and the Federal Reserve is what creates currency."

"Doesn't that create a deficit?" his colleague asked.

"That's correct; it's called deficit spending. But what's worse is that the workers, who earn the currency through that government spending, deposit their money into the banks, which in turn lend that money out for more spending. Thus, the money supply is exponentially increased. The amount of money in the market is what creates inflation or deflation, which the Fed was created to manage."

It was a hard concept for anyone to understand, and he was frequently asked for help when it came to the country's financial dealings.

He knew the process was further complicated by the 1913 constitutional amendment that allowed the government to collect personal income taxes. That income collected by the IRS is turned over to the Treasury so it can pay off the principal and interest on the bonds it has issued, which ultimately were bought by the Federal Reserve with money it never had. This process requires an ever-increasing debt ceiling because there is never enough money in the system to pay off the debt.

Who benefits in this process? That was the question that bothered Welsh. The deeper he looked, the more bewildering it became. On the surface, it appeared that the banking system was the benefactor. The banks earn funds by selling the Treasury bonds to the Federal Reserve at a profit, by earning interest on that newly created money through loans, and finally through their 6 percent dividend as stockholders of the Fed.

The damn banking system, Welsh initially thought, but the more he learned, the more irritated he became. He began to believe there was more to it. He knew the quote from Mayer Amschel Rothschild (1744–1812), the founder of the Rothschild family dynasty, and believed today's modern bankers still followed that belief: "Permit me to issue and control the money of a nation, and I care not who makes its laws." He was also familiar with John Maynard Keynes, the British economist known for his Keynesian economics, who wrote, "By continuing a process of inflation [deficit spending], government can confiscate, secretly and unobserved, the wealth of the people, and not one man in a million will detect the theft."

As a senator, Welsh was familiar with the US Constitution and realized that this process, driven by a debt-ridden paper currency, was unconstitutional. Article 1, Section 10 of the Constitution says, "No State shall enter into any Treaty, Alliance, or Confederation; grant Letters of Marque and Reprisal; coin Money; emit Bills of Credit; make any Thing but gold and silver Coin a Tender in Payment of Debts." Yet in 1932, Congress passed the Glass-Steagall Act, which authorized the Federal Reserve to issue loans in the form of paper notes (Federal Reserve Bank Notes) to its member banks, even if those banks did not have the required gold backing.

This process of monetary policy and fiscal policy, which has continued year after year, drove Welsh to look for a solution. He knew it was the reason the country was kept in a state of mild chaos. He also felt it was a well-orchestrated strategy that was deliberately started in 1913 with the implementation of the Federal Reserve. But why?

In 1934, the Treasury Department created the Exchange Stabilization Fund (ESF) through the Gold Reserve Act. Its funding came from the paper profit of the US government raising the price of gold, and its purpose was to act as a stabilization fund. It provided for three functions: currency swaps with other countries, bailouts of international corporations, and interventions in the currency markets to prop up the US dollar.

Unofficially, Welsh learned that some believe it had funded CIA's dark operations worldwide, including the drug trade, money laundering, and the CIA's worldwide propaganda network, in which more than four hundred journalists in the most prominent sectors of the media provide disinformation to the United States and the world.

Privately, one of his fellow senators asked, "Why can't we do something about it?"

Welsh explained, "The ESF has no oversight committee. It's above any laws and purposely maintains an air of secrecy. Essentially, it's a Ponzi scheme—a giant slush fund." He tried to explain more, but the senator just shook his head.

Welsh knew that in July 1944, the Bretton Woods Conference, driven by the ESF, established the International

Monetary Fund and the organization that became the World Bank. It basically established an international exchange rate based on the US dollar instead of gold, thus furthering the ESF's reach.

The ESF performs its actions with maximum anonymity to protect—so it says—US interests worldwide and to maintain the value of the dollar as the world's reserve currency. Many historians believe that it has authorized and performed an enormous number of illegal activities to accomplish its goal. In the United States, the monetary policy and fiscal policy are secretly driven by the goals of the ESF. The ESF, in turn, is run by the office of the US Treasury through the Federal Reserve Bank of New York.

Thus, the Federal Reserve Bank of New York, as the lead bank in the Federal Banking System, controls not only the Federal Reserve System but also the Exchange Stabilization Fund. Its chairman has ultimate power over the US financial system and, by extension, the worldwide financial system. Senator Welsh believed this person held far too much power.

He frequently vented his frustrations with his wife. She would patiently listen, and after a while, she would lean over in bed and give him a sweet kiss. "Time to go to sleep," she'd whisper. It always softened his heart, and he slept well. But when she died, he had many sleepless nights.

What was not known by historians, investigative journalists, and Senator Welsh, who had all uncovered this ripping-off of the American public, was that it was actually driven by a small, elite group whose sole purpose was to maintain its wealth and power. Although the original ancestral members of this group have passed on, their wealthy heirs have secretly maintained this mild state of chaos in the country via policies, laws, politics, caucuses, groups, and any ideologies that keep the flow of money into their pockets and increase their power.

The Republican Party, the Democratic Party, Congress, the Federal Reserve, the banks, corporations, individuals such as VP Locker and Senator Benn, and even the ECC were all but cogs in this wheel of corruption and domination of the American people driven by these few powerful individuals. It was a well-hidden secret, but these elites knew their livelihoods depended on an ongoing state of mild chaos in the country and did everything they could to maintain it.

Conspiracy theorists believe these elites are the secret members of the Illuminati.[50] Originally, the Illuminati were keepers of the knowledge of the Holy Grail, but like the Knights Templar, they grew into a large organization. In 1785, the Bavarian government issued an edict that banned all secret societies, and the Illuminati went underground and splintered. Only a handful had the HGT knowledge and knew the organization's original mission. The larger body occasionally heard rumors of abilities and powers but had no firsthand knowledge. Eventually, this took a negative turn.

Today, it is believed that the Illuminati conspire to control industry and governments worldwide. Historical events in the United States, including World War I and World War II, are

---

50 The official historical record reports that the Illuminati were formed in Bavaria (what is now known as southeast Germany). Some historians believe they existed far earlier. According to the confidential HGT tradition, they originally protected and promoted its purity while opposing abuses of power by governments.

believed to have been orchestrated by Illuminati to increase their power and wealth.

Their symbol—which they pirated—is the all-seeing eye that is on the back of the US one-dollar bill. It is known as the Eye of Providence and is located at the top of the pyramid on the left-hand side of the bill. It is part of the great seal of the United States.

In 1782, the symbol was adopted with the recommendation of three committees. Members of those committees are believed to have been Freemasons who were also keepers of the HGT knowledge. The eye was meant to represent the all-knowing and all-seeing properties of pure consciousness, the Holy Grail of all life: the consciousness of Jesus, which was one and the same with the consciousness of God.

The pure side of the Illuminati merged into history, and the original meaning of the Eye of Providence was lost. Instead, it became associated with the power-hungry side of the Illuminati. Today, that symbol is associated with the Eye of Lucifer and the supernatural powers he has—the complete opposite of its true meaning. It can be seen in the logos of universities and fraternities, the seal of the state of Colorado, and even the DARPA logo—a new, hidden message that only the elite few comprehend.

Additionally, the mottos surrounding the Eye of Providence pyramid—*annuity cœptis* (favor our undertakings) and *novus ordo seclorum* (new order of the ages)—have also completely lost their original meanings. The HGT members of the original adopting committee knew of the Meissner effect—not by that name, because science had not discovered it yet, but through their deep understanding of the power of pure consciousness. They knew that it could create a *new order of the ages* and that God would *favor our undertakings*.

Senator Gregory Welsh had not known these original meanings nor had knowledge of the conspiracy theory of the modern Illuminati or the true history of the Freemasons. But he had grasped the cycle of negativity that kept the country in a state of mild chaos. His research showed him that. Additionally, he believed there was more to it—hidden details he couldn't uncover. The result was that he understood that a completely different approach had to be taken to get the country back onto a secure financial path. So he commissioned the Meissner study. He felt that only by increasing society's level of consciousness as a whole could true prosperity be created for the population. Unfortunately, it cost him his life.

CHAPTER 37

"'You are not here merely to make a living. You are here in order to enable the world to live more amply, with greater vision, with a finer spirit of hope and achievement. You are here to enrich the world, and you impoverish yourself if you forget the errand.' Those words were spoken by another President Wilson," the current President Wilson said. "President Woodrow Wilson, and they couldn't be more appropriate. Congressman John Moore exemplified those principals in his life. He was a great congressman, a loving husband, and a devoted father. He will be missed by all. Thank you, and God bless." President Wilson finished and slowly walked away from the podium.

It was the second time in less than two months that the president had given a eulogy. The service was delayed because of scheduling difficulties and conflicts and was overdue, but the Moore family was grateful. Most members of Congress were in attendance, along with Representative Moore's acquaintances and close friends. On his way out, the president stopped one more time to give his condolences to the family and briefly talked with Locker.

Jeff Catson remained extra alert in the background during the eulogy. For the past several days, while he was escorting the VP, he sensed she was being watched. He passed this alert on to the other agents, and their threat level went up. He also told the VP.

"Madam, our alert level has gone up a notch."

"Thank you, Agent Catson. I'll stay alert. I trust you have my back?"

Jeff understood the two sides to that question.

On the way out of the cemetery, as he escorted Locker to her limo, Jeff spotted Caesar's two goons. He understood why he had sensed the VP was being followed. It wasn't her they were following; it was him. *Damn Caesar.*

Instead of returning to her office, the VP had her driver go to Constitution Avenue north of the Capitol and head to the Russell Senate Office Building to pay a visit to Senator Benn. The Russell building, which is the oldest congressional office building, was first occupied in 1909. The Dirksen addition was built in 1958, and the Hart addition in 1982. Senator Benn's office was in the older part of the Russell building. He liked the historical characteristics and felt it fit his personality. Besides, he had one of the nicer office layouts.

As Andrea Locker entered his office suite, Senator Benn's staff rose and welcomed the VP. She was not expected, and the staff was at a loss. The senator had not returned, so they offered the VP some refreshments. While they waited, the VP described the funeral service, and the staff passed along the latest congressional gossip.

About twenty minutes later, Senator Benn arrived. He was surprised to see Jeff Catson standing outside.

"I don't believe you are on my schedule today," Benn said.

"No, but the vice-president is," Jeff replied.

Benn stared a moment at Catson and then entered his office. "Good afternoon, Madam."

"Afternoon, Bill. There are some things I'd like to talk to you about. I was hoping you could spare some time for me this afternoon."

It wasn't a question. "Of course. Please come in." Just before closing his office door, the VP asked the nearest assistant to have her Secret Service agent join her and the senator.

Jeff entered the office, closed the door, and remained standing. "What's up?" he asked.

Vice-President Locker began. "Two days ago, a man entered my office unannounced. He said he had information on *you*"—she pointed to Jeff—"and Senator Welsh that I needed to know about."

"What information?" Jeff asked.

"Just before I was about to ask him that, the president called, and I asked him to step out. When I finished with the president, he was gone."

"What do you mean, gone?" Benn asked.

"Gone! As in left."

"Did you get his name?" Jeff asked.

"No, but there should be security video."

"Do you think he knew about us?" Benn asked.

"What else could it have been?"

"There's no way anyone could have connected me to Senator Welsh," Jeff said emphatically.

"Well, I don't know what else it could be," Locker retorted.

"OK, can we find out who this guy is?" Benn asked.

"I can track down the security videos. Madam, would you be able to identify him?" Jeff asked the VP.

"Yes, I'm pretty sure I can."

"All right, if we can track him down, I'm sure I can get answers from him. And we can decide what to do from there. Agreed?"

"I don't see what else we can do," Benn said.

"All right, Jeff, get it done," the vice-president ordered.

Later that day, Jeff alerted his coagents that he had spotted two suspects who were following the VP. He lied because he had his own agenda in mind. They set a trap for that evening.

"I think they're looking for a slipup in our security to get at the VP. She's impenetrable at home. So I suspect it's when we're traveling with her that they'd make their move. Thus, they're probably following us to learn our routines. Let's give them a perceived security slipup and see what happens," he told his agents.

They agreed to have dinner together. After that, they would split up and give the impression that Catson was going to pick up the VP by himself. They figured with only one agent protecting the VP, whoever was following might take that as an opportunity.

Outside the restaurant, they said their good-byes and split up. About fifty feet away, Catson turned and yelled, "Oh, I forgot to tell you. I'm going back to pick up the VP. No need for you guys to come."

He didn't know where Caesar's goons were, but he was certain they would hear the message. As he walked back to the parking lot, the other agents turned around and secretly followed. Sure enough, the two thugs were following Catson. The other agents quickly confronted them.

They admitted to nothing, but they were carrying guns and did not have DC concealed-carry permits—theirs were from Florida—so they were arrested. The District of Columbia requires all gun owners to register with the Metropolitan Police Department. DC also does not recognize permits that the states issue. As a result, all nonresidents are prohibited from possessing handguns.

They spent an uncomfortable night in jail before Caesar's attorneys got them released on bail. Catson was waiting. He did have a legal DC concealed-carry permit, but what he was about to do was far from legal. He confronted the men with his weapon. He walked them to a Dumpster in a side alley, bound their wrists and ankles together behind their backs, gagged them, and not so carefully lifted them up and dropped them into the Dumpster.

"Tell your boss respect goes both ways!"

Later that day, the driver of the garbage truck that was lifting the Dumpster noticed it shaking.

"That's odd," he told his partner. He lowered it back to the ground. His partner got out to inspect.

"Whoa! Get out here!"

The two garbage collectors freed the two smelly guys, who immediately left without a word of thanks. The garbage collectors stared at each other in disbelief.

When Caesar learned of the escapade, he laughed. "That Catson's smarter than I thought."

CHAPTER 38

Jeff Catson entered the security control center of the Eisenhower Executive Office Building and asked to review the video from the day the VP had had an unexpected visitor. He fast-forwarded the digital recording to the lunch hour. It wasn't until 12:37 p.m. that he saw a man enter. No one else entered until 1:14 p.m., so he assumed the 12:37 man was the one he must find. He cropped out the clearest frame to show the VP, but he was confident he had the right person.

After e-mailing the photo to the VP, he printed out a copy for himself. Then he went to the guard station to ask for the entry log for that day.

"You work through the lunch hour, right?" He already knew the answer from the video.

"Ah, sure. Why?"

"May I look at your entry log?"

"Of course." The guard pulled out the manual log and handed it to Jeff. Although signatures can be electronically captured, a handwritten signature in pen is less likely to be modified or deleted "accidentally."

Jeff flipped through the pages. There was no record for the 12:37 man, as Jeff was now calling him. "Do you remember this guy?" he asked the guard after showing him the photo.

"Oh yeah. There weren't many guests that day. He had an appointment with the vice-president."

"Then why isn't he logged in?"

"What do you mean?"

"There is no entry for him."

"That's impossible. Let me see." The guard looked at the entries and then flipped the pages. "I don't understand. He couldn't have gotten in without me registering him and giving him a visitor pass."

They both looked at the photo: 12:37 clearly had a visitor pass. The guard was dumbfounded. Jeff was suspicious. He went back to look at the video again. On the video, 12:37 walked up to the guard, who then turned to his computer. He appeared to check it, but he turned back too quickly. He waved the man through the scanner and gave him a guest pass without having him sign in. Jeff left the security room and went to the VP's office.

"Good morning, Mr. Catson," the assistant said.

"Do you remember this gentleman?" Jeff asked, showing the photograph. "He apparently had an appointment with the vice-president."

"Yes, he was in the other day, but he didn't stay very long."

"What do you mean?"

"Well, he was with Ms. Locker for only a minute or two before the president called. Then she asked the gentleman to step out of her office while she took the call. He asked me where the restroom was, but he never came back."

"May I see the appointment log?"

"Of course, Mr. Catson." She pulled up the VP's online schedule. "Something's wrong. I don't see his appointment, but I'm sure it was there."

Jeff leaned in to view the screen. "Is the VP in?"

"Yes, but she's in conference."

"Thank you." He left the office and the confused assistant.

There was just no explanation for it. Perhaps the VP's assistant had deleted the appointment entry by mistake, but she didn't do anything really wrong. On the other hand, 12:37 should never have been allowed in the building without a log entry and valid appointment. As a result, the entry guard was put on suspension pending further investigation.

Jeff received confirmation from the VP that 12:37 was the man who had visited her. That was the confirmation he needed before he went to the FBI. He explained the situation and asked to have 12:37's image run through their facial-recognition database. It took some time, but no matches were found.

Damn. The vice-president was not going to be happy, not to mention Senator Benn. He left to see the senator.

Senator William Benn was quietly working in his office. He was expecting Jeff Catson to arrive when he got the call.

"Hello, Bill," the voice said.

"Yes?"

"How's the progress on the defense system bill coming?"

"I'm making good progress," he lied. "I believe I have nearly enough votes to get it passed."

"Very good. I'll be in touch." The phone went dead.

Benn was worried and fuming. He was tired of this ECC guy. He was also eager to hear what progress Jeff had made in locating Caesar, but now he needed a drink. In fact, he had a few scotches before Jeff showed up.

Jeff was greeted by the senator's assistant. "Welcome, Mr. Catson. He's waiting for you. Please go in."

"Afternoon, Senator," Jeff said as he took a seat.

"Would you like a drink?"

"No thank you." Jeff noticed the strain on Benn's face. "You seem a little shaken."

Benn got up from his desk and paced back and forth. Jeff sat silently. "Have you made any progress on my request?"

"You're talking about the ECC problem?"

"Yes. What else would I be talking about?" The anger on Benn's face was clear.

"I've been able to make some good progress." That part was true. "But I haven't been able to track him down as yet." That part wasn't.

Benn remained silent. There wasn't much he could do.

"Maybe I'll have that drink after all," Jeff said.

"Please help yourself." Benn pointed to the cabinet with the liquor.

"I've also not been able to find out who that guy was who saw the vice-president," Jeff confessed after taking a swig.

"The one we believe knows about the killings?"

"Well, we don't know what he knows, but it seems logical."

"He wasn't on the security videos?"

"Oh yes, he was on them all right, but he doesn't match any facial profiles in any database. There was no record of him coming or going. Andrea's assistant, Barbara, couldn't find the appointment entry, even though she swears there was one. The entry guard had no record of logging him in but believes he did. That guard has been suspended. I personally believe that the guard and Barbara are both innocent. Something is very wrong, and I can't figure it out."

"Have you told Andrea yet?"

"No."

"I can understand why."

CHAPTER 39

Kevin took Sheely to have sushi. Locals liked to make fun of people ordering seafood in the mountains. "You should order elk or buffalo." But the Frisco Sushi Bar shipped in fish via overnight carrier. Besides sushi, it offered traditional Japanese nigiri, sashimi, and specialty rolls—all favorites of Sheely.

Sheely purposely dressed sexy in dark, tight leggings with Sorel boots that had overflowing furry tops and a beige turtleneck with a loose-cut, light-red sweater. Kevin thought she looked stunning and was doing his best not to stare. He was wearing faded jeans and an old but nice plaid shirt. *Maybe I should have dressed better.*

They were talking shop. Sheely's PSIA certification exam was quickly approaching, and Kevin was prepping her.

"Remember that if you're asked what causes a ski to turn, it's not rotary motions in the body," Kevin said. He explained that a turn is a change in linear direction. Rotary mechanisms produce torque or a change in angular motion—in other words, twisting. The two forces that create a turn are gravity and deflection. They change the skier's linear motion, the direction of the skis. They must work together.

"Gravity," he continued, "is what pulls you down the hill." Then he explained that without deflection, the skier would just go straight. Deflection is created by tipping the skis on edge. Therefore, it's the interaction of edging and pressure against the snow, which is deflection, along with gravity, that causes the ski to turn.

Sheely was getting glassy-eyed.

"Rotary does not have to be involved at all. The ski will turn based just on its side cut. If you want to tighten the turn, then rotary comes into play."

"So if I kept the skis flat on the snow and just used rotary, I would be doing pivot slips down the hill because of gravity," Sheely concluded, proud of herself for finally putting it together.[51]

"Yes, that's exactly right. That's how pivot slips are done. I'm confident you'll do OK, but there's one thing the examiners will nail you on in the skiing demonstrations. Do you know what that is?"

"I don't have the best pivot slips."

"Yes, but they're passable. What is it you're not doing well enough, not only in pivot slips but also in your turns?"

She thought for a moment. "Oh, flattening my skis."

"Yes. You understand the concept, but you tend to resist the hill."

"You mean I fight gravity?"

"Yes. How does our HGT meditation work?"

---

51 A pivot slip is a maneuver in which the skier uses only rotary mechanics to sideslip vertically down the hill, pivoting the skis back and forth across the hill without creating a change in direction.

"What does that have to do with skiing?"

"Just go with me for a second."

"Well, we use a special sound, and it just goes."

"You're so funny."

"What?"

"Your auntie knows all the technical details, but you just go by your heart, don't you?"

Sheely smiled broadly. "You're really getting to know me, aren't you? But I'll have you know I *do* know some technical HGT stuff. Auntie keeps repeating it over and over, so it's hard not to pick up some knowledge."

"Your auntie is a special lady."

"So how does our meditation relate to skiing?"

"Just like we don't control our special sound, which allows the mind to take its own direction toward greater joy, and the greatest joy is the experience of pure consciousness. So pure consciousness acts as gravity for the mind, pulling it inward."

"Yes, yes, I know all that. Auntie has drilled that into me, but how does it relate to skiing?"

"You need to let go of the hill and—"

"Not fight gravity," Sheely said.

"Exactly, and you do that by flattening your skis. You're experienced in letting go internally. Now transfer that skill externally."

"Don't fight nature."

"Yes, again. Just like in life, we allow nature to work for us. We flow with it, not against it."

"And we direct it with our desires."

"Now you're catching on. In skiing, let gravity pull you down the hill and then manage it. Don't fight it."

"OK, I've got it. Can we talk about something else?"

"Well, one more thing."

"Oh, great." She reached for another bite of sushi.

Kevin went on to explain that all she had to remember were the steps in the teaching cycle, the different teaching styles, the five skiing fundamentals and the movements that produce them, the differences among men, women, and children in their stance and basic mechanics, the four ways of producing turns, basic movement analysis, DIRT,[52] class-management skills, teaching methods, progressions, and the concept of guest-centered teaching.

"Did I leave out anything?" Kevin smiled.

"Yes, your sushi is still *out* on your plate."

"Sorry, I tend to rattle on when it comes to skiing. Not a good characteristic of an effective lesson. I always have to remember that students are taking lessons to ski, not just to listen to me."

"You're a great instructor, Kevin."

"We can always improve."

They were enjoying each other's company more and more. Kevin normally wasn't very good at carrying on a conversation, yet words seemed to flow easily with Sheely. But Kevin needed to interrupt that flow; there was something special he wanted to give her. He was nervous, but the feeling seemed right. He finally got up the courage.

"Sheely, I have something I want to give you."

Sheely smiled.

---

52 DIRT: Duration, intensity, rate, and timing.

"I wrote a poem for you." Kevin reached into his pocket and retrieved a folded piece of paper. He handed it to her.

"Read it to me," she said.

"No, no, no." Kevin suddenly became shy.

"OK, I'll read it." Sheely unfolded the paper and read it out loud:

Because you are an inspiration
A spark of life
A glowing example
A star flickering and shining
Strong and bright
Alive
Blooming like flowers
One in each eye
Each eye a birth
Each blink unfair.

Her bright blue eyes became misty. Kevin blushed. She reached across the table and squeezed his hand. "It's wonderful," she said.

They were silent for a while and then naturally and comfortably started chatting again. They could have talked all night. After the waiter came by three times to take the check, Kevin finally got the hint.

"Let me help," said Sheely, reaching into her purse.

"That's OK. Thanks for offering, but I'll get this. I know you're perfectly capable of taking care of everything, but helping you from time to time gives me a sense of…of being a man."

"You're definitely a man," Sheely said with a laugh.

"I know, I know…just that…oh, never mind."

Sheely got up, walked around the table, and gave him a kiss. "Take me home, and I'll fix you some warm herbal tea to help digest all this food in that manly stomach of yours."

Kevin paid the bill, and they left for the short ride back to Sheely's home. Sitting next to her on her couch, Kevin could not help himself and silently stared into her eyes. Sheely gazed back, and before they knew it, they were in a passionate embrace. Sheely finally broke away, got up, and reached out for Kevin's hand.

"Come," she whispered.

And they went to her bedroom.

CHAPTER 40

As nice as that evening was, they both had to get up early and go to work. It was a normal day on the hill, except for the pleasant memories that occasionally distracted them.

They got together again after work. Sheely invited Kevin over for dinner, and they both had similar expectations for the evening. Unfortunately, a knock at her door interrupted their dinner. Kevin got up to answer it.

"Brad? Hi! What are you doing here? Come in, come in."

"Brad! Hi!" Sheely went over to give her cousin a hug and a kiss. "Yes, what *are* you doing here?"

"Well, let me take my coat off. Ooh, that looks good," said Brad, eyeing the food on the table. "Do you have any more of that?"

"Yes, here, sit down."

Sheely set up a place setting and served Brad. She had fixed a special meal for Kevin with a fragrant coconut sauce that immediately caught Brad's senses.

As they settled in, Brad explained why he was there. "I went to see Vice-President Locker."

"Was she concerned?" Sheely asked.

"Um…" Brad raised his hands as if about to speak. His mouth opened, but nothing came out. He put his hands back down and slightly shook his head. Kevin and Sheely gave him a puzzled look.

"OK," Brad said. He took a deep breath. "I had to use special abilities to get in to see her. When I told her I had information she needed to hear about her Secret Service agent and Senator Welsh, her whole demeanor changed. Her aura went dark, and a flood of images and thoughts transferred to my head. At the same moment, the president called, and I was asked to leave. And that's exactly what I did. I got out of there as quickly as possible."

"Images?" Kevin asked.

"Yes, and words. So much it completely overwhelmed me." Brad paused to gather his thoughts. "In a nutshell, what I learned is that the VP knew her agent was involved in the murder of Senator Welsh. And another senator, William Benn, was also somehow involved."

"Holy shit!" Kevin said.

"Exactly."

Brad detailed his entire visit to the VP's office. Kevin and Sheely asked him about being identified, and he told them it would be virtually impossible. He explained that he couldn't understand Senator Benn's involvement and had done some research. He found that Benn had questionable campaign contributions and that he headed up a finance committee, but that was it. Then he started looking into Senator Welsh and stumbled upon the Meissner study. He knew his cousin and Kevin would be interested in it and explained what he knew.

"I wonder if my auntie knows about this effect," Sheely said. "She would be very interested in the science behind it, but I bet she would know the historical context as well."

"If this study is true and it was implemented on a massive scale, then a lot of issues would be resolved, *and* we might actually get a working Congress," Kevin said.

They all laughed. Brad continued. "The bill that could authorize funding for the study was championed by Senator Welsh. After his death, the House representative who was pushing the bill flip-flopped and killed it. However, Representative John Moore apparently reintroduced the bill over his coworker's objection."

"Wasn't John Moore that congressman who died in a car accident?" Sheely asked.

"Yes, but the FBI believes it may not have been an accident."

"Really?"

"Sheely, where've you been? It's been all over the news," Kevin teased.

Sheely made a face at him and then asked her cousin, "Are you suggesting that Representative Moore was murdered to kill the bill?"

"It's possible. This article I read suggested that the closeness of all the events seemed too coincidental. And given what we know, it kind of fits. But here's the kicker: Senator Benn was a strong opponent of the bill. Could Senator Benn, Vice-President Locker, and Jeff Catson be involved in some plot to kill these people, including your friend, just to make sure this bill didn't pass?"

"Whoa, this is even bigger than I could have imagined," Kevin said.

"But why wouldn't anyone want this bill to pass?" Sheely asked. "If it does what it claims, it'd be really good."

"What if somebody or some group does *not* want things to change? What if they're making money or increasing their power or something due to the confused state of affairs our country has slipped into?" Brad proposed.

"I can't imagine that," Sheely said.

"I can," Kevin said. "Remember the nonsense that just occurred over the funding of Homeland Security? The Republicans essentially were blackmailing the president. They wanted his immigration programs killed before they would refund the department. It's so typical of Congress to play politics instead of getting real work done. All they do is kick the proverbial can down the road of indecision."

"But what does that have to do with the killings?" Sheely asked, confused.

"It's the same thing but just on a more corrupt scale," Kevin said.

"From my agency perspective," Brad offered, "I believe there is a bigger picture here that is way out of our hands."

Now what? was the question hanging in the air.

Brad had taken off early from work to catch the flight to Denver and rented a car to get to Sheely's. What he had to say had to be said in person, but he couldn't stay. He was involved at work and had to return. His flight was early the next morning. They all decided to take some time before making any further decisions. Kevin returned home, and Brad and his cousin spent a couple of hours chatting.

"Can I tell you something?" Brad asked Sheely.

"Sure."

Brad paused. "You're lucky to have a boyfriend in our tradition."

Sheely smiled.

"My girlfriend, Kathy, is not. She's wonderful, and I've fallen in love with her, but…"

"But she's not into meditation and everything else we can do," Sheely said.

"Yes."

"I had a boyfriend like that once. We finally went our separate ways. But it doesn't have to be that way. My mom knew nothing about our tradition. Dad told me that he was just patient and loving. He had the ability to know a person's heart, and my mom's heart was pure gold. Eventually, my mom started meditating, and the rest is history."

"Does your mom know everything about our tradition?"

"Of course. She has never been able to develop any of the special abilities, but she fully understands everything."

"Your dad taught her?"

"My mom actually gets teary-eyed when she talks about it. Having my dad share such personal and intimate knowledge opened her heart even more."

"How'd your dad die?

"He had a genetic heart condition, and one day, well, it took him."

"I'm so sorry."

"Thanks. Have you told Kathy about us? I mean, meditation and everything?"

"We've talked about meditation a lot but only in very general terms about the other abilities."

"Well, I can tell you care a lot for her, so don't give up."

CHAPTER 41

After work the following day, Kevin called his grandfather to let him know he was coming to visit. His grandfather had a meal waiting when he arrived.

"You're not going to believe this," Kevin said. He explained everything Brad had done and the conclusions he had drawn.

"Now that's something to be concerned about," Grandfather said.

"What do you think we should do? Should we do anything? Is there anything we *can* do?"

Grandfather sat silent for a while. Kevin remained silent as well. He knew his grandfather was deeply immersed in the fathomless level of consciousness that the HGT tradition had brought to his life. From that enlightened level of pure knowledge, he knew his grandfather would intuitively receive guidance.

"First, nature calls for justice, and we can help promote that with the knowledge you have of the killings. Second, we need to see that the Meissner study bill is passed to promote justice for society."

"Great!" Kevin said mockingly. "I knew that."

Grandfather smiled. "You are already on the way. 'Well begun is half done' is a popular saying. Just continue, and nature will support your efforts." He had full confidence in Kevin.

At the same time Kevin was talking with his grandfather, Sheely was talking with her aunt through Skype—Brad would have been highly irritated. Sheely first asked about the water damage.

"Fortunately, it's not too bad," Auntie said. "They had to open up a wall to fix the leaking pipe, but everything else dried up nicely. Well, at least better than I expected. Some spackling and painting, and all will be back to normal."

"I'm glad to hear that." Sheely got to the real reason for the call. She relayed Brad's story and said she couldn't believe how mean and evil people could be. Her aunt reminded her that there is no source of evil, no source of darkness in the world, only a lack of light. Of course, she backed that up with an example from science and religion.

"I've explained how the unified field underlies all life. It's the home of all the laws of nature. Everything in the universe is just vibrational waves of this infinite field. Nature is structured in layers. Wait a minute; I'm going to draw you a diagram." Auntie grabbed a piece of paper and drew a diagram of the structure of creation.

She held it up to the webcam.

"Yes, I remember all that," Sheely said. "I also remember you saying that everything is just energy, and you gave the

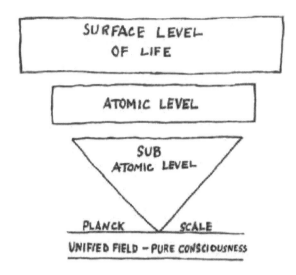

example of electrons. We commonly call them particles, but actually, they're some sort of wave energy. What'd you call it?"

"Wave functions. They're actually an excited state of the electromagnetic field. Just like waves on the ocean are excited states of the field we call an ocean."

"That's right. I remember. Everything is actually an excited state of the unified field."

"That's right, dear. It's a field of pure knowledge, unbounded, infinite, and silent. But that doesn't mean it's hibernating. It's full of dynamic potential. It's like an arrow drawn back on a bow. It is silent yet full of potential. In spiritual terms, the unified field is a field of pure consciousness. We know this from our HGT tradition. It's what we experience."

She explained what Sheely more or less already knew, but her niece was happy to get a review. She reminded her that in religious terms, the unified field is the consciousness of God.

She quoted the Bible. "In the beginning was the Word, and the Word was with God, and the Word was God." She explained that the "Word" in scientific terms was the energy that created the big bang.

"Like you said, the universe is nothing but the expression of energy. God is a creator, and by his very nature, he creates. So the dynamic silence of the unified field had no choice but to expand into life as we know it. You can think of it as the light of God expanding everywhere. Even here on Earth, darkness comes because the sun goes away, not because a source of darkness overtakes the sun. There is no source of evil in people, just a lack of the light of pure consciousness."

Sheely was always amazed by the depth of Auntie's knowledge and had to admit to herself that Auntie was right. Nevertheless, she couldn't understand why there were bad people in the world. Auntie's explanation of the Meissner effect, on the other hand, was fascinating and fulfilling.

She explained the 1 percent principle in nature and gave examples. A laser beam is created by having approximately 1 percent of the photons align themselves, and then the rest of the photons spontaneously fall into alignment. The same thing occurs in the creation of a magnet. About 1 percent of the iron atoms line up, and suddenly all the rest fall into line. Crystals form the same way. "It's not surprising that the same phenomenon exists in human behavior. When about 1 percent of a population is contacting the unified field, the field of pure consciousness, through a meditation technique, they would generate waves of coherent energy that would affect the surrounding environment."

She called it a field effect and explained that it's like a radio tower broadcasting its signal: receptors called radios pick it up.

In this case, she told Sheely, it would be waves of coherence being generated from the coherent state of people's minds, and those receptors called nervous systems would pick up on it and start acting in a more coherent, positive fashion.

"It makes perfect sense. Jesus said it first: 'For where two or three are gathered together in my name, there I am.' That is, coming together even in the name of pure consciousness generates a field of purity that prevents negativity. That's what going to church is all about. That's what this Meissner study wants to prove and then implement in society. I think it is a great and needed plan."

"That's wonderful, Auntie, really, but what should we do with all these bad, negative, incoherent waves of energy we've uncovered?"

"Exactly what you are doing. Well begun is half done. Just continue, and nature will support your efforts."

The HGT tradition runs deep.

CHAPTER 42

Brad had mentioned he could get his hands on a highly sophisticated bugging "thingamajig," as Sheely called it. They did a three-way conference call, and speaking in general terms, they agreed that Kevin would go to DC and place the device in Senator Benn's office. They were confident VP Locker was involved and knew about the killings, but they did not know Senator Benn's connection or level of involvement. Thus, they agreed he seemed the obvious choice for bugging. As anxious as they were, Kevin had to wait until the spring-break season was over to get more time off. Finally, he flew into DC and stayed with Brad.

Brad had been in the Russell Senate Office Building a couple of times. He knew the general layout and educated Kevin about it. The bug, which Brad was able to obtain through his connections in the spy business, was an advanced model not available to the general public. It was about the size of a match-box, it was voice activated, and it could store a terabyte of voice recording at 128 kilobits per second. That's about seventeen thousand hours—far more than they would ever need. Its electronic signature was tiny. A detection device would have to be about an inch away to locate it. It was powered by a highly classified sodium-ion (Na-Air) battery built with nanopores that had been proved to last nearly five hundred hours when voice activated and almost indefinitely when idle, which should be sufficient for the month-long plan.

Kevin was nervous. He had the ability to become invisible on cue, but he had done so only for fun or to support his research with consciousness during meditation. He wasn't 100 percent certain he could pull it off under pressure, especially for the length of time needed. The only exception was after he witnessed Senator Welsh's murder. Brad and Sheely were reassuring, but that went only so far.

The plan was to hide the device behind some books. All congressional offices had shelves of books to give a scholarly impression, Brad and Kevin assumed, and these books were rarely, if ever, removed. The backup plan was to hide the bug behind a wall picture or under Benn's desk. The device had a self-sticking pad using a strong adhesive that could be removed easily and quickly.

On the chosen day of execution, Brad dropped off Kevin at the Bethesda Metro Station. It was the closest station to his home and one of the busiest in the DC area's rapid transit system. At its completion, it had the longest escalator in the country. Traveling down it, Kevin thought of the task ahead. *I hope this goes down just as smoothly*. He rode the Red Line to Union Station in the center of downtown DC.

Going up to the main hall, he paused to admire the beautiful arched ceiling. He walked out through the center of the three arched columns on the front of the building and into the sunlight. He had never been to DC, so he stopped to take a look. Turning 180 degrees, he spotted six statues standing proudly on the facade of the entrance. He wondered who they were.[53] Turning back around, he entered Columbus Circle. Columbus Circle manages the intersection of six streets. In the center of the circle is the Columbus Fountain with a statue of Christopher himself.

"Here we go," he said out loud, as he started the two-block walk down Delaware Avenue to the Russell Senate Office Building. Suddenly, he picked up on a thought form. It didn't have a clear articulation, but the message seemed to say, *Can you help?*

Kevin looked around and didn't see anyone in distress.

Can you help? He heard again but could not determine its source.

"Woof!" The dog lying on the short patch of grass to his left sat up and announced himself. *Can you help?*

"You?" Kevin asked the dog.

I ran away.

Kevin was stunned. *I can hear you!*

"Woooooof!" The response was loud and clear.

Kevin was aware of this ability, but he didn't know he had it. Understanding the language of all creatures was one of the special abilities of the HGT tradition.[54] His grandfather told him about it, but its implementation had been lost to time.

---

53 The six statues are called "The Progress of Railroading" and were designed by Louis St. Gaudens. They were installed between 1909 and 1911, and their iconography represents the US railroad industry.

54 This ability is clearly described in the ancient Vedic tradition. Patanjali wrote about it in the third chapter of his aphorisms. It is sutra 17, and Aunt Jennifer Shannon probably knew about it.

Kevin stopped dead in his tracks and stared at the scraggly mutt in disbelief.

Can you help?

Where's your home? Kevin's thought somehow transferred and was understood.

Ran away. Mean. Hurt me.

Kevin didn't know what to do.

Hungry.

How long have you been gone?

Long time.

The dog continued saying what Kevin thought was, *Wandered city, eating out of garbage cans.*

Kevin reached down to pet the dog. "What's your name?" he asked out loud, and somehow it transferred.

Tucker.

Well, Tucker, where's your collar?

Neck thing other dogs have?

Yes.

Never had.

"Well…" Kevin looked in the direction of the Russell building. "I guess my plans for the day have changed." He looked back in the direction of Union Station and the waiting taxis.

When Brad arrived home that evening, he was greeted by a growl.

"Whoa! Kevin!"

Kevin came running to the front door. "Sorry." Looking at Tucker, he transferred, *He's my friend. He's good.*

Tucker sat and offered his paw. Brad, shaking his head in confusion and wonder, cautiously shook Tucker's paw.

"You should have seen him before I bathed him," Kevin joked.

Brad just stared in return.

"I guess you want an explanation."

They sat down, and Kevin told the story. Brad had mixed emotions. He was hoping to hear that the bug had been successfully placed. At the same time, he was excited to hear about Kevin's new ability, but not exactly thrilled to have a dog in his home.

"I've had some time this afternoon to think about this. I'm going to bring him home with me. My grandfather could use a pet. Even though he's fulfilled and quite happy, I think he could use a companion. Since my grandmother passed, he hasn't had anyone to talk to."

"Does your grandfather have that ability?" Brad asked.

"Not that I know of, but I'm sure he could develop it. I'm not even sure how I got it. Maybe Sheely's aunt will know more about it."

"That's a good thought. I'd like that ability as well."

"Well, if I learn how it's happening, I'll teach you. We should go out and get some real dog food. I cooked up some of the hamburger you had and threw in some carrots for good measure, but some real dog food would probably be better."

Your food good, Tucker said. Kevin laughed.

CHAPTER 43

Invisibility has been the subject of science fiction and fantasy for as long as literature has existed. Potions and spells, magic amulets, Frodo Baggins's ring, and Harry Potter's cloak are prevalent in literature and fairy tales. The Greek hero Perseus is said to have had a cap that, when worn, produced invisibility.

There are also stories of invisibility in ancient Indian literature. In the *Kathasaritsagara*,[55] the Brahmin Gunarsarman had a magic ointment that, when put in his eyes, would produce invisibility. The *Ramayana*, an ancient Vedic text attributed to the saint Vyāsa, talks about invisible *Rakshasas*.[56] Also, *Vimanas*, or flying machines with the ability to become invisible, are mentioned in several other Vedic texts. There are even instructions for what to do in case one of these invisible flying machines collides with birds. A story in the *Mahabharata* tells of Krishna "killing" a *Vimana* with a weapon that sought out its sound.[57]

---

55 The *Kathasaritsagara* is an eleventh-century collection of Indian folk tales.

56 *Rakshasas* are demons in Vedic literature.

57 The *Mahabharata* is another ancient Vedic text attributed to Vyāsa. The central part of the *Mahabharata* is the well-known spiritual text the Bhagavad Gita.

Today, we have stealth technology. Stealth planes avoid detection by preventing radar, a form of radio waves, from bouncing back to the source. In 2014, two scientists from the University of Rochester demonstrated optical invisibility using ordinary lenses.[58] The technique is to bend the light around an object. It is similar to water flowing around a rock. If an imaginary eye was upstream of water flowing around a rock, then the eye would not see the rock because there would be no reflection. The water does not bounce off the rock but instead flows around it.

In 2006, an invisibility cloak was produced using microwaves that hid a copper cylinder, and again in 2009, a Turkish university research center achieved invisibility using nanotechnology.

From gross forms of stealth technology to finer levels using nanotechnology, scientists are discovering that, at finer levels of creation, the possibility of invisibility exists. If one could act at the finest level of creation—the Planck's scale, which is ten million, million, million times smaller than the nucleus of an atom—then one could theoretically change the statistical probability of events and could prevent light from reflecting off a body, thus producing the effect of invisibility.

Through the HGT process passed down through generations and learned from his grandfather, Kevin was perfecting this ability. Aunt Jennifer recognized it as Patanjali's sutra twenty-one. This was the skill Kevin hoped would stay with him as he entered the Russell Senate Office Building.

---

58 Joseph Choi and John Howell.

Kevin's initial plan that he and Brad had worked out was to enter via the accessibility entrance on Delaware Avenue closest to Constitution Avenue. They figured that might be the less-restrictive way to get in. They discovered that Senator Benn's office was room 386, which they assumed was on the third floor. They were not able to get a detailed layout of the interior. All they knew was the general description from Brad's previous visits.

It was a pleasant day, not too warm or cold, which psychologically helped Kevin as he walked down Delaware Avenue. It wasn't too busy; everyone seemed to be focused on their own thoughts. He waited until he was some distance away, checked to see if anyone was paying attention, stopped, closed his eyes, and created the desire. He waited a moment before opening his eyes.

Whew! I did it.

In his concealed state, he continued walking toward the Russell building. A lot of people were entering the door closest to C Street. This entrance was restricted to staff personnel until 10:00 a.m. Kevin checked his watch; it was 8:10 a.m. He changed his plan. Instead of using the accessibility entrance, he approached the staff entrance and followed the next person into the building.

He paused to watch the flow of people. Each staff member swiped a badge through a reader and walked through a scanning device. Although he couldn't be seen by human eyes, he did not know what would show up on the scanning device. He looked around for a way to bypass the scanner. There was none.

He walked closely behind a heavyset man. No buzzers went off when they went through, but the guard monitoring the device noticed an anomaly and asked the man to wait. The operator called over another guard, and they seemed to be looking at a replay. Kevin didn't wait to find out.

This was a basement entrance, so Kevin quickly found some stairs to the next level. He walked down a hallway and found himself in the rotunda of the historical entrance on the southwest corner of the nearly square building. He checked out the statue of Senator Richard Russell, for whom the building was named, and continued on to a stairway. He climbed up to what he thought was the third floor, but it turned out to be the second floor. The size and majesty of the three-story rotunda had confused him.

Great. I'm already screwed up. Kevin started to swear but then relaxed and silently laughed at himself. He found the third floor but had no idea which way to go. Instead of spending the morning wandering the hallway, he decided to ask for directions. He waited until no one was around and materialized. He didn't have an identification badge, but he thought he could get away without one for a quick encounter. A woman turned a corner and approached him.

"Excuse me; I must have made a wrong turn. I'm new to Senator Benn's staff. He's in room 386. Could you point me in the right direction?"

"Hi, I'm Maggie."

"Peter."

"Nice to meet you, Peter. You're close. Walk down here and around the corner. You'll find his office on the left."

"Thank you." He started walking away. As soon as she turned around, he disappeared. *Whew, that was lucky.*

If he and Brad had done more research, Kevin would have been smiling at the irony of his visit. In the 1970s, the Russell Senate Office Building was featured in the TV shows *The Bionic Woman* and *The Six-Million-Dollar Man*. Today, it was *The Invisible Man*.

He found the door labeled 386. Now, how to get in? He couldn't just open the door—that would be too spooky—so he knocked. When an assistant to the senator opened the door and stepped into the hallway, puzzled, Kevin walked inside.

"Who was that?" another assistant asked.

"No one was there. Do you think someone is just goofing on us?"

"Who knows? Anything is possible in this building." They both chuckled.

Kevin surveyed the reception area and found the door to the senator's office open. He looked in; no senator. Entering, he considered where to put the recording device. He checked out the bookshelf, but it seemed too far away from the senator's desk. He decided to put it under the desk. The front of the desk had a panel hiding the opening for a chair. He went to the rear of the desk, pulled out the chair, and looked underneath the desk. The back of the top center drawer did not go all the way to the front panel. There was just enough room to stick the device there. It would be close to someone sitting at the desk and to anyone sitting in the chairs just in front of the desk.

Just as he finished securing the bug, he heard someone enter the room. The person stopped and asked, "Liz, would you please get the folder on Senate Bill 456 for me?" Kevin started to escape from under the desk.

Damn! He almost said out loud. He forgot to activate the bug. He quickly turned back, pushed the tiny lever to *on*, nearly bumped his head, turned again, and this time tripped over the desk chair just as the senator moved it to sit. The chair's sudden jerk surprised the senator. He looked at the floor to see what it hit. Seeing nothing, he ignored the anomaly and sat down, with the chair creaking under his weight.

"Here's the file, sir," said Liz. Kevin was still recovering his composure. He rushed to the door, but the assistant had closed it on her way out. *Now what?* If he opened the door, the senator and his assistants were sure to notice. Knocking on it didn't seem to be a good idea either. He decided to sit on the floor near the door and wait. He leaned against the wall and made himself as comfortable as possible.

Senator Benn was reviewing papers and writing notes. He made a couple of phone calls about Senate business. He finally got up and walked around his desk. *Finally*. Kevin got ready to exit. Unfortunately, Benn just went to the bookshelf to retrieve a book. *Glad I didn't put it there.* Kevin settled back down against the wall. About an hour and a half went by before Liz stuck her head in the door to announce the senator had a visitor. Kevin had almost dozed off but managed to quickly get to his feet.

"Please bring him in," Senator Benn replied.

Liz held the door open. As the man entered, Kevin quickly exited and almost brushed against him. The main office door was closed. Liz was still in the senator's office, and the other assistant was nowhere to be seen. Kevin opened the door to the hallway and exited. Two people in the hallway who had just walked past heard the door close. Kevin held his breath. *I should have closed that more softly.* They turned, saw nothing, and continued walking. Inside, Liz heard the noise as well but kept her attention on the senator. Kevin's rapid change in metabolic rate from nearly asleep to rushing out the door caused his heart rate to increase rapidly. He was now breathing hard. He hurried down the hall.

Shit! He was losing it. He was no spy. *I'm just a dumb ski instructor. What the hell am I doing?* He nearly said out loud. Unfortunately, his nervousness caused a shift in his physiology, and he swiftly became visible. *Damn!* He took a few deep breaths and continued walking. In the stairwell, he heard steps coming up toward him. "Stay calm," he whispered to himself.

"Afternoon," Kevin said to the person as he passed.

The person happened to be a guard, and he noticed two things: it was still the morning, not the afternoon, and the young man he encountered was not wearing an identification badge. The guard quickly turned around and confronted Kevin.

"Where's your ID?"

"Ah, shoot, it must have fallen off," Kevin said.

"Who are you, and where are you going?"

"I'm…I'm John Adams." As soon as it was out of his mouth, Kevin couldn't believe he had said it.

The guard didn't buy it. "Come with me." He grabbed Kevin by the arm and escorted him down one flight of stairs, through a couple of hallways, and into a small room. He told him to sit and put his arms in front of him. The guard brought out a zip tie from his pocket and fastened it around Kevin's wrists. "Wait here," he said before leaving and closing the door.

Kevin tried the door; it was locked. "Shit! Shit! Shit!" He took a deep breath. "OK, get it together." He didn't know how much time he had. He sat down in one of the chairs, closed his eyes, and began to meditate. Because of the advanced state of his nervous system, he was able to reacquire his HGT consciousness. Even so, it wasn't happening fast enough. Kevin swore silently. Finally, he let go and eventually felt the subtle shift in his molecular structure that told him he had left the visible range. Now all he had to do was wait. Fortunately, he didn't have to wait long.

Two guards entered the room. Kevin didn't waste any time and left through the open door as soon as they entered. He had not seen a security camera in the room. There may have been some in the hallways, but he couldn't worry about that now. He guessed which direction to go, ran into a few people talking about an early lunch, and followed them to the exit.

Once outside, he slowed his pace and gathered his thoughts. His hands were bound, so he couldn't materialize without raising suspicion. He managed to get out his cell phone, turn it back on, and call Brad.

"Brad, I have a problem," he announced without explaining any details. He just needed to be picked up.

Brad sensed the tension in his voice, so he did not question him. He knew he could do that later. "OK, it's usually about a half-hour drive, but it could take me longer to get there depending on traffic. Why don't you hang out in front of Union Station where that monument to Christopher Columbus is located?"

"Is that who it is?" Kevin asked.

"Yep, our so-called discoverer of America. It's a fitting place for you to hang out as our new discoverer of American intrigue."

"Very funny."

"There's a circular drive in front of it. You'll recognize my Mustang when I get there. Materialize, and I'll pick you up."

It was a relatively nice day, and Kevin didn't mind waiting outside. As he approached the monument in Columbus Circle, he found a sweatshirt lying on the marble. No one was around, so he figured someone must have forgotten it. He grabbed it, tucked himself more or less out of sight into one of the corners of the monument, and became visible.

Now with the sweatshirt covering his wrists, he found a nearby step and sat down to wait. He figured he saw more people and cars than he'd see in a month in Frisco. He also wondered if the statue would soon be replaced with one of an American Indian, as many communities were beginning to call Columbus Day "Indigenous Peoples Day."

Brad finally showed up, and Kevin got into the passenger seat. Noticing the zip tie on Kevin's wrists, Brad laughed and said, "There must be a good story here."

Kevin glared at him.

"Well, were you successful or not?" Brad asked.

"Yes, it's placed."

"And?"

"And can I get this off?" Kevin asked, pushing his wrists toward Brad's face.

Brad found a safe place to pull over, reached into the glove compartment, and retrieved a small knife. Kevin was still visibly shaken, but he settled down once the zip tie was off. Brad wisely remained silent. Kevin closed his eyes for a while. Thoughts of Sheely passed through his mind, and he drifted off. When he opened his eyes, he looked over at Brad.

"Feeling better?" Brad asked.

Kevin began to tell the story.

CHAPTER 44

Kevin stayed at Brad's another day. He found good therapy in walking and playing with Tucker. He drove Brad to work, so he had the car for the day. He made good use of it. He and Tucker found a park where they played catch for more than an hour. They also went to a pet store and bought a travel crate for Tucker. He explained the upcoming plane ride; Tucker was nervous about it but up for the adventure.

When he and Tucker picked up Brad from work late that afternoon, he learned that Brad had arranged for the two of them to meet Kathy for dinner that evening. Brad had talked briefly about his girlfriend a couple of times, and Kevin looked forward to meeting her. Brad had explained to Kathy that Kevin was in town on personal business and that he had offered to have him stay at his home.

Before they left for the restaurant, Kevin told Tucker they would be gone for a few hours. Kevin sensed the other day, when Tucker had been left alone, that he was worried about being abandoned. Kevin felt bad about that.

"We'll be back, I promise, and I'll have a nice treat for you," he told Tucker. He gave him a nice hug before he left. Kevin could sense Tucker's smile, and they both felt better.

Kathy met them at the restaurant. The first thing she noticed was that Kevin was younger.

"You didn't tell me your friend was still in college," Kathy said.

Kevin and Brad looked confused. Then Kevin took it as a compliment.

"Oh, thanks. I'm actually twenty-six. I've been out of college for a while."

"You look so young."

"Well, next to this guy, maybe." Kevin gave Brad a jab in his side.

The playfulness continued from there, and the evening turned out to be pleasant. Kathy liked Kevin. She noticed he had the same wonderful energy about him that Brad had.

"Do you meditate?" she asked Kevin.

"Yes. Brad and I both meditate. It's one of the things that brought us together."

"Ah."

Brad explained that Kathy was still thinking about it. Kevin encouraged her. "We'll see," she said and then asked about Tucker. The boys tapped danced around that. The conversation continued on a light note with Kathy asking more questions, especially about Sheely and Kevin. When finished, they had their leftovers put in a doggie bag for Tucker. Outside the restaurant, Kathy gave them both hugs, and they headed home.

Tucker was waiting.

"Hold on! I've got to get it out of the bag."

Smells good!

It cost an extra $200 to have Tucker flown, but they managed to get home without much difficulty. He called Sheely the evening of the mission to briefly relay its success, but Sheely was so eager to see him and hear the details that she was over at Kevin's home within minutes of his arrival call.

As soon as Kevin opened his door, she gave him a big hug and kiss.

"I should play James Bond more often," he said.

"I was so worried. I'm afraid I didn't give the best ski lessons while you were gone. My mind was just not there," Sheely admitted.

"I'm sure you did fine. Can I get you anything? Not that anything is here."

"No, I'm fine. Oh, hi, Tucker." Tucker nuzzled up to Sheely. "He's so cute!"

She smells nice! Kevin laughed.

The three of them settled in on Kevin's couch, and he told Sheely all the details of his trip. She was fascinated about how Kevin and Tucker met. "I'll have to ask Auntie how to do that," she said, as she scratched Tucker behind his ears.

After some silence, Sheely leaned in and gave Kevin a kiss. "Well, you're not quite a James Bond, but you did OK. Now we just have to wait a month, right? And then you have to retrieve it?"

"Yes. That should be a lot simpler, since I won't be nearly as nervous. Hopefully, we'll get some answers."

Kevin yawned. "I've got to go to bed. I'm exhausted. Oh, wait, I've got to walk Tucker first. Want to come on a walk with us?"

They took a short walk around Kevin's complex. On the way back, he walked Sheely to her car.

"What are you doing?" she asked.

"I'm going to open the door for you."

"The only place I'm going tonight is your bed."

Sheely had to go to work the next morning, but she took Tucker for a short walk before she left to allow Kevin to sleep in. She kissed him good-bye, gave Tucker a nice head rub, and left the two of them to fend for themselves.

Kevin later sat up and meditated. It felt good to be home. He wasn't looking forward to the next phase of their plan, but he knew it wouldn't be as nerve-wracking as what he had just accomplished. What was going to be nerve-wracking was explaining the extra unscheduled days off from work. He showered, dressed, and scrounged up some breakfast for himself and Tucker from what little he had in the kitchen. Then he headed to his grandfather's. He was looking forward to surprising him.

On the way, he explained to Tucker what was about to happen. *You mean my job will be to take care of him?*

"Yep."

Tucker tried to jump into Kevin's lap.

"Whoa, boy! Not while I'm driving."

Tucker was clearly excited about having such an important responsibility. He had always been treated poorly, and now he was going to have a real job.

CHAPTER 45

Time passed slowly but normally for the HGT band of amateur detectives. Kevin and Sheely taught for the last couple of weeks of the ski season and grew closer. Kevin had yet to go into detail with his mom about his relationship with Sheely. He would just say he was dating a nice lady when his mom asked. Centennial, where his mom lived, was about an hour and a half away, and like any loving son, he visited her from time to time.

Sheely, on the other hand, had a close relationship with her mom. They talked frequently. She told her mom everything—well, almost everything. Her mom was excited about Sheely's relationship with Kevin and was quite inquisitive at times. Sheely didn't mind. They both moved through life with their hearts.

Neither Sheely nor Kevin told their moms about the investigation.

Brad kept in touch. Auntie's home was repaired and back to normal, and Grandfather was enjoying his new buddy. As the end of the ski season approached, it was time to retrieve the bug.

Still, Sheely had her PSIA level-two exam coming up. She had taken the last required elective—the Teaching Exam Preparation Clinic—and felt prepared but nervous. Kevin had prepped her well, but it helped to get the general feel of the exam from an actual clinic examiner.

Even with all the required training, some candidates fail the level-two exam. Sheely took a deep breath and told herself, "I'm ready."

The exam was held at Vail Resort, which Sheely knew well. Day one focused on movement analysis, which she struggled with a little. The first part was pointing out ski performance and body performance from one phase to another in a turn. That was not easy for her; sometimes she guessed. The second part was to construct cause-and-effect relationships, and the last part was to give a prescription for change. She had to do this from watching both a video and a live skier. She had her fingers crossed the whole day.

Day two consisted of the skiing section, including the highlighted tasks of controlling rotational, edge, and pressure movements in specific maneuvers. Sheely felt confident that she had passed them.

Day three was mock teaching. She was judged on safety, identification of motives and needs, creating a goal statement, and facilitation or giving the lesson. For Sheely, this was the fun part of the exam.

At the end of day three, all thirty-two candidates waited in a room until the examiners finished their scoring and paperwork. Everyone waited patiently, but tension and anticipation filled the air. Sheely was a strong contributor to that. The examiners finally walked into the room to announce the names of the twenty-four who had passed. Sheely's name was the sixth one called. She bounced out of her chair with a small yell and collected her pin and certificate. *I can't wait to tell Kevin!*

Kevin took Sheely out to dinner to celebrate.

"I'm really proud of you," he said.

"Thanks. I'm proud of me too."

"How'd you do on the MA?"

"I was really nervous about that. I just barely passed: four out of six. As you know, four is the lowest passing score. Four is passing at a satisfactory level, five means you're better than the required level, and six means you're a supergirl. I don't know how anybody can get a six."

"Passing is passing. Level two is a hard exam. The examiners don't pass you unless you've met all requirements, so don't feel bad. You've earned that level-two pin," Kevin said.

"Thanks," Sheely said with a broad smile.

While they were enjoying the meal, Kevin remembered a comment Sheely had made about different types of meditation.

"Hey, remember when you mentioned that only our HGT meditation causes transcending? What do the other techniques do?"

"You forgot already? We talked a little bit about this when you came over after I got the e-mail from my friend Todd."

"Oh yeah. I forgot, but I could use a review."

"Well, according to Auntie, all meditation types fall into three categories: concentration, mindfulness, and transcending. They have different brain-wave rhythms. Concentration produces gamma waves. Mindfulness produces theta, and transcending produces alpha. I think she said it was specifically alpha1."

"So what does that mean, exactly?"

"The brain," she said, reaching over and tapping Kevin on the head, "produces five distinct wave patterns, and they are associated with distinct activities. Beta waves are created by normal activity. What we are doing right now. Delta waves are created when we are asleep…are you falling asleep on me?"

Kevin had pretended to doze off, and Sheely softly whacked him.

"No, no. I'm paying attention."

"You looked a little dazed."

"Well, it gets a bit technical."

"You're the technical one!"

"Well, yes, when it comes to skiing. How do you remember all this?"

"Guess."

"Auntie." They both laughed. "That's right. I forgot."

"When you hear it over and over again, it tends to stick." Sheely explained that focusing or concentrating causes gamma waves. A meditation technique that uses concentration or just studying hard for a test causes gamma to be produced. Theta waves come from dispassionately watching an activity, such as watching one's breath or the flow of thoughts through the mind. "That's what mindfulness meditation produces," she said, "and transcending produces alpha."

She said the distinctions produce different results in the mind and the body. "In concentration and mindfulness techniques, you are directing the mind." She said it didn't matter whether it was done actively or passively, but giving direction causes the mind to remain on the surface level.

"My grandfather drilled that into me as well," Kevin said.

"As you know, in our technique," she continued, "we keep the mind active but not directed. This allows the mind to follow its own direction and experience finer levels of thought. The mind transcends to the HGT level—that is, pure consciousness—by its own nature without resistance, without trying, and without effort. This is the secret that is misunderstood in all other techniques."

"And that's what you did in your exam, right?" Kevin asked with a sly grin.

Sheely stared blankly at him for a moment. "Oh, flattening my skis and not resisting the hill, not resisting gravity. Yes, I did that. And, in fact, the examiner commented on it. He liked the way I made it look so natural." She paused. "Just like transcending."

Kevin high-fived her.

"OK, but how do we know that our technique produces alpha?" Kevin asked.

"Oh, good point. Auntie was curious about that, so she sought out a neurologist and had her brain wired up. She sat and meditated while the neurologist measured her brain waves. It turned out that she had the purest and strongest alpha1 waves he had ever seen."

"Cool."

"He wanted to know how she did it, but Auntie just left him guessing."

"So, this transcending…"

"This transcending gives our body a deep state of rest that allows a lot of stress to be dissolved, which in turn keeps us healthy. According to Auntie, no other technique produces this level of rest because no other technique produces transcending. Auntie also says other meditation techniques are misunderstandings due to the passage of time."

"Wait…didn't you say once that there's another technique that's supposed to be like ours?" Kevin asked.

"Oh yeah, you're right. I forgot. Auntie did tell me that once, but I don't remember what it was."

"Well, thanks, I think, for the explanation." Kevin smiled. "I've done a lot of research on the history of our technique, but I've mostly ignored others. My granddad always told me they were a waste of time."

"You apparently ignored a lot of stuff in your training."

"Yeah, Granddad told me many times that I wasn't always the best student, but he has complimented me as well." He paused. "I wonder if Brad has explained all this to Kathy. I know he'd like her to start meditating."

"Yeah, he mentioned that to me as well," Sheely said. "I'm sure he must know some of this. We can always get Auntie to talk to her." They laughed at that. "Changing the subject, are you ready to go back to DC?"

"As ready as I'll ever be."

Back home, Sheely got a call from Brad. "When's your last day of teaching?" he asked.

"Sunday, April nineteenth."

"Will Kevin be ready to go?"

"Yes, we've already talked about it. He was supposed to call you. He's planning on flying out on the following Tuesday. Will that be OK?"

"Yeah, that's good."

"I'll remind him to call you."

"Thanks. I'm looking forward to getting this over."

"Me too."

CHAPTER 46

The day arrived, and Kevin was confident he could pull it off without any hitches this time. He got through the scanner without difficulty, but again, it created a hiccup. This time, he stuck around to watch. *Just for the fun of it.*

"Look, it did it again," the guard said. "Mr. Daniels, I need you to go back through."

"OK. I swear I'm clean," Mr. Daniels said jokingly.

"Yes sir, but I need you to go back through."

Mr. Daniels backed up through the scanner and waited, ready to go through again.

"Please stay there a moment," the guard commanded. He and the other guard reviewed the output from the scanner. "Something is wrong with this. It's showing what looks like two bodies. Like a shadow or something."

"It did this before, right?" the other guard asked.

"Same thing as before. Mr. Daniels, please walk through again."

Both guards viewed the screen. "That's weird. Now it's gone. We need to have the technician come and check this out. Mr. Daniels, you're OK to go."

"Thank you."

Ah, so it can see me. Kevin started down the hall and easily found Senator Benn's office. He had to pull the same knock-on-the-door trick to get into the reception area.

"I'm going to find out who's knocking on this door and then running away," Liz said to her coworker after finding no one there.

"Didn't that happen a month or so ago?"

"Yes. It's pretty childish, if you ask me."

"Pay no attention to it. There's enough nonsense in this place as it is."

"Girl, you can say that again."

The door to the senator's office was closed. Kevin wondered if the senator was here working. *That wouldn't be good.* He carefully sat in one of the guest chairs and waited. Finally, he heard one of the assistants on a phone call say the senator would be back later. He got the idea to knock on the door. He got up and walked over to the door, but this time, he knocked down low, mimicking, he hoped, something falling against it.

"What was that?" Liz asked.

"I don't know. I'll check. Sounds like something hit the door," Liz's coworker said. She opened the door and walked inside, looking around the room and behind the door. Meanwhile, Kevin entered.

"It's your ghost," she said. "There's nothing here."

"You're sure?" Liz asked.

"Come look for yourself."

"No, I believe you. What's the number for the Ghostbusters?" Liz joked, shaking her head as her coworker closed the door.

Well, at least I'm in. Kevin was a little anxious, but the bug was still there. One amazing thing about real invisibility is that anything that essentially attaches itself to the body, as if becoming a part of it, also becomes invisible. Movie depictions of invisible men inaccurately had to have them naked. The full functioning of invisibility is currently beyond the understanding of physics, but that doesn't mean it's beyond the laws of nature.

Kevin put the bug in his pants pocket and waited patiently for the office door to open. He didn't think it would be a good idea to use the knocking trick again, so he settled into one of the guest chairs in front of the desk, closed his eyes, and meditated.

Kevin wasn't sure how much time had passed when the office door opened and he heard two people enter. It startled him because he was deep in meditation, and his chair moved slightly. Still invisible, he managed to get out of the chair and quietly move to one of the side walls. This time, the chair movement went unnoticed.

"Have you located Caesar yet?" a voice asked.

"Not yet, but I'm close."

Kevin recognized Senator Benn but wasn't sure who the other person was.

"Well, please keep at it. Oh, by the way, the rumor is that the FBI still believes the NRA was responsible for the death of Senator Welsh, even though they can't prove it. You did a marvelous job of that scalping."

"Thanks. It was a little messy."

Holy shit! That's Catson! Kevin was surprised he didn't recognize him right away.

"Whose idea was that, anyway? Yours or the VP's?" Catson asked.

"Well, we kind of came up with it together."

"Again, I apologize about the screw-up with the witness. I could have sworn there was no one there when I shot Welsh, but I took care of it as you asked and eliminated the witness."

"No problem. What's done is done."

I hope this thing is still working. He recalled that he forgot to turn off the bug.

"You never told me why you and the VP wanted Welsh out of the way," Catson said.

"Actually, that's above your pay grade," Benn said mockingly, "but in general he would have caused problems for a few highly placed individuals." Senator William Benn, Republican from New York, didn't know the half of it.

Catson, on the other hand, suspected that Caesar was involved, and he was right. Caesar pushed Benn to have the Meissner study killed even before Vice-President Locker got involved. Fortunately, the VP was of the same thought, and when she brought in Catson, it turned to his advantage. Neither Catson nor Benn caught the irony of "highly placed individuals."

The conversation lightened up and went on for a few more minutes. Kevin stood silently in the background, fascinated and horrified at the same time. Finally, Catson said, "So you called me here just to find out if I've found Caesar? You could have done that over the phone."

"I could have, but it's important for you to know who's in charge," Benn said.

Catson nodded, got up, and left, with Kevin closely on his tail.

CHAPTER 47

That evening, Brad uploaded the bug's encrypted data to his computer. Using its decryption software, he was able to expand the data into a usable form. The total file size was much smaller than he had anticipated, which worried Brad. *Maybe it hadn't worked properly.* He scanned through it and listened to segments here and there.

"He must not be in his office very often," Brad thought out loud.

"Or he doesn't talk much when he's in there," Kevin added.

Brad scanned the file for a few more minutes and concluded it was OK. "It seems to have worked," he told Kevin.

"Go back to the end and see if it caught the conversation when I was there today."

Brad chose a spot in the displayed wave spectrum and clicked play.

"What's that?" Kevin asked.

"Remember, you didn't turn it off when you retrieved it. That's probably subway noise."

"Oh yeah, but it's a good thing I forgot."

Brad clicked on an earlier segment.

Thanks. It was a little messy.

"Stop!" Kevin said. "That's where I recognized it was Catson, the Secret Service agent."
Brad continued.

Whose idea was that anyway? Yours or the VP's?

"That's Catson," Kevin said.

Well, we kind of came up with it together.

"That's Senator Benn."

Again, I apologize about the screw-up with the witness. I could have sworn there was no one there when I shot Welsh, but I took care of it as you asked and eliminated the witness.

No problem. What's done is done.

You never told me why you and the VP wanted Welsh out of the way.

Brad stopped the recording. "Wow."
"Yeah, wow," Kevin echoed. They were silent for a moment. "We should transcribe this."
"I'll let you and Sheely do that," Brad said. "My job keeps me busy enough. Besides, you two are unemployed at the moment, right?"

Kevin laughed. "No problem. We'd be happy to do it."

Brad made a copy, broke the file into four parts, and downloaded it onto four 128-gigabyte USB flash drives. He kept the original.

Back in Colorado, Kevin and Sheely each took two flash drives. They transcribed for a week, taking some time off now and then. The work was tedious. Most of the recorded voice data, especially the phone conversations, were one-sided and boring. Some of the meetings in Benn's office were eye-opening. Kevin and Sheely were learning the business of Congress. Unfortunately, little of it gave them the incriminating evidence they sought.

There were several conversations between Benn and the vice-president regarding the Meissner study, but only a few directly implicated them in the murder of Senator Welsh. They hoped that was enough. One conversation between Senator Benn and Jeff Catson cleared up a suspicion Kevin had—that someone or some group wanted things to stay the way they were. It started with Catson's voice:

Why did you want Representative Moore killed?

Why do you care?

Just curious. You paid five hundred thousand dollars for it. So it must have been important.

Again, like I said before, certain highly placed individuals did not want a certain bill he was pushing to go through.

You mean the VP.

And others.

Several other conversations between Benn and Catson centered on someone named Caesar. They didn't say so explicitly, but it seemed they wanted him killed. It turned out that some of the best evidence was recorded the day Kevin retrieved the device.

When they were almost finished, they notified Brad, and he made arrangements to fly out to join them on the weekend. He had them combine their separate Word documents into one and, along with each conversation, add the megabyte location so the recorded data could be retrieved easily. Then Brad had Kevin create a shorter, edited version with just the conversations that implicated Senator Benn, Secret Service Agent Catson, and Vice-President Locker.

He showed them how to handle the paperwork, print and address the documents, and remove fingerprints so none of it would be traceable. They put a full copy of the contents of the four USB flash drives on each of their computers for safety. Then they carefully put the flash drives, the full transcribed document, and the shortened highlighted version in an eight-and-a-half-by-eleven-inch manila envelope addressed to the president. They considered sending it to the FBI, but at this point, they didn't trust anyone. They also understood, through their HGT training, the principle of "seeking the highest first," and in this case, there was no one higher than the president. They decided to deliver it personally.

Since they had no legal authority for the recording, they did not want to be associated with it. Kevin assumed he would use his special skills to get into the Oval Office and leave it for the president clandestinely. He was the only one who could get in unseen, but Brad insisted on going with him.

"Who knows what could happen? You may need my skills. And besides, you can't have all the fun," Brad said.

Kevin thought it was a dumb idea, but Brad's assertion that he might need his skills was logical. He said Brad could ride piggyback to keep both of them invisible.

"Can't we just hold hands?" Brad asked.

"That would be great, but I can't just touch things to make them invisible. I have to grab them and sort of make them be like a part of my body, like clothes. So if you're on my back, that'll work."

Brad was smaller than Kevin—shorter and lighter. They thought it would be doable but a challenge given the distance they would have to cover.

"You guys should practice," Sheely said with a smirk, knowing it would be fun to watch.

Brad and Kevin looked at each other. They both had the same thought: *In front of Sheely?*

"She has a point," Kevin finally said.

Brad hopped onto Kevin's back and nearly knocked him over. Kevin let go as Sheely laughed.

"Let's try that again," Kevin said.

This time, he was solid. They walked around the room several times. Kevin jostled Brad around to get him into a more comfortable position.

"Whaddaya think? Doable?" Brad asked.

"It will be a little challenging, but I can do it."

With that out of the way, they spent the rest of Brad's time there working out the basics of a plan.

CHAPTER 48

This time, they were more prepared. During his time as a CIA field agent, Brad had been in the Oval Office and knew the layout of the building. He was there to debrief the president and his senior security advisers on a connection between the Shiite Hezbollah rebels and a Colombian cartel. He worked briefly with a team of agents who had extensive experience with the ins and outs of that relationship. It was an exciting time in his career, and at times he missed it. What he was involved in now, though, he thought was pretty cool.

Back in DC, Kevin and Brad refined their plan.

"The Oval Office is in the West Wing of the White House complex known as the Executive Office Building. We should enter the West Wing via the less-impressive side entrance off West Executive Avenue," Brad said. He explained that entering via the West Wing's north-facing entry portico was a poor choice. "That's more of a ceremonial entrance and doesn't get used as often. We might be waiting forever to follow someone in. Also, if the president is in, there's always a marine sentry standing guard outside." He said the west entrance was the one the workers use, so they wouldn't have to wait long to follow someone inside. It was on what could be considered the base-ment or ground floor. The Oval Office, he told Kevin, is on the first floor. "So we'll have to go up some stairs. Can you handle that?"

"Well, we'll see." That got an uncomfortable stare from Brad. "Yes, I can do it."

The first obstacle, Brad told Kevin, would be the security at the entrance. Kevin wasn't as concerned about that as Brad was. He'd been there, done that.

Brad was able to determine that the president would not be in his office. "Though that could always change," he told Kevin. Although they would be invisible, not having the president in-house made their plan less complicated. The Oval Office has four doors. One enters into the room where the president's secretary sits, another enters into a dining room/study suite, the third exits onto the Rose Garden, and the fourth enters into the hallway of the West Wing. The only accessible one for them was the West Wing hallway door.

"If we even make it that far," Brad said.

"Not to worry. I'm an experienced ghost."

There was some tense laughter, but they were ready.

The next day, they awoke early and had a good breakfast. "I hope this isn't our last good meal," Brad said, half joking. Brad wore a small backpack carrying the manila envelope with the evidence. They got on the Metro's Red Line at the Bethesda station and took it to the Farragut North stop. From there, it was a little over four blocks to the White House.

They walked the half block to Farragut Square. Along the sidewalk was a long line of food vendor trucks.[59] They ducked

---

59 Farragut Square is a popular lunchtime area on warmer days. It has eight sidewalks that crisscross the square lined with benches surrounding eight grassy areas, all of which can be crowded on nice days with people taking a break from their workdays.

between two of them, Brad hopped onto Kevin's back, and they disappeared.

"Damn the torpedoes, full speed ahead!" Brad whispered.

"What?" Kevin said.

"Never mind. I'll explain later."

They had walked about fifty feet when Kevin whispered, "This is too soon. I won't make it." When Kevin ducked again between two trucks, Brad hopped off. "What was that you said?" Kevin asked, now visible.

"Oh, see that statue over there?" he said, pointing to the center of the square.

"Yeah."

"That's Admiral David Farragut. He was in the Civil War and is famous for saying, 'Damn the torpedoes, full speed ahead!'"

"OK, I get it. Very funny," Kevin said. They walked the next two blocks past I Street and H Street Northwest looking for a place to "disappear." The sidewalks were busy.

"There." Brad pointed to the McDonald's on the other side of the street. They jaywalked across the street, entered the restaurant, and went into the men's room. They pretended to use the facilities. As the current occupant turned to exit and pushed open the door, Brad climbed onto Kevin's back, and they disappeared. They quickly and silently exited while the bathroom door remained open and followed another patron out of the restaurant.

"So far, so good," Kevin said quietly. It was a half block to Pennsylvania Avenue Northwest, where the road became a pedestrian walkway. They turned left onto it, walked about a half block, and turned down West Executive Avenue Northwest, which is just a parking lot for the West Wing and the Eisenhower Executive Office Building. Another half block, and they were at the entrance.

As they approached the exterior fence along the side of the building, they paused just before the canopy covering the entrance. A guard was standing outside; they weren't expecting that. They leaned against the fence and waited. It didn't take long. A well-dressed man and woman approached. Kevin and Brad followed closely behind. As the couple's credentials were checked, they waited and then followed them into the lobby.

They were a little concerned about the security in the small lobby but more concerned about what they were carrying if they got caught. Brad distracted that guard with a thought transfer, and they were in.

"This way," Brad whispered and gently pushed Kevin's head toward the hallway. As they approached the intersecting hallway, where the stairway to the first floor was, two workers quickly rounded the blind corner. The guys immediately backed into the wall, just missing them.

"What was that?" the worker closest to the wall said after he heard a thump. The two of them stopped for a moment and listened again. They heard nothing.

"Who knows?" They turned back around and continued down the hall.

"Whew, that was close," whispered Kevin, once the other men had passed. The stairway to the first floor was right next to the entrance to the Secret Service office, so they moved as quickly as possible. They made the left turn into the hallway in front of the office and after a few more steps entered the stairway.[60]

---

60 To view a detailed floor plan of the White House West Wing, go to https://whitehouse.gov1.info/visit/tour.html and scroll down to the West Wing tour map.

Kevin struggled a little on the stairs; he was getting tired. The top of the stairs was right next to the Cabinet Room on the first floor. What was waiting for them at the top, they didn't know, so they cautiously stepped off the top step. The hallway was empty. They turned the corner and started down the hall to the Oval Office.

"Hey, jump off a moment. I need a quick rest," Kevin said. He also made himself visible to give his senses a break. Just then, a man stepped out of the Oval Office. It was Jeff Catson. Kevin reached out to grab Brad, but he was too late.

"Hey!" Jeff said as he ran up and grabbed Brad by the arm. "You're the guy who snuck into the VP's office, aren't you?" Turning to look at Kevin, he said, "And I bet you're the one from the Russell building. Well, well. Isn't this a coincidence?"

Brad and Kevin remained silent.

"What's this you're carrying?" Jeff grabbed Brad's backpack, spun him around, and ripped it off. He opened the backpack and pulled out the envelope. Brad and Kevin started to break away, but Jeff pulled out his gun.

"Oh no you don't," Jeff commanded. They saw the gun and stopped. Jeff inspected the rest of the backpack. Seeing that it was empty, he threw it back to Brad. Then he opened the envelope and saw its contents. "I'll keep this," he said, guessing what it might contain.

Jeff walked them across the hallway and into the empty Roosevelt Room, using the door closest to the lobby. The Roosevelt Room was named after Teddy Roosevelt, who was responsible for building the West Wing. Kevin didn't care what it was called. To him, it was a jail, but Brad had an idea.

Jeff kept the door to the Roosevelt Room open. He turned and reached across to open the door to the lobby in order to call out to the guard. The moment he looked away, Brad jumped onto Kevin and whispered, "Now!" They disappeared. Brad guided Kevin around the long table in the center of the room and had Kevin open the door on that side. Kevin started to exit.

"No, turn back," Brad said firmly but quietly, twisting Kevin around.

"What the fuck?" Jeff yelled as he turned and saw the room was empty. Out of the corner of his eye, he saw the door on the other side of the room move. He quickly ran around the center table, through that door, and into the hallway, assuming that was the way they had left. As Jeff circled through the room, Kevin and Brad quietly but quickly circled in the other direction, back toward the first door.

The guard in the lobby was immediately distracted by Jeff's temper and ran into the Roosevelt Room, colliding with Kevin and Brad as they were about to exit. All three men were thrown backward. Stunned and confused, the guard got back up and looked around. For a moment, he thought he saw something, but then nothing was there. He shook his head in disbelief. After gathering his thoughts, he followed after Jeff.

Brad was momentarily thrown from Kevin in the collision. Kevin kept his wits about him and grabbed Brad. While the guard was distracted, Brad hopped back onto Kevin's back.

They made it to the lobby of the north-facing portico and left the building through the front entrance. The marine guarding the door looked concerned when the door opened by itself and no one came out, but the guys didn't wait to see his reaction.

"The president must be in," Brad said as Kevin carried him across the lawn to the pedestrian gate next to the driveway entrance. At the entrance, two guards were chatting outside.

"What do we do?" Brad whispered.

Kevin knew the answer. He violently shook the vehicle gate at the driveway entrance. The guards noticed but did nothing. Kevin shook it again, and that got the guards' attention. One walked over to check it, couldn't see anything wrong, and returned to his buddy, raising his hands indicating he had no idea why it shook.

"Better check to see if it's working," the other guard said. It was, and Kevin and Brad left through it undetected. They cut through Lafayette Square toward Connecticut Avenue. Once on the avenue's sidewalk, Kevin frantically looked for a place to unload Brad. He was exhausted, but the sidewalks were too busy to just magically appear. Across the street, he spotted the entrance to an underground parking garage. He entered, found a dark corner, and started to tell Brad he could hop off. Brad beat him to it.

"That was close," Brad whispered. "That was as scary as anything I did as an active spy. How'd you know shaking the gate would work?"

"Experience." Kevin left it at that. "Now what? Catson has all the evidence."

"You got me. I guess we start over," Brad said.

That evening, they called Sheely using the speaker capability on Brad's cell.

"That was dumb luck. I'm sure glad you guys made it out," Sheely said. "But they might have a security recording of what happened."

"No doubt," Brad said, "but they haven't been able to identify us yet, so let's keep our fingers crossed."

"What are we going to do?" Sheely asked.

"I'm not sure," Brad said.

"Why don't we just sit it out awhile and see if anything materializes? I doubt it will, but who knows?" Kevin said.

"Brad, can you keep your eyes and ears open at the CIA?" Sheely asked.

"Can do, but I probably won't hear anything."

Kevin stayed a couple of days at Brad's. Nothing more materialized. Dejected, he flew home.

CHAPTER 49

Secret Service Agent Catson did not waste any time. He saw the envelope was addressed to the president but decided to check out the contents before handing it over to him. After reading the transcript and listening to the audio, he knew precisely what to do, and it wasn't giving them to the president. He did not know where Caesar hung his hat, but he had his phone number. It turned out it went to one of his lieutenants, who made the arrangements to pick him up.

They met in a local café, and once again Jeff had to submit to being blindfolded. It annoyed him, but there was nothing he could do about it. He swore to himself he would find out where this secret location was. It could prove useful someday.

After the short ride, he was escorted up to the same room where he had been before. They waited at the open door while Caesar had a conversation with another man.

"That Meissner bill has been killed?" the man asked.

"Yes, Benn finally managed that. So he was able to get something done," Caesar said.

"It seems like he's becoming less useful."

"Yes, I agree," said Caesar. "He has yet to get that defense bill we want, passed."

"We need to get that done. Do you have anyone to replace the senator?"

Who was this guy? Jeff wondered.

"Well, interestingly enough, I'd like you to meet Jeff Catson." Caesar pointed in Jeff's direction and nodded to the escorts to let Jeff enter. "Jeff's not a direct replacement, but he's with the Secret Service, assigned to Vice-President Locker, which gives us another window of opportunities."

Jeff extended his hand. "And you are?"

"Clayton Howard," the man said. "Jeff, you're new here, aren't you?"

"Jeff's a new addition to the family," Caesar said.

"Nice to meet you," Clayton said.

"Thank you, likewise," Jeff responded.

"Yes, I can see interesting opportunities here," Clayton said with a smile.

"So, what's so important that you had to join us this morning?" Caesar asked Jeff. "Oh, and by the way, I got your Dumpster message."

Jeff nodded in acknowledgment. "I have audio that proves Senator Benn and Vice-President Locker authorized the killing of Moore and Welsh."

"Really?" Caesar smiled.

"What?" Clayton was looking back and forth between Jeff and Caesar.

"Jeff was the hit man," Caesar said.

"Oh, now I see." Clayton was catching on to the bigger picture.

"How'd you come about this audio?" Caesar asked.

"Well, apparently, there was a bug in Senator Benn's office, and for a month or so, everything that took place in there was recorded. A few mysterious things have been going on that I can't explain." He paused. "Anyway, I just happened to catch two guys, who I can't seem to identify, about to enter the president's office carrying this envelope. How they got in I wasn't able to figure out, and how they escaped is an even a greater mystery, but they were carrying this envelope addressed to the president." Jeff explained in detail what it contained and handed the envelope to Caesar.

"*Very* interesting," Caesar said while looking through the envelope's contents.

"Yes, I thought you'd find it useful. What I propose is for you to have someone edit it to remove any reference to me and then anonymously forward it to, let's say, the FBI."

"You're saying this directly implicates Senator Benn in the murders of Welsh and Moore?" Clayton Howard asked.

"Yes, and the vice-president as well," Jeff said.

"This could solve our problem with the senator," Clayton told Caesar.

"It may do more than that," Caesar said.

When Jeff got home, he googled Clayton Howard to learn who he was. There was a guy who had just earned his PhD, another who was a professor, and some Facebook entries. He was about to give up when he paged forward and found Clayton Howard, member of the Board of Governors of the Federal Reserve.

"I wonder..." Jeff mumbled to himself.

Reading further, he discovered that this Clayton was the president of the Federal Reserve Bank of New York. As such, he was a permanent member of the board committee. There was information about something called the ESF, which Jeff skipped over. He went to the Federal Reserve website to look for a photo. Sure enough, it was the same man he had met at Caesar's.

"Why would such a man be involved with Caesar and the ECC?" Jeff wondered out loud. He was curious but really didn't care. He felt he was now safe and was looking forward to seeing Senator Benn and the VP get their due. He knew he would be questioned, being the VP's top agent, and perhaps temporarily suspended during the investigation, and he was a little concerned about that. Nevertheless, he felt comfortable with his arrangement with Caesar.

Jeff didn't have to wait long. Three days later, he received a call from Caesar.

"Good morning, Jeff."

"Morning, sir." Jeff recognized the voice.

"I've got some good news and some bad news."

"OK."

"The good news is we successfully edited the data you gave us and will have it delivered to the FBI in the morning."

"That's great news."

"Well, not completely. You see, we edited out the references to Vice-President Locker but not yours."

There was a long moment of silence.

"What are you saying?" Jeff asked cautiously.

"Because we respect you, I am giving you twenty-four hours' notice."

"You set me up?"

"I'm sorry about that, Jeff, but there's a bigger picture here."

"You son of a bitch!"

"I suggest you leave immediately if you don't want to spend the rest of your life in prison. Good luck, Jeff." There was a moment of silence. "Oh, and by the way, there'll be a reference letter waiting for you if you ever make it to Havana." He told Jeff how to retrieve it, and the phone went dead.

Jeff was stunned. Angry didn't even come close to what he was feeling. It took a good half hour before he calmed down and began to plan his next move. Several scenarios ran through his head, but nothing appealed to him. He finally decided he first had to get to his account in the Cayman Islands. From there, he wasn't sure. *Something will develop.*

CHAPTER 50

It took a mere twenty-four hours for the FBI to process the data, and with the addition of the $500,000 transfer they were already following up on, they had a solid case against Senator Benn. They were able to get search warrants for both his office and home. They were also able to get warrants for Jeff Catson's home and work area. Checking ahead, they discovered the senator was in his office, but Catson had not reported to work. Three agents were sent to Catson's home, and three were sent to Senator Benn's office.

The agent showed his badge. "Is the senator in?" he asked Liz, who was sitting at the reception desk of Benn's office.

"Yes sir. He's in a meeting."

The agents went directly into Benn's office without asking for permission.

"Senator Benn?"

"Who are you? I'm in a meeting. You need—" Benn was agitated, but the agent cut him off.

"I'm Special Agent Jennings." He showed his credentials. "This is Special Agent Bowman and Special Agent Miles. Senator Benn, you are under arrest for the murders of Senator Gregory Welsh and Representative John Moore."

"What?"

"Please don't resist, Senator. We already have enough proof to put you away for life." The agent read Benn his Miranda rights.

"What's going on, Bill?" the guest senator from the meeting asked.

As his hands were cuffed, Benn asked, "Is this necessary? I won't resist." He got no response. "My coat!"

One of the agents grabbed his coat, and Benn was escorted out.

The agents assigned to Catson acquired a key from his condo association's management company. They knocked before entering. There was no answer, so they used the key and entered. The condo was empty. They called headquarters and put out an APB.

Jeff wanted to fly directly to Miami, but all those flights were full. He had to settle for a Southwest flight to Fort Lauderdale. He used a fake ID he'd had for years. From there, he rented a car and drove to Miami International Airport, where he took the first flight to Cancun. In Cancun, he had a two-hour layover before he took an Aero Mexico flight under his assumed name to Havana, Cuba. He figured it would take a few days to track him down. That would give him enough time to make his way to the Cayman Islands. From there—well, that was still up in the air.

Agents also approached Vice-President Locker. She put on a surprised face. She said she had no idea about Agent Catson's hidden life, and of course she knew who Senator Benn was, but ordering killings, she couldn't believe that.

"This is shocking!" she told the agents. "What can I do?"

The questioning went on for several minutes.

"Any idea where Mr. Catson might have gone?"

"Where did he vacation?"

"Does he have a second home?"

"Any girlfriends?"

Eventually, the agents apologized for interrupting her day and asked her to call if she thought of anything. When they left and closed her office door, she let out a long breath of air.

Oh my God! How did all this happen? She gathered her thoughts and went directly to the president.

It took several days for the news agencies to piece together the story, which forced the director of the FBI to hold a news conference. He confirmed the arrest of Senator Benn and the outstanding arrest warrant for Secret Service Agent Catson. He outlined the details without giving specifics because the investigation was still in progress.

Bradley Grant heard about the arrests before the news broke to the public. He immediately called Kevin. Kevin called Sheely. Sheely called Auntie. Kevin called Grandfather.

Grandfather Keith recorded the FBI director's press conference. Kevin and Sheely drove down together to watch it.

"We're just a bunch of amateur goofs!" Kevin was angry at himself after watching the recording. "We should have gone to the FBI. What were we thinking?"

"Well, two out of three ain't bad," Grandfather said, "and besides, you guys developed a wonderful fellowship."

"*What?*"

"Come on now, Kevin. The three of you aren't exactly James Bond. Considering everything, I think it worked out pretty well. Who knows what Mother Nature has up her sleeve? Senator Benn will get his due, the Secret Service agent will probably be found, and you still have all the evidence on the vice-president." Grandfather paused. His deep, inner wisdom kicked in, and he chuckled to himself. "I think your adventure is *just* starting."

Kevin just shook his head.

Grandfather put his arm around Kevin. "Nature knows best; just follow her lead."

Sheely smiled at the James Bond comment. She went to Kevin and hugged him. "We did the best we could, and we do have a nice fellowship—you, me, and Brad."

"Yeah, but now what?"

EPILOGUE

It was near the end of June, and the snow in the mountains was nearly gone. Kevin and Sheely were hiking up Peak One, just outside of Frisco. The hike consisted of three peaks: Mount Royal, Mount Victoria, and Peak One. Mount Royal and Mount Victoria were two smaller humps on the way to the top of Peak One. The trail passed the remains of Masontown, an old mining village partway up Mount Royal. Folklore said that as the occupants of Masontown were celebrating one winter evening in Frisco, an avalanche broke loose on the mountain and wiped out the village. However, the facts showed that the village was deserted long before the 1926 avalanche.

Once above Masontown, they passed the Mount Royal cutoff and headed up the steep trail toward Mount Victoria. On the way, they passed the old "grandfather" tree, as Kevin called it. It had to be several hundred years old. The first time Kevin had climbed Peak One, he had noticed the tree and spent time admiring it. It wasn't tall, but it was wide and handsome in a gnarly way. Now it was all brown. It had survived all these years only to be murdered by pine beetles. Kevin and Sheely blessed it and went on.

The summit of Mount Victoria was above the tree line at 11,785 feet and opened up to a nice meadow. A few of the more than seven hundred species of Colorado wildflowers were in bloom. They sat on a large rock and took in the view. Kevin was nervous. He had an announcement to make.

"I know we've been dating only a few months, but there is no one else I ever want to be with," Kevin said bravely. He paused, took a breath. "I love you, Sheely."

"I love you too."

"I want...I want..." Kevin closed his eyes for a second and mustered his courage. He looked directly into her eyes. "Will you marry me?"

"Kevin..."

They looked at each other. Her eyes got misty, and she broke into a broad smile. "Where's my ring?"

"We haven't even met each other's moms. I thought I should ask your mom's permission first."

"That's very noble and old-fashioned of you." She paused, her eyes now sparkling. "But I'd like to just surprise her."

"I was hoping you'd say that." He reached into his pocket and pulled out a ring.

Sheely reached over and gave Kevin a long, wet, passionate kiss. "Yes, I'll marry you!"

Kathy finally asked Brad to teach her how to meditate, which surprised and thrilled him.

"What convinced you?" he asked.

"You."

"What do you mean?"

"Who you are. Everything you've told me and everything I've read and researched is all good and dandy, but it's you. Your inner self, your energy, your inner Being, to use yoga-speak."

Brad laughed at that, but it also tickled his heart. He taught her the HGT method of meditation. It took a couple of days for the journalist in her to comprehend the depth of her experience, but then all she could do was smile.

Brad also noticed a greater warming of her already wonderful heart and reflected on his conversation with Sheely about her mom. He was feeling good about his relationship with Kathy and hoped he could tell her more about everything soon.

Aunt Jennifer and Grandfather Keith were delighted to hear the news of Kevin and Sheely's engagement, as were the moms, though they were quite surprised. Auntie, true to her nature, had spent some time doing research in the quiet depths of her expanded consciousness and figured out Patanjali's saṃyama technique of understanding the language of animals. This she taught to Keith, who thoroughly enjoyed conversing with Tucker. In fact, Tucker had to ask him at times to please be quiet because he wanted to sleep.

Because of Tucker, Grandfather Keith turned into a regular hiker. On his walks with Tucker, he would frequently run into a grandmother named Amy with her dog, Daisy. Tucker and Daisy became great friends and looked forward to playing with each other. Keith and Amy also became good friends. His grandfather would deny it, but Kevin knew they were dating. They often shared dinner together and went to movies, and their favorite activity was, of course, hiking with the dogs.

Jeff Catson was eventually tracked to the Cayman Islands due to the account information VP Locker gave the FBI, but from there his trail was lost. The money from Catson's now-closed account enabled him to settle comfortably in Colombia. He was considering making contact with the drug lord who had taken the place of Colombian kingpin Jose Evaristo Linares-Castillo after his arrest in 2013. He had the reference letter from Alfonso Cesare, which he'd picked up in Cuba. He figured the letter could help establish a position for him with the cartel, but he was still enjoying his clandestine freedom, especially the beautiful women like the one he had this evening.

"Thank you, Señor Jeff," the young lady said as Jeff handed her cash. "Will I see you again?"

"We'll see." The call girl quietly exited and threw him a kiss.

Jill Hill, democratic representative from Utah, reintroduced the bill to fund the Meissner study. The deaths of Senator Welsh and Representative Moore and the horrendous acts of Senator Benn softened the mood of Congress. Although many still did not believe in the Meissner effect, they were beginning to understand that changes were needed. The bill was passed, and Jill also got funding for the national parks in Utah as well as all other national parks.

Still, she was concerned. The revelation about Benn, Catson, and the murders was certainly upsetting, but she felt there was more to it. The Congress and the country were so divided. "It shouldn't be this way. What's going on?" She'd ask herself over and over. She called Russell Kelly and asked him to keep at it.

Senator Benn was denied bail. He was assigned to the Federal Correctional Institution in Cumberland, Maryland. He was held in isolation. On his third day, a guard he didn't recognize came to his cell.

"Mr. Benn, I've been asked to pass on a message."

Benn sat up.

"It is recommended that you do not involve the vice-president in any way. If you do, you will not make it to your trial."

Benn's eyes and mouth opened wider. *What? How?*

"Do you understand?"

Benn couldn't move.

"Do you understand?"

Benn nodded and the guard left.

Russell Kelly, Boston private investigator, was at first surprised as anyone about the actions of Secret Service Agent Catson.

Yet, shortly after hearing the news, he remembered a feeling he had when he first met him. That raised his curiosity. He called his reporter friend, Byron Pierce, at the *Summit Dispatch*.

"Byron, congratulations on your story. You started a flood of investigative reporting."

"Thanks. It was my fifteen minutes of fame."

"The reason I'm calling is I believe there is more going on here than what's being reported."

"What do you mean?"

"I met Agent Catson when I worked for the FBI in DC. When I first met him, I felt something negative about him: his mannerism, his words, his energy. There was just something. I couldn't put my finger on it. Later, I had the opportunity to work with him on an investigation, and he was very professional. I completely forgot about my earlier intuitive feeling. But now, my intuition has kicked back in."

"What are you saying?"

"I think there is more going on than what is being reported and that feeling is shared by a member of Congress."

"Who in Congress?"

"Sorry, that's confidential. But this person believes the murders are just the tip of the iceberg, so to speak."

"OK. Then do you think the FBI is hiding information?"

"Don't know. Probably not. But there is just something."

"Cool."

"Anyway, I wanted to let you know there may be more to report on."

"I'll be waiting with bated breath."

Russell laughed. "Well, I'd take a breath or two. It may be a while!"

Vice-President Andrea Locker had settled into her normal routine, but she was still brooding over the passing of the Meissner bill. The only joy she felt over that whole incident was the arrest of Senator Benn. That made her chuckle every time she thought about it. Triple P had worked in a way she could not have imagined.

She gave a few interviews, saying how blessed she felt. "I'm ashamed to say I was fooled by both Senator Benn and Agent Catson. It could have been a lot worse for me, having a murderer supposedly protecting me. I feel blessed not to have been hurt." The public soaked it up, and her ratings went sky high—giving her another ego boost.

One morning, as she sat in her office at the Eisenhower Executive Office Building enjoying her morning coffee, she got a phone call.

"Good morning," she answered.

"Hello, Ms. Locker?"

"Yes, this is Andrea. Who's this?"

"That's not important," said the voice. "What's important is…"

The End

AUTHOR'S NOTE

The Meissner effect is real. It can be and has been produced by meditators practicing Patanjali's yoga sutras. For a detailed description of its theoretical foundation and scientifically proven effectiveness in creating peace, visit the Global Union of Scientists for Peace at www.gusp.org.

www.rgreynovels.com
www.facebook.com/themeissnereffect